P9-DDL-632

WINGS
OF
FIRE

BOOK ONE
THE DRAGONET PROPHECY

BOOK TWO
THE LOST HEIR

BOOK THREE
THE HIDDEN KINGDOM

BOOK FOUR
THE DARK SECRET

BOOK FIVE
THE BRIGHTEST NIGHT

BOOK SIX
MOON RISING

BOOK SEVEN
WINTER TURNING

BOOK EIGHT
ESCAPING PERIL

BOOK NINE
TALONS OF POWER

LEGENDS
DARKSTALKER

WINGS OF FIRE

TALONS OF POWER

by
TUI T. SUTHERLAND

SCHOLASTIC PRESS
NEW YORK

For Adam, my OTP and the
only person I would trust with
absolute magical power.

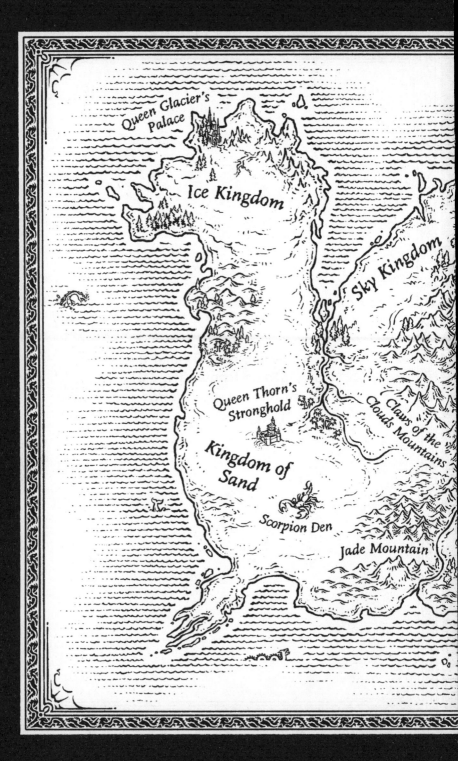

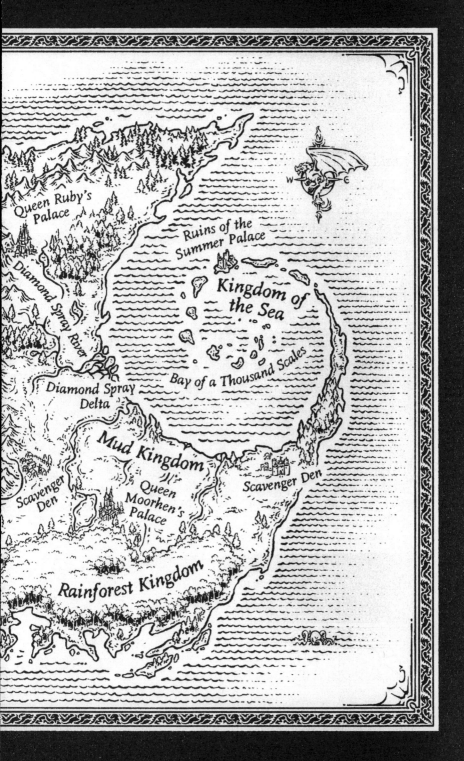

Ice Kingdom

Kingdom

A GUIDE TO THE
DRAGONS

Sand

Scorpion Den

Jade Mountain

OF PYRRHIA

UPDATED AND EDITED BY
STARFLIGHT OF THE NIGHTWINGS

WELCOME TO THE JADE MOUNTAIN ACADEMY!

At this school, you will be learning side by side with dragons from all the other tribes, so we wanted to give you some basic information that may be useful as you get to know one another.

You have been assigned to a winglet with six other dragons; the winglet groups are listed on the following page.

Thank you for being a part of this school. You are the hope of Pyrrhia's future. You are the dragons who can bring lasting peace to this world.

WE WISH YOU ALL THE POWER OF WINGS OF FIRE!

JADE WINGLET

IceWing: Winter
MudWing: Umber
NightWing: Moonwatcher
RainWing: Kinkajou
SandWing: Qibli
SeaWing: Turtle
SkyWing: Carnelian

GOLD WINGLET

IceWing: Icicle
MudWing: Sora
NightWing: Bigtail
RainWing: Tamarin
SandWing: Onyx
SeaWing: Pike
SkyWing: Flame

SILVER WINGLET

IceWing: Changbai
MudWing: Sepia
NightWing: Fearless
RainWing: Boto
SandWing: Ostrich
SeaWing: Anemone
SkyWing: Thrush

COPPER WINGLET

IceWing: Alba
MudWing: Marsh
NightWing: Mindreader
RainWing: Coconut
SandWing: Pronghorn
SeaWing: Snail
SkyWing: Peregrine

QUARTZ WINGLET

IceWing: Ermine
MudWing: Newt
NightWing: Mightyclaws
RainWing: Siamang
SandWing: Arid
SeaWing: Barracuda
SkyWing: Garnet

SANDWINGS

Description: pale gold or white scales the color of desert sand; poisonous barbed tail; forked black tongues

Abilities: can survive a long time without water, poison enemies with the tips of their tails like scorpions, bury themselves for camouflage in the desert sand, breathe fire

Queen: since the end of the War of SandWing Succession, Queen Thorn

Students at Jade Mountain: Arid, Onyx, Ostrich, Pronghorn, Qibli

MUDWINGS

Description: thick, armored brown scales, sometimes with amber and gold underscales; large, flat heads with nostrils on top of the snout

Abilities: can breathe fire (if warm enough), hold their breath for up to an hour, blend into large mud puddles; usually very strong

Queen: Queen Moorhen

Students at Jade Mountain: Marsh, Newt, Sepia, Sora, Umber

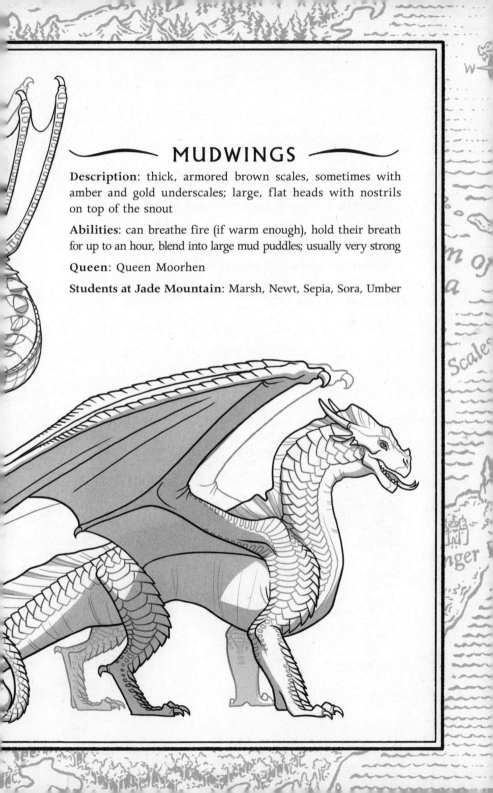

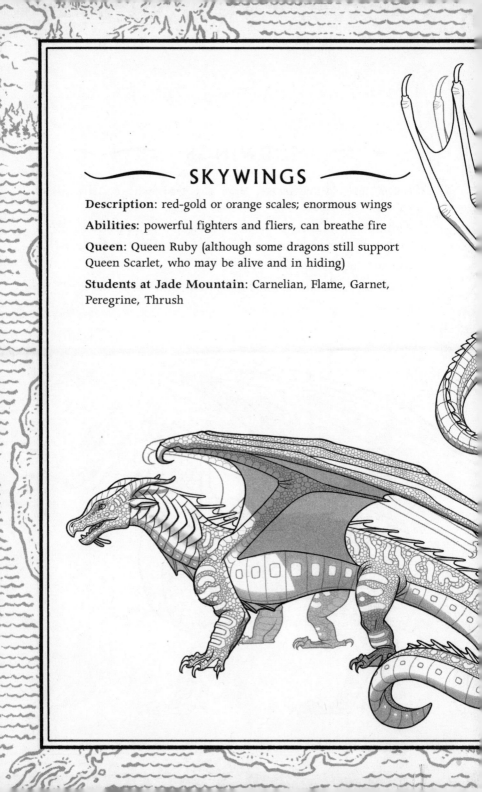

SKYWINGS

Description: red-gold or orange scales; enormous wings

Abilities: powerful fighters and fliers, can breathe fire

Queen: Queen Ruby (although some dragons still support Queen Scarlet, who may be alive and in hiding)

Students at Jade Mountain: Carnelian, Flame, Garnet, Peregrine, Thrush

SEAWINGS

Description: blue or green or aquamarine scales; webs between their claws; gills on their necks; glow-in-the-dark stripes on their tails/snouts/underbellies

Abilities: can breathe underwater, see in the dark, create huge waves with one splash of their powerful tails; excellent swimmers

Queen: Queen Coral

Students at Jade Mountain: Anemone, Barracuda, Pike, Snail, Turtle

ICEWINGS

Description: silvery scales like the moon or pale blue like ice; ridged claws to grip the ice; forked blue tongues; tails narrow to a whip-thin end

Abilities: can withstand subzero temperatures and bright light, exhale a deadly frostbreath

Queen: Queen Glacier

Students at Jade Mountain: Alba, Changbai, Ermine, Icicle, Winter

RAINWINGS

Description: scales constantly shift colors, usually bright like birds of paradise; prehensile tails

Abilities: can camouflage their scales to blend into their surroundings; shoot a deadly venom from their fangs

Queen: Queen Glory

Students at Jade Mountain: Boto, Coconut, Kinkajou, Siamang, Tamarin

─ NIGHTWINGS ─

Description: purplish-black scales and scattered silver scales on the underside of their wings, like a night sky full of stars; forked black tongues

Abilities: can breathe fire, disappear into dark shadows; once known for reading minds and foretelling the future, but no longer

Queen: Queen Glory (see recent scrolls on the NightWing Exodus and the RainWing Royal Challenge)

Students at Jade Mountain: Bigtail, Fearless, Mightyclaws, Mindreader, Moonwatcher

THE
JADE MOUNTAIN
PROPHECY

Beware the darkness of dragons,
Beware the stalker of dreams,
Beware the talons of power and fire,
Beware one who is not what she seems.

Something is coming to shake the earth,
Something is coming to scorch the ground.
Jade Mountain will fall beneath thunder and ice
Unless the lost city of night can be found.

PROLOGUE

Three Years Ago . . .

The Royal Hatchery was supposed to be a warm, safe, peaceful place for eggs to rest quietly until it was time to hatch.

It was not supposed to be a death trap that gave you the creeps.

"It's not a death trap!" Coral would protest whenever Gill brought this up. "SeaWing princesses and princes have been hatching there for thousands of years. *I* hatched there, and it was safe and beautiful. It's part of our heritage. It's a SeaWing tradition. There's nothing wrong with the hatchery — the problem is our useless guards."

"They're doing their best," Gill objected. "You can only expect so much of a dragon."

"I'm not expecting the three moons in a bowl," Coral growled. "All they have to do is *protect my eggs* until an heir hatches. WHY IS THAT SO HARD?"

Gill didn't know the answer to that. He didn't know why they'd lost six female eggs in the last five years. He didn't know how his other three daughters had died. Coral was sure there was an assassin in the palace, but Gill didn't understand who would want to kill so many little princesses.

His heart ached as he swam through the Deep Palace, thinking about all the dragonets they had lost. Coral was trying so hard to hatch an heir that she was having eggs every year now. The palaces were overflowing with all the sons who had survived the many hatchings. SeaWing princes were everywhere, to the point where an entire wing of the Deep Palace had been set aside for them to live in.

Gill tried hard to remember all their names and tell them apart — Coral didn't bother — but there were twenty-four of them already, plus three more waiting to hatch. He sometimes wished they didn't have the animus-touched balance that indicated male versus female eggs. He wondered if they were making it easier for the assassin, separating the eggs so clearly in the hatchery. But then he wondered if it didn't matter; without a way to tell them apart, perhaps the assassin would just have destroyed *all* the eggs.

His wings took him toward the hatchery, as they did all the time now, sometimes five times a day. So far Coral's latest plan had been working — it wouldn't be much longer before the eggs hatched, safe and sound. And then they could be taken out of the Royal Hatchery, which would be a relief to Gill . . . although, given what happened to the other princesses, he wasn't really sure they would be safe anywhere.

The new Council Chief of Dragonet Care was

nervous but dedicated. Abalone had a deputy chief to help him, and together they rotated in and out of the hatchery, so someone was watching the two princess eggs at every moment. Abalone and Snapper were two of Gill's most loyal soldiers; he had talonpicked them himself.

And yet, and yet . . . he couldn't stop checking on them. Just to be sure. Just to be safe.

He slid open the door and swam inside the dark, egg-shaped room. His wings fluttered in the bursts of warm water that bubbled through the hatchery, keeping it at the perfect temperature for the eggs.

Abalone? he flashed in Aquatic. It was very quiet. The marble statue of his daughter Orca loomed over the nests, watching over her future brothers and sisters. Gill wished the statue could protect them as fiercely as her face suggested. He wished Orca were still alive, so she could protect them herself.

But if she were alive, Coral would be dead. He shook his head. He would never understand why Orca challenged her mother for the throne at such a young age. If she had only waited . . . they could have had so many more years together as a family.

Unless the assassin killed her, too. He shivered and swam farther into the room.

Abalone was slumped over the nest with the two princess eggs in it, his wings covering them.

Abalone? Gill hurried over, worried. Abalone never slumped; he hardly ever even sat down. He was always on full alert, always a model soldier.

Gill shook his friend's shoulder. With a soft groan, Abalone sat up, and Gill realized that the council chief was a strange white color around his gills. His eyes were bloodshot and there were flecks of foam rising from his scales.

I'm sorry, Abalone flashed with the phosphorescent scales under his wings. *I've been waiting for someone to come. But I won't leave the eggs — I won't — they'll be safe, I promise.* He reached to cover them with his wings again and staggered sideways.

You're sick, said Gill, catching him before he could land on the eggs. *You shouldn't be here. I'll go get help.*

Yes — no! Abalone flashed. *Afraid I'll . . . drift off . . . everything spinning.*

Can you make it to the healing room on your own? Gill asked. *If I stay here to guard the eggs?*

Maybe. Abalone tried to paddle forward, shifting his wings, and instantly violent tremors shook his whole body. He gasped and curled into a small ball on the smooth floor of the hatchery.

All right, stay here. Watch the eggs and don't fall asleep. I'll grab someone and send for help. Gill swam to the door as fast as he could and powered up the ramp to the main floor of the palace.

Three little dragonets, all about two years old, were wrestling in the entrance hall, kicking and squeaking gleefully. Three of his sons, Gill realized — the ones from two hatchings ago. (There was only one female egg in that group, and she didn't even make it halfway through incubating, he remembered with a fresh stab of grief).

He flashed his scales at full brightness to get their attention. They turned toward him, blinking, and he flashed, *I need help. Who's going to help me?*

The princes glanced at one another nervously, and then one of them paddled forward a little bit.

Me! he flashed. *I'll do it, Father!*

Good, said Gill. *Thank you . . .* He hesitated.

Turtle, the dragonet flashed. *I'm Turtle.*

I know, Gill answered, although he hadn't been sure. *Turtle, this is very important. I need you to go find Snapper and send her to the Royal Hatchery. Tell her to hurry as fast as her wings can swim. Can you do that?*

Sure. Turtle nodded, his green eyes wide.

I'm counting on you, Turtle, Gill said, touching his son's shoulder. *It's really important. I know you can do this. I'll be waiting. All right?*

Yes, sir, Turtle answered, shivering a little.

Go, then. Hurry!

Turtle swam away toward the kitchens with what felt like agonizing slowness. Gill reminded himself that Turtle was a prince. He wouldn't fail. He'd find

Snapper, Abalone's deputy chief, who could watch the eggs while Gill took Abalone to the healing room.

Gill rushed back down to the hatchery. Abalone was still awake, crouched by the eggs with his front talons pinned across his chest. Gill realized with alarm that there was now a growth on Abalone's neck — a large, round lump that hadn't been there a few moments ago. He touched it lightly and Abalone flinched away. It was blazingly hot.

Gill had no idea what kind of disease this was. *Is it safe for him to be here? Could he infect the eggs?*

He needed to get Abalone out of the hatchery. For the safety of the eggs, but also because Abalone looked closer and closer to death every moment.

Hurry up, Turtle.

They waited in painful silence.

Was the growth getting bigger?

Turtle, where are you?

Come on, come on.

The lump *was* expanding, little by little, pushing Abalone's silvery blue scales into strange jagged shapes. It looked as if it might explode any moment now.

You'll be all right, Gill flashed at Abalone. *Help is coming.*

Help didn't come. Time crept by, dragging its long, long tail. Nobody came.

Abalone started making a low whimpering sound, ragged, like claws scrabbling up the inside of his throat. His gaze was fixed on the eggs and he kept his wings tucked in close to him, rocking softly.

Turtle, Gill thought with helpless fury. This was his own fault. What a useless command he'd given. He should have sent all three dragonets to find Snapper. No — he should have told them to find *any* other adult dragon, or to summon one of the healers. Or he should have swum straight to the healing chambers the moment he saw that Abalone was ill. Now he could see there would have been time to make it there and back with a healer. But with each moment that passed, Abalone looked closer and closer to collapse.

The truth was he should have done anything other than what he did. He'd made a terrible mistake.

But *where was Turtle?* Couldn't *he* figure out a smarter option, if he couldn't find Snapper?

Somebody come. Please, please, somebody . . .

Finally it became unbearable. Abalone would die if he didn't reach a healer soon — it might already be too late. Gill couldn't wait any longer.

Don't leave, Abalone flashed weakly as Gill moved toward the door.

I can't let you die like this, Gill flashed back. *Just stay awake until I get back.* He hesitated in the doorway, worrying. Abalone was no match for an assassin in this condition. But Gill would only be gone a short time — it would be truly uncanny terrible luck for the assassin to show up during those few moments.

He swam. He swam for Abalone's life, and his daughters'. He burst through the palace like a typhoon, swooping up to the healing chambers. His sons were gone from the main hallway; he saw no sign of Turtle or Snapper anywhere.

HELP, he flashed at full brightness as he reached the healing floor. Dragons came pouring into the hall, curious, and a flurry of bubbling gasps went up as he explained Abalone's condition to the healers. Three of them grabbed their kits and swam after him, back down, down, down to the Royal Hatchery.

They found Abalone unconscious, his wings drifting in the current of the jets. For a moment Gill thought his neck had been slashed; then he realized that the blood running down Abalone's scales came from the growth, which had burst.

The healers hurried toward him, then stopped, turning heartbroken faces to Gill.

No. Gill's scales flashed without him realizing it. *No. No.*

The two eggs had been crushed, apparently by huge, heavy talons. The dragonets inside were dead.

Two more lost princesses.

Gill roared his pain and fury, roared until his throat gave out, and then he whirled and swam away. He never wanted to see the Royal Hatchery again.

Find my son Turtle, he snarled at one of the gawking dragons in the hallway.

Upstairs, he saw a group of dragons approaching through the gardens — Queen Coral, returning from the Summer Palace and her meeting with Blister.

How could he tell her what had happened . . . what had happened *again*?

But she saw it on his face as he swam out the door toward her. She sank suddenly, as if a boulder had been dropped on her, touching down amid the coral and anemones. Her wings came forward and she covered her eyes with her talons. She didn't want to see him spell it out in Aquatic.

I'm sorry, he flashed anyway. *I'm sorry.*

She didn't move, didn't look up.

A movement caught Gill's eye and he turned. Some distance away, there was Turtle, swimming slowly through the garden of the wounded, peering at each recuperating dragon's face. His brothers were behind him, joking and laughing and shoving one another back and forth.

Gill tore across the gardens, seized Turtle's wing, and flung him around to face him.

WHERE HAVE YOU BEEN? Gill roared.

Turtle flinched and shielded his eyes from the intensity of Gill's scales. *I can't find her,* he flashed nervously. *I'm — I'm still looking.*

Out HERE? Gill waved his talons at the nearly empty section of the coral reef, where injured soldiers were taken to rest and recover surrounded by color and beauty. Gill wanted to rip that beauty to shreds; he wanted to tear apart the coral reef and kill all the creatures that lived on it.

Well, I — I couldn't find her in the palace so I — I didn't know where to look! I'm trying!

It's too late, Gill growled. *Your new sisters are dead, and it's your fault.*

Turtle blanched. *But — how — I didn't —*

You were too slow. Gill backed away, glaring at the other two princes, who were huddling behind an outcropping to watch with wide eyes.

I'm sorry. Turtle bowed his head, fiddling with a piece of coral in his claws. *I . . . I don't know what Snapper looks like. And nobody knew where she was —*

You shouldn't volunteer for things you're incapable of doing, Gill said harshly. *You shouldn't offer to help if you're going to be* useless.

I really tried, Turtle said, wringing his talons. *I really, really did. I promise, Daddy.*

You failed. Gill stared down at him. He felt a small pang of guilt at the crushing despair on the dragonet's face — but his anger was too strong to hold back right now.

I am very disappointed in you, he said.

Maybe one day he would forgive Turtle. Maybe one day he'd be able to think clearly again. Even now, he knew deep down that blaming a two-year-old dragonet for his own mistakes was wrong. One day, when his grief had subsided, maybe he could find the words to tell his son that.

But not today.

Gill turned away from Turtle's stricken face and swam back to Coral. She was watching him with vacant, sad eyes.

What did he do? she asked dimly.

I sent him for help, and instead he flapped around looking in all the wrong places and goofing off.

He's only a prince, she said. *What can you expect?* She reached out and seized one of Gill's talons. *The next one is going to live, Gill.*

Oh, Coral, he said. *Maybe we shouldn't —*

I'll stay with her this time, Coral said fiercely. *No one else can do it except me. I was right about our incompetent guards.*

It wasn't Abalone's fault, Gill protested.

Doesn't matter, she said, flicking a claw at the palace. *I sent word to have him and Snapper both executed.*

Coral! Gill cried, appalled. He tried to pull away, but she gripped his talons even tighter.

I'm going to keep our next daughter alive, Coral said. *I'll stay in the hatchery with the egg to keep it safe. But I need you to run the kingdom for me.*

I'll do anything, he promised sadly. He couldn't argue with her in this state, not right now.

I'll keep her by my side all the time. Her whole life, if I have to. Coral's eyes glowed, reflecting her scales as she spoke. *I'll never leave her alone. She's going to be perfect, Gill, you'll see.*

She glanced down at the spot where she had landed, at the sea anemones waving long, pinkish-blue tendrils over her claws.

And we're going to call her Anemone.

Ice Kingdom
Sky Kingdom
Queen Thorn's
Stronghold
Claws of the
Clouds Mountains
Kingdom of
Sand
Scorpion Den
Jade Mountain

PART ONE

A DRAGON AWAKES

CHAPTER 1

The nightmare rose out of the mountain, vast and glittering.

Turtle had never seen a dragon so large; he'd never seen eyes so sharp. He knew instantly that this dragon could and would happily kill him in a heartbeat.

Terror pounded through him like waves in a storm, building higher and higher.

I need to hide. I need to hide.

He desperately wanted to disappear, to vanish into the dark sky as if he'd never been there. He wished he could melt away like a camouflaged RainWing.

Why did I ever let anyone notice me? I'd be safe if I'd stayed boring and forgettable. This is what happens — when someone sees you, soon everyone will see you.

And one day that "everyone" will include a dragon who wants to kill you.

He couldn't have explained how he was so sure. Darkstalker was smiling at the dragonets below him. In fact, he looked absolutely delighted, not particularly murderous.

And yet — as his eyes darted past Turtle, Turtle thought he saw a flash of hatred there, deep and fierce.

For some reason, this legendary dragon, the most powerful NightWing who'd ever lived, loathed Turtle with all his heart. Turtle was sure of it.

He's going to kill me the first chance he gets.

This wasn't how he'd expected his story to end.

Turtle had always loved stories. He loved histories and animus tales and stories of war, of skyfaring pirates or enchanted treasure, of scavengers who could speak the language of dragons, of lost tribes in faraway lands.

But his favorite stories were about heroes — especially the ones in the scrolls his mother wrote. Since she was so busy with running the kingdom, writing her scrolls, and protecting her heirs, Queen Coral didn't have much time or interest to spare for any of her thirty-two sons. Reading her stories was as close as Turtle could ever get to her.

He loved scrolls about brave dragons who saved the day and stopped the forces of evil. One of his favorites was about a dragon named Indigo, who'd rescued the entire tribe from a deranged killer. Another starred an insignificant gardener named Droplet, who'd discovered a secret invasion of MudWings and fought them off before they found the hidden palaces.

The more Turtle read these stories, the more he imagined a story of his own: a story where Turtle was the hero.

A story where Turtle battled squadrons of SkyWings and storms of SandWings all on his own. A story where

Turtle stood at the gates of the palace and swung his spear in ferocious arcs, stabbing their enemies, as strong as a whale, while his older brothers and the rest of the tribe cowered inside.

A story that ended with his parents cheering and hugging him. And then his mother would write a scroll that was all about *him*.

Turtle the Strong and Mighty
Turtle: A Tale of a Hero Heroically Doing Hero-Type Things
How Turtle Saved the Entire Kingdom with His Awesomeness

Sometimes, when Turtle had a moment alone, or when he wasn't paying attention in class, he would secretly write pieces of this story on scraps of slate he kept hidden in his room. He dreamed that one day he'd have a whole manuscript to show his mother, and then she might say, "Oh, son, I know one of my daughters will run the kingdom eventually — but you are the true heir I've been waiting for: the next writer in the family."

A hero or a writer. Or both, why not? That would be Turtle's place in the world.

But then, too soon and disguised in a confusing shape, his chance came. His one opportunity to save the day and be a hero in his parents' eyes — but he didn't even know it until it was over, and he'd failed.

He failed, and they hated him, and he'd never get that chance again.

That night when he'd failed to find Snapper and save his unhatched sisters, Turtle destroyed every bit of writing he'd ever done and swore he would never write again. He'd stop dreaming; he'd stop imagining that a useless dragon like him could ever save the day or make something wonderful.

He wasn't the hero, and he wasn't the storyteller. He was the idiot who fell over his claws in the first chapter, had to be rescued in the fourth, nearly ruined the whole plan in the ninth, and ran away at the end, or died, if he was really extra stupid.

So he hid his one power and stayed exactly where he was supposed to: under the surface of the water, in the middle of his pack of brothers. Ordinary, unmemorable. A dragon nobody would expect anything from, and so nobody could ever be disappointed by him again.

And that had worked for quite a long time, until he made the mistake of caring about some other dragons and trying to do a couple of little things to help them, and where did that lead him?

Right to the feet of the most terrifying dragon the world had ever known.

This is the part where I die pointlessly. The one who gets sacrificed so the real heroes can get on with saving the day.

His wings were shaking so hard he couldn't stay in the air. He dropped down beside Moon and Qibli, clutching the ground with his talons. Winter and Peril were still hovering in the sky, their wings beating, silver and gold flashing in the moonlight.

I need to hide, Turtle thought. But how could anyone hide from the most dangerous dragon in the world — a mind reader, an animus, *and* a seer who knew the future?

He can't read my *mind, though.* Turtle's gaze dropped to the three remaining skyfire stones in his armband, which shielded him from mind readers. Maybe he had a millisecond to do something, anything, before Darkstalker foresaw it and stopped him.

He scrabbled his talons along the ground, keeping his eyes on the towering NightWing. His claws closed around something small and rough — a broken stick from one of the trees that had fallen when the mountain cracked open.

Hide me, Turtle thought at it frantically. *Hide me from Darkstalker.*

Darkstalker stretched his vast wings and grinned at Peril. "Ah, that's infinitely better," he said. "Nice to finally meet you, Peril. Thank you so much for your help."

Peril roared furiously and threw herself at him, claws outstretched and flames blazing from her mouth.

"Peril!" Moon shrieked as fire engulfed Darkstalker's face.

"Oh, no, no, no," Darkstalker said, waving away the smoke. He pressed one of his front talons into Peril's chest and held her at arm's length while she struggled and tried to bite him. "Peril, very brave, but tsk-tsk. First of all, I'm your friend, although I realize you're new to that whole concept. Second of all, invulnerable scales over here! Didn't you know that? Surely that detail came up at some point in the great scary legend of Darkstalker. There's nothing you can do to me, little firescales. So settle down and let's start over."

Peril fell back, breathing heavily and brushing at her scales where Darkstalker had touched her. The smoke rising from her wings twisted into the thin clouds in the sky overhead.

Turtle's heart was still pounding. Darkstalker turned toward Moon, and his eyes went right past Turtle as though the SeaWing prince was not there. But Turtle still didn't feel safe, not completely hidden, not yet.

Darkstalker paused with a slight frown. "Weren't there . . . more of you?" he asked, touching his temple. "Wasn't there someone I particularly wanted to see?"

Moon glanced around, confused.

"Particularly wanted to see" — *does he mean ME? I need a better spell,* Turtle thought in a panic. He gripped the stick harder. *As long as this stick is near me or touching me, I enchant it to hide my entire existence from Darkstalker. That means he cannot see me or hear me; he cannot remember that he's ever heard of me; he cannot hear about me in other people's minds or conversations; and he cannot see me anywhere in his futures. I enchant this stick to completely erase the dragon holding it from Darkstalker's awareness.*

The furrow disappeared from Darkstalker's forehead. "Moon!" he cried, beaming at her. "We're finally meeting!

Isn't this amazing? Wow, you're a lot smaller than I thought you'd be."

"That's you, actually," Qibli said, finally finding his voice. "You're . . . a lot bigger than you probably remember."

Darkstalker looked down at the ground, held out his talons, and flicked his massive tail, knocking a shower of boulders down the slope. He wasn't really as big as the entire mountain, although it had seemed that way to Turtle at first. But he was at least three times as big as the biggest full-grown dragons Turtle had ever seen.

"I really am," Darkstalker said, delighted. "Two thousand years of slowly growing. I must be the hugest dragon that ever lived. Also the oldest — by all the shining moons, I'm *ancient*, aren't I?"

"Beware the darkness of dragons," Moon said, taking a step back. "Beware the stalker of dreams . . ."

"Oh, that's not me!" Darkstalker said. "Moon, come on, you know that. I don't slither about in the dreams of other dragons, apart from fixing your nightmares. I'm guessing that part of the prophecy was about Queen Scarlet, who, you might remember, was chock-full of darkness. On the other talon, 'something is coming to shake the earth' — that's totally me! Watch this." He stomped one foot on the ground so hard that tremors shuddered out in all directions. Turtle stumbled, and the closest small tree fell over.

Darkstalker grinned at Moon. "Pretty impressive, right?" He paused, thinking. "I guess being this big is the upside of being alive for two thousand years, even if I slept through it all. BY THE CLAW-SHAPED MOONS, I am SO HUNGRY. Does anyone have any food?"

"How did you get out?" Winter demanded.

The look Darkstalker shot at Winter was as unfriendly as the one he'd given Turtle. *He doesn't like IceWings either,* Turtle realized.

But Darkstalker's answer was cordial. "Oh, that was all Peril here," he said, tapping the SkyWing on the head. Peril's blue eyes were blinking fast and her claws kept clenching and unclenching.

"When she set my scroll on fire," Darkstalker explained, "all my magic returned to me, so I could use it to free myself. Wasn't that kind of her?"

Peril's wings slumped. She looked as though she'd just rescued a baby dragonet from a trap only to watch it immediately get eaten by a great white shark.

Turtle wished he could make her feel better. He wanted to fly up and tell her this wasn't her fault, but his wings were still shaking too hard for him to take off. Also, he hadn't completely convinced himself that the magic was working. What if Darkstalker could see him, after all? He didn't want to draw the NightWing's attention, just in case.

"Wait," Moon said. "That means — you *lied* to me." She unfurled her wings and pointed at Darkstalker. "You told me to destroy the scroll if it looked like it would fall into evil talons. You made it sound like then you'd be trapped forever, but it would be worth it to protect everyone else. But you *wanted* me to destroy the scroll all along. You *knew* that would send your power back to you! You were tricking me!"

"Yes, that's true," said Darkstalker, "but lucky for me that I did, right? Otherwise you might never have freed me. Not very kind, Moon. I'd say I did the right thing." He looked at her without a smile for the first time, his eyes odd and glittering.

"You called us friends," Moon said in a low voice. "You shouldn't trick your friends."

"Yes, well, you also shouldn't leave your friends trapped under a mountain for the rest of their immortal lives," Darkstalker said briskly. "Good *point*, Darkstalker. Listen, I can't even talk anymore, I'm so hungry. Let's all catch something to eat and then you can show me around Jade Mountain! There are some dragons there I can't *wait* to meet." He lifted off into the air, then turned to beckon at Moon. "Come on, Moon! I just want to have friends again, to use my voice, to hunt and fly. Can't we save the 'oh, no, but you're so sinister and evil' talon-wringing for later? What do you say — give me a chance?"

Moon glanced at Qibli, looking torn.

"*I'm* not going with you," Peril said. "You're not the queen of me!"

"Me neither," said Winter. "The IceWings have legends about you. We know what you did to us. And I don't take orders from —"

"I'm not ordering you to do anything, Prince Winter,"

Darkstalker said, turning to look at Winter. The IceWing fell silent. "But I think you know that those old legends don't tell the whole truth. You know that a dragon should not be judged by what other dragons say about him. And the more time you spend with me, the more I think you'll find that I'm really an absolutely wonderful dragon." He smiled with all his teeth.

Winter touched his temples for a moment, then stared at Darkstalker with something new in his blue eyes.

"You're right," he said. "Let's start over."

"Winter?" Qibli said sharply. He darted into the sky and up beside Winter, brushing the silver dragon's wings with his own. "Are you all right?"

"Of course," said Winter. He tipped his head toward Darkstalker. "I am trying not to judge dragons too quickly anymore. Let's hear him out."

"That doesn't sound like the Winter I know," Qibli said to Moon. "Does this seem weird to you?"

"You don't know me *that* well," Winter objected, snorting a tiny cloud of ice crystals. "Dragons can change! *I've* changed. Maybe he has, too."

"Without question," Darkstalker said, nodding. "I've had a lot of time to think about my mistakes."

Qibli backed away from them, worry spilling across his face. "Moon . . ." he said carefully, as though he were reaching for the only island in a vast, empty sea. She flew up beside him, ducking her head to look into Winter's eyes.

"Did you do something to him?" Moon asked Darkstalker.

"Of course I didn't!" Darkstalker protested, and, "No! He didn't!" cried Winter at the same time.

"Darkstalker," Moon said. "You have to promise me — you cannot put spells on my friends."

"I'm *really* offended by this," Winter said haughtily. "I'm *such* an open-minded dragon."

Peril and Qibli snorted in unison.

"Moon," Darkstalker said reasonably. "I wouldn't waste my animus magic — and my soul — on some tiny hush-up-an-IceWing spell. I mean, seriously. Don't you remember the whole point of my scroll? That *I* made?"

"To keep your soul safe," Moon said hesitantly. She swooped around Winter, studying him. "But —"

"Stop worrying so much!" Darkstalker nudged her with one of his giant wings. "Boy, you remind me of someone I used to know. Can't you be excited for me? This is a great day! Let's go celebrate! Tell you what, I promise if I feel the need to use animus magic, I'll let you know."

"And you promise not to hurt my friends?" Moon asked.

Darkstalker sighed gustily, sending a hurricane of leaves swirling around Turtle's feet. "*I'm* hurt that you even need to ask me that," he said. "But of course. If it makes you feel better, I promise that these three are officially the safest dragons in Pyrrhia." He waved his talons at Qibli, Winter, and Peril.

Moon opened her mouth, then closed it. She and Qibli simultaneously looked down at Turtle.

Turtle crouched lower, pressing his underbelly into the ground, and shook his head at them.

"Let's hunt now, as Darkstalker suggests," Qibli said, nudging Moon, "and figure out what to do next after that." He shot a significant glance at Turtle.

Oh no. That glance had a meaning, a message. Qibli was expecting Turtle to do something, and Turtle had a bad feeling that "something" wasn't "Turtle flying all the way back to the Kingdom of the Sea, finding a deep trench, and staying there forever." A queasy, tense feeling started bubbling through Turtle's stomach.

"Good idea," said Winter.

Moon nodded, and then *she* gave Turtle a meaningful look, too.

By all the moons, what did they think he was going to do? Attack Darkstalker, like Peril had? Obviously that wouldn't work. If Peril couldn't hurt him, Turtle certainly wouldn't be able to.

Did they want him to hide them as well? He winced. He should have thought of that sooner. A good friend, a better dragon — a hero — would have thought to protect everyone instead of just hiding himself. *But they all wanted to talk to Darkstalker, didn't they? I just wanted to hide. That's what I always do.*

As the dragons flew away, veering southwest, Qibli twisted in a spiral, looked at Turtle again, and flicked his tail in the direction of Jade Mountain.

Oh, Turtle realized. *They want me to go warn the school.*

I can probably do that without messing it up.

I think.

For a moment, Peril hovered mutinously in the sky behind them, and then she swooped down to Turtle.

"Aren't you coming, too?" she asked. "Don't we all have to follow his grand mighty lordship SinisterFace?"

Turtle shook his head and held out the stick. "He can't see me," he whispered. "I hid myself from him."

Peril's face lit up. "Of course!" she said. "That's awesome! You have animus magic! *You* can kill him!"

"Oh," said Turtle, flustered. "No, I — I don't really — kill anyone." A brief flash of scales and blood darted through his mind, and when he looked down, he saw his claws curling dangerously. He jumped and shook them out until they looked like his own talons again. "That's not my thing," he said, tamping down a wave of panic.

"I know, I know, it's my thing," Peril said, "but I *can't* kill him, because of his *stupid* magic, GROWL. So you have to. Don't worry, it's not that hard, and it would be such a relief — for me, I mean — because I'm having this feeling — I don't know what to call it, but it's kind of big and heavy and annoying? And it's filling me all up inside like everything is awful and it's all my fault? Like maybe all the bad things in the world are my fault? I really don't like it, so if you can make it stop, that would be the greatest."

"I think what you're describing is what we call guilt," said Turtle, "but it's not your fault he tricked us. I still think you did the right thing, burning the scroll."

"Well, thanks, but the universe disagrees with you," Peril said, jerking her head at the enormous crack in the side of the mountain.

"Peril!" called one of the dragons in the distance.

"Good luck," Peril whispered. "Make it something really cool, like his insides exploding. Or his face falling off. I'm kidding! I'm a little bit kidding. I mean, insides exploding would be pretty cool, right? Never mind, it's up to you! Destroy him and save the world! Three moons, I wish I could do it!" She took off and flashed away, fast as a firework.

Turtle shivered.

Save the world?

That's not my thing either. I would definitely mess it up. That's way, way too much pressure.

I'm clearly not a hero.

He raised his eyes to the shadowy peaks of Jade Mountain.

But I know where I can find some.

CHAPTER 2

The sun was starting to sneak over the mountains, nervously spilling little beams around the peaks as if it were making sure Darkstalker was gone. Clouds were visible in the north, with the gray haze of distant rain below them, but Jade Mountain was still dry and clear and sunlit.

Turtle tucked the broken stick — knobbly and half-stripped of its bark, the most ordinary, insignificant-looking thing in the world — carefully into the pouch around his neck. He tied the pouch shut twice as tightly as usual and put his front claws over it as it rested on his chest. Anxiety twisted inside him.

I'd better not lose this.

He'd lost other animus-touched objects before. It was a little embarrassing, actually. When he was three, his (many, many) older brothers used to make fun of him for being the slowest SeaWing prince in the ocean. "Guess somebody gave *you* the right name, ha ha!" "Careful, or a clownfish will catch you!" "You swim like a sea cucumber!"

So Turtle had enchanted a strand of purple kelp, wound three times around his upper arm, to make him just a bit faster than some of his brothers. He couldn't make himself the fastest — that would attract attention. Attention was the last thing he wanted. But he could be faster than the other two from his hatching, Octopus and Cerulean. He could be a tiny bit faster than a couple of the four-year-olds, and that's where he'd stop. Then he'd be nothing remarkable, and his brothers would move on to teasing someone else.

It worked — they got bored and left him alone after a couple more races. But he still wished he hadn't lost the kelp a few weeks later; it drifted off in his sleep one night, and he often wondered if there was a startled sea horse tangled up in it somewhere out there, speeding along the ocean floor.

He knew he should be smarter about what he enchanted — he should pick things he couldn't lose, things that would last a while. But usually he didn't spend enough time thinking about his spells beforehand to plan them that carefully. His spells were all so little, just small magic to make his life easier, and he generally used whatever he could grab with his claws when he needed one.

Like the very ordinary-looking river stone in his pouch, bumping along with the stick. It could heal surface wounds and aches and pains, and he'd enchanted it to make himself feel better after a long day of flying. But it was a silly thing to enchant; Peril was right about that. If he ever lost it, he'd never find it again. Same with this stick . . . so he had to be careful.

He flew toward the main entrance of Jade Mountain, where he had landed on his first day as a new student. He remembered how excited he had been. A new school! Nobody knew him here. It was the perfect place to be a background character in other dragons' stories. No one would expect anything of him. He'd be far away from Octopus and Cerulean, who knew about his biggest failure and surely must think about it all the time, even if they never mentioned it.

Here he could blend in, be ordinary . . . and keep an eye on his little sister Anemone, who had been acting strangely ever since the attack on the Summer Palace.

None of that had quite worked out the way he'd planned. It was his own fault. If he hadn't chased after the other dragons in his winglet, he could be sound asleep with the rest of the SeaWing students right now.

A splash and a peal of laughter caught his attention, and he soared over Jade Mountain, following the sound to an opening in the roof of a cave.

Down there was the underground lake — and there were dragons swimming in it even now, at the crack of dawn. Turtle never woke up early if he could help it. But Anemone was often up at sunrise, which meant one of those swimming dragons might be her.

I should warn her — her more than anyone.

He tucked his wings into a dive and arrowed through the hole, but he somewhat misjudged his speed, and ended up smacking into the cold lake like a hippo dropped from a great height.

"Yow!" he yelped, surfacing and rubbing his eyes, his scales stinging from the shock.

"Turtle?" said a voice nearby. "Turtle! You're back!" Wet wings were flung around his shoulders, dunking him underwater in a cascade of bubbles. Anemone's glow-in-the-dark scales flashed happily at him in Aquatic as she dragged him up into the air again.

"Hi," he sputtered at his sister.

"Hey! You nearly landed on the princess!" Pike shouted in his ear. The skinny gray-blue SeaWing had always been a little louder and more aggressive than Turtle thought was strictly necessary. But he'd been much worse since they'd arrived at Jade Mountain Academy, thanks to some secret instructions from Queen Coral. Turtle knew from eavesdropping that Pike was here specifically to be a covert bodyguard for Princess Anemone.

Anemone, of course, had no idea. She never seemed surprised that Pike was so easy to boss around. In her mind, that was how all SeaWings were supposed to behave around her.

"Oh, shush, I'm fine." Anemone splashed water up Pike's snout and he backed off, shaking his head irritably. "Turtle, where have you been? I had the weirdest nightmare just before I woke up — I thought there was an earthquake, but nobody else felt it. Did you find your winglet? Are they here, too?"

Turtle seized her front claws in his. "Anemone, I need to talk to you."

"You *are* talking to me, fishface," she said. "Did you find the RainWing you were moping about?"

"You mean Kinkajou?" A little RainWing was sitting in the shallows of the lake, tilting her ears toward them. Her scales were spiraling pale peach and citrus green, except where they were covered by swathes of bandages and streaks of black scorch marks. A poultice of damp leaves was tied over her eyes. "Is Kinkajou all right?"

"I'm sure she's absolutely fine, Tamarin," Pike said kindly. He jabbed Turtle in the shoulder with one claw, much less kindly, and jerked his head toward Tamarin, scowling.

Turtle hesitated. The last time he'd seen Kinkajou, she was lying in a hospital bed in the town of Possibility, unconscious. Her usually bright, shifting rainbow scales had turned white and still. She had hardly looked like Kinkajou at all.

But how could he say that to her best friend — to Tamarin, who was suffering from her own injuries after the explosion that rocked Jade Mountain Academy?

"She was alive when I saw her a few days ago," he hedged. "I'm sure she'll come back to Jade Mountain just as soon as she can."

If it's still here when she wakes up.

"Oh," Tamarin said softly. "Good."

."Anemone," Turtle said. "Come flying with me?"

"You are being such a jellyfish right now," Anemone sighed. "I don't *want* to fly; I want to swim. Can't you just say whatever it is right here? Pike and Tamarin won't care."

Oh, they might, thought Turtle. But he could see that Anemone wasn't moving. This was Anemone's new stubborn, petulant personality, the princess who'd risen to the surface after she was cut free from Mother's harness. This Anemone made him feel nervous.

This Anemone made him feel guilty.

"All right, fine," he said. "You're in danger, and you need to leave Jade Mountain right now."

"What danger?" Pike barked, swiveling his head to glare around the dark cave.

"And go where?" Anemone demanded. "Home? Back to harnesses and boredom and Mother staring at me all the time? No, thank you, I'm staying here." She scrambled up on one of the boulders that jutted out of the water and coiled her tail around her talons.

"But there's a big, scary dragon coming," Turtle protested.

Anemone looked archly down her snout at Turtle. "Who *are* you talking about?" she asked. "I thought our illustrious teachers defeated all the bad dragons."

"This is a new one." Turtle glanced anxiously up at the sky above them, which was shifting closer and closer to full daylight. "His name is Darkstalker and he's been trapped underground for two thousand years and he just escaped — I don't really understand the whole story, but I know he's a mind reader and an animus and he *seems* nice on the surface but —"

"An animus!" Anemone cried, interrupting him. She stood up, flaring her wings. "Really? A real animus?"

"Yes," Turtle said cautiously. "But a *bad* one, like Albatross."

"Oh, how would you know?" Anemone scoffed. "I've been dying to meet another animus! I visited the old fossil living in this mountain and he was *useless*. His great helpful advice was that an animus dragon should never use her power. I mean, come on! He was all, 'but look what happened to meeeeeee,' wheeze moan glug, and I wanted to be like, 'didn't you put this dopey stone-scales spell on yourself? What use is your perfect soul if you can't move a muscle?' So pathetic. If there's a *real* animus coming here, I want to meet him!"

"No!" Turtle protested. "He'll probably kill you! He's really smart! He'll see another animus dragon as a threat!"

"If he's really smart, he'll see that I'm awesome and want to get to know me," Anemone said, tossing her head.

"Princess, I think your brother is right," Pike interjected. "This sounds like a dangerous situation. You should hide while I assess this stranger."

"What?!" Anemone threw her wings up in disbelief. "I'm not going to hide like some kind of nervous shrimp! Three moons. Turtle, did you actually see him kill anyone?"

"No, but according to history he killed his dad and —"

"'According to history,'" she said dismissively. "Has he hurt anyone since he 'escaped'?"

"No — but he probably will — he doesn't like IceWings and he doesn't like me."

"Well, I'm not an IceWing, and I'm not the most boring prince on the planet," she said, "so I think he'll like me just fine. Pike, shut up." Pike closed his mouth and ducked his head. Anemone clapped her front talons together. "This is so exciting! Another animus to talk to!"

Guilt wormed through Turtle's heart again. He had thought about telling his sister his secret a hundred times. If he had ever admitted that he was a fellow animus . . . would she be more willing to listen to him?

Should he tell her now? Would that stop her from wanting to meet Darkstalker?

Probably not.

And to tell her in front of Pike and Tamarin . . . it just didn't seem like a good idea. Pike was one of Queen Coral's most loyal followers; he'd definitely report back to her the first chance he got. Even Anemone . . . would she keep his secret?

He wasn't ready. Better to stay hidden and keep quiet. Safer that way.

Anemone dove off her rock and paddled to the tunnel that led back to the school. "Last one to the main hall is a rotten oyster!" she called, galloping away into the dark.

Pike hissed softly, twisting between the disappearing princess and the injured RainWing by the lake.

"It's all right, Pike," Tamarin said. She waded out of the water, limping, and rested one talon lightly on the wall. "I can find my way back to the infirmary on my own."

"Can you go with her?" Pike asked Turtle. He was halfway to the tunnel already. "Make sure she gets safely to the infirmary?"

"I can *take care of myself*," Tamarin said through gritted teeth, limping another few steps.

Turtle nodded, and Pike leaped out of the lake to run after Anemone.

"I know you two were making secret faces at each other," Tamarin said as Turtle climbed out of the lake beside her. "I don't like it when dragons do that around me."

"Sorry," Turtle said. "I was only responding to *his* secret faces."

"So is Kinkajou really all right, or were his faces making you lie to me?" she asked. She set off toward the tunnel, stepping cautiously but confidently along the rocky lakeshore.

Turtle winced. "She did get hurt," he admitted, following her. "Pretty badly — she's still unconscious, as far as I know. But the doctors in Possibility thought she'd be all right, if she wakes up soon."

"Oh, poor Kinkajou!" Tamarin cried. She stopped and pressed her talons to her face. "I knew it was too dangerous for her out there. She's always running straight at the bad things instead of hiding, or at least *thinking* first."

That's true, Turtle realized. That was one of the things he liked about Kinkajou . . . that she was nothing like him.

"Queen Glory sent RainWing healers to watch over her," he said. "She's not alone."

"I wish I could go to her," Tamarin said with a sigh. She set off along the main passageway. After a moment, she said quietly, "I didn't know Anemone was an animus."

Turtle felt like an idiot. He'd been so worried about hiding his own powers, he'd forgotten that Anemone's were supposed to be kept secret, too. "The other tribes aren't supposed to know," he said. "Tsunami's friends do, but they swore not to tell anyone."

"I won't say anything," Tamarin promised. "That must be hard on Anemone, keeping a secret like that."

"I guess," Turtle said uncomfortably. He'd been keeping the same secret his whole life, but from everyone. Was it hard? Maybe sometimes — like whenever something happened that he knew his magic could fix, but he had to go ahead and leave it broken.

Like Tamarin's eyes. *I could fix them. I could do it right now . . . I could enchant that bandage so when she takes it off, she could see for the first time in her life.* That was the kind of thing he wished he was free to do, and it felt awful to have to stop himself.

But he still figured it was a lot easier to be a secret animus than an animus everyone knew about.

"I wouldn't want to be an animus," Tamarin said. She paused at a spot where the tunnel branched into three directions. "I don't know how anyone could stay a good dragon with all that power."

"What if they only used it for good things?" Turtle asked, a little stung.

"But who gets to decide what's a good thing?" Tamarin asked. "Dragons would always be asking for spells, or telling you your choices are wrong. And I think sometimes it's hard to tell what's good and what's just easy."

Turtle gave her a puzzled look. "Aren't those the same? What's wrong with trying to make life easier?"

"It depends," Tamarin said. "For instance, an animus dragon might think, *I'll make all our medicinal herbs appear magically in the healers' treehouse, so we never have to go looking for them again.* That seems obviously good, right? But then we'd stop learning how to look for them, and we'd stop experimenting with new ones to see how those might help dragons in different ways. We'd stop thinking about it at all, because everything would be too easy. Don't we lose something when everything is done for us?"

Turtle blinked at her, confused. "I thought RainWings were all lazy," he said. "I thought your lives *were* easy and you liked them that way."

"Not mine," Tamarin said, gesturing to her eyes. "Not Kinkajou. Maybe we're a little different from the others." She shrugged. "Anyway, I can see why Anemone wants another animus to talk to about it."

"Right," said Turtle. His thoughts had snagged on Kinkajou and how she wasn't anything like the RainWings he'd read about in Mother's stories. He hadn't thought about that before, because he didn't think *RainWing* when he saw her; he only thought *Kinkajou*.

"I'm really fine from here," said Tamarin, flicking her tail at one of the side tunnels. "You go find Clay or Tsunami with your news." She strode off to the left, limping as fast as she could, as if she wanted to prove she didn't need help.

Turtle took the path all the way to the right, winding up through the mountain toward the Great Hall. Halfway there, he heard voices coming from one of the caves.

Instinctively, he slowed down and snuck closer on quiet talons. He'd always been good at eavesdropping. It made his life easier, knowing what other dragons whispered about behind closed doors. He'd avoided several palace scandals and feuds that way.

This might be the kind of thing Tamarin is talking about, he realized uncomfortably. *A way I make my life easier that's not exactly "good."*

"Mother feels terrible," said one of the voices quietly. "She can't figure out how they escaped."

"Can she trust her guards?" asked another voice, which Turtle recognized as his sister Tsunami. "Maybe she needs to replace them all with Outclaws — everyone knows their undying loyalty to Thorn."

"But she needs her best Outclaws in other parts of the kingdom," said the first voice. *That must be Sunny,* Turtle realized. "There was an explosion at one of our western oases a couple of days ago. Two dragons were killed, and we have no idea why."

"Was it one of those viper-licking cactus bombs like the one here?" asked Tsunami, growling.

"Seems like it." Sunny sighed. "But it makes no sense that a SkyWing would be out that far west or targeting these dragons. Anyway, Mother has enough problems, and now she's worried that Glory will be mad at her. She won't be, right? Glory knows how tough it is being a new queen."

"Of course," said Tsunami. "On the other talon, Thorn *did* promise to hang on to those prisoners for her. And who knows *what* they'll do now that they've escaped. I bet they'll go try to kill Glory. Or you! They hate you, too, don't they?"

"See, this is why I come to you with my problems," Sunny said. "Because you're always so comforting."

"I can make a stab at comforting!" Tsunami joked. "Let me try . . . um . . . hey, it's only two dragons, right? Ah, they won't be able to do anything. Deathbringer will totally stop them if they go anywhere near her. I mean, that is his entire purpose in life, as far as I can tell. And if they kill *him*, Glory will take them down with her magical death spit. So don't worry, pat pat pat."

"Hmmm," said Sunny. "That was very . . . stabby comforting."

There was the scrape of claws against rock, and Turtle realized they were coming toward the cave entrance. He backed up to act as though he was walking along the corridor when the two dragons emerged.

"Turtle!" Tsunami's face lit up with such delight that he felt ashamed of spying on her. "By all the moons,

Sunny, look — a student from the Jade Winglet is actually HERE! At SCHOOL, where they're SUPPOSED to be! What a glorious honor. Is it my hatching day? Or am I hallucinating?"

"All right, enough sarcasm," Sunny said, elbowing her in the chest. "Turtle, we've been really worried! Is everyone else back, too?"

"Well . . . they're coming," he said. "I'm here to warn you — they're coming with someone else. Maybe a bad someone else. Have either of you ever heard of Darkstalker?"

Sunny jumped and gave him a startled look. "I have! When I was chasing Fierceteeth and the others — I heard them talking about this ancient NightWing legend, a dragon called Darkstalker. They were *crazy* scared of him, like he might actually be hunting them right that minute even though he died, like, centuries ago."

"Um. So. That's the thing," said Turtle. "He didn't so much . . . exactly die."

"What?" Tsunami demanded, lashing her tail.

"He's woken up," Turtle said. "And he's on his way here right now."

There was a gasp from farther up the tunnel. They all turned and found a NightWing dragonet standing there, staring at Turtle, with his face contorted in terror.

CHAPTER 3

"Mightyclaws," Sunny said, holding out her talons. "Wait, don't overreact. We don't even know —"

"I have to warn the others!" he cried. He bolted up the tunnel toward the main hall.

"Oh, good," said Tsunami. "School-wide panic. We haven't had any of that in at least two days."

"Mightyclaws!" Sunny called, running after him. "Wait!"

"Tell me everything," Tsunami said to Turtle. He hurried to keep up with her as they strode along the winding stone tunnel. The violet and rose glass lights overhead reflected off her thoughtful expression.

He didn't tell her *everything*. He didn't tell her about his own magic. He sort of skimmed over the part where he hid from Darkstalker, implying that tall bushes and fallen trees were involved. But he had to tell her about Moon's powers, although he felt as though that should have been Moon's secret to share. Still, there was no other way to explain the prophecy and how Moon had been communicating with Darkstalker.

"Arrgh, *no*," Tsunami said, sweeping her tail across the floor. "More powers and prophecies? Seriously? I thought we were all done with that!"

Turtle had told Sunny about Moon's prophecy before, after his winglet left, but he'd left it up to her to decide who else to tell. Apparently Tsunami hadn't been on that list.

"I hate prophecies," Tsunami muttered darkly. "All cryptic and demanding. Most useless way to communicate in the history of the world. Is Darkstalker as terrifying as he sounds? That NightWing student looked like he'd just been bitten by a ghost shark."

"He scared *me*," Turtle admitted. He felt a little better now, here in Tsunami's shadow. The dragonets of destiny could deal with Darkstalker. He didn't have to do anything. He could leave saving the world in their talons.

"Let's swing by the library and ask for a lecture," Tsunami said, grinning at Turtle. "It'll make Starflight's day."

They took another branch of the tunnel and soon came to the wide, open cave lined with scrolls. One of the leaf windows had been torn apart when Icicle leaped out of it, and it still hadn't been fixed, allowing a burst of bright sunbeams to cut across the otherwise cool green light. Starflight was behind his desk with Fatespeaker, nudging scrolls into three different piles. His forehead was creased with worry, as it often was.

Turtle liked Starflight. He was quiet, and better yet, he let other dragons be quiet. After the rest of Jade Winglet left the school, Turtle would often sit in the library by himself, and Starflight never asked questions or made him talk.

"Hey, Starflight." Tsunami tapped the desk lightly so the blind librarian would know where she was. "Don't explode with joy or anything, but I have a historical question for you."

"Really?" Starflight's face lit up, turning toward the sound of her talons. "Which era?"

"I have no idea," Tsunami snorted. "Is there an Era of Sinister Bad Guys? What do you know about a dragon called Darkstalker?"

Something clattered to the floor across the room, and Turtle realized there was a trio of IceWings studying over by the windows. They'd dropped their scroll when they heard Tsunami's question, and now they were leaning toward Starflight with sharp, curious expressions.

"He was a very powerful animus NightWing who disappeared over two thousand years ago," Starflight said cautiously. "The stories say he was betrayed by his friend, a SeaWing animus named Fathom, and perhaps also by his girlfriend, Clearsight. But nobody knows exactly what happened to him."

"He didn't really disappear," said one of the IceWings. "He spent years lurking in the shadows and killing IceWings."

"And you're leaving out the part about him killing his own father," said another IceWing, flicking her wings back. "Who was an IceWing prince, *by the way.*"

"Whoa, really?" Tsunami said, giving Turtle a worried look.

"That story has been highly oversimplified," said Darkstalker, poking his head in through the broken window. "I mean, don't *any* of the scrolls mention that he totally deserved it?"

The IceWings shrieked in unison, loud enough to break glass. They scrambled over one another to get away from the oversized NightWing, knocking down an entire shelf of scrolls in the process. Paper unfurled across the cave in cascading fountains.

Turtle froze, trying to sink into the floor. How had Darkstalker gotten here so fast? Was he already done hunting? Where were Turtle's friends?

"What's happening?" Starflight cried. "Who was that?"

"A really, really, *really* big NightWing," Fatespeaker yelped, clutching his arm. "I haven't had any visions about this! This seems seriously vision-worthy! Powers, help me out!" She closed her eyes. "Oh, no! I see . . . darkness ahead!"

"That's because you have your eyes closed, you ninny," Darkstalker said pleasantly.

"Who are you?" Tsunami demanded.

"You already know," he said, startled. "This is amazing. How in Pyrrhia did you know I was coming?" He paused. "I can't even find the answer to that in your mind. What in the world? A fascinating mystery."

Don't think about it too hard, Turtle prayed. *Don't figure out there's a secret to uncover here.*

"So you *are* Darkstalker." Tsunami lashed her tail. "You'd better not hurt any of my students."

"What?" Starflight sputtered. "Darkstalker? How?"

"Why would I hurt any of your students?" Darkstalker protested. "There's literally zero motivation for me to do that. Dragons today, so full of mistrust and hostility. Now, in *my* time — no, wait, we were exactly the same." He poked at the ragged green edges of the leaf windowpane. "That's one of the many problems I was going to fix."

"It's the Darkstalker!" shouted one of the IceWings. "Die, you monster!" She leaped across the cave, blasting frostbreath in Darkstalker's face, landed in a roll right in front of his snout, and slashed her serrated claws across his nose.

All of which, of course, did nothing to him. The IceWing staggered back, shaking her arm as if she'd just smashed it into a rock.

Darkstalker gave her a bored look, then reached one of his long talons through the window and casually pinned her to the floor.

"All right," he said. "*Now* I'm a little motivated to hurt somebody."

Tsunami started toward him and he chuckled. "Oh, I won't," he said. "I promise! No need to get all ferocious with me, Tsunami. But you might want to add a manners class to your curriculum. Or is it fine with you if your students attack innocent visitors?"

"Let her go," Tsunami growled.

Darkstalker lifted his claws and the IceWing scrambled away. All three ice dragons bolted out of the cave as fast as they could run.

"I don't think I'll fit through the tunnels to get in here," Darkstalker said regretfully, glancing around the library. "But I love what you've done with the space, Starflight. Could you please bring any scrolls you have about Clearsight and meet me in the main entrance hall?"

"Scrolls about Clearsight?" Starflight echoed. "Your, uh — the dragon you —"

"Yes," said Darkstalker. "The dragon I loved. Specifically about what happened to her after . . . well, after our . . . unfortunate misunderstanding."

"But nobody knows," Starflight blurted. "She disappeared at the same time you did."

"Maybe there's a clue somewhere," Darkstalker said. "You're a terrific librarian. If anyone can find it, you can." His eyes narrowed. "Perhaps it would also be useful to bring any scrolls about what happened to Fathom."

"I — I —" Starflight stammered, moving his claws along the desk. Fatespeaker grabbed one of his talons and leaned in to him.

"Thanks ever so much," said Darkstalker. "Now, if you'll excuse me, someone is trying to attack my tail." He swung his head out the window and Turtle heard him say,

"Seriously? You too? Does everyone believe everything they read these days?"

Tsunami hurried over to the window. Turtle managed to breathe again, managed to move one foot slowly in front of the other to follow her.

Outside, two small NightWings were dive-bombing Darkstalker, shooting trails of flame across his scales. Turtle saw his friends hovering in the sky not far away. Moon was trying to call to the NightWings, but they weren't listening to her.

Darkstalker lifted off from the mountainside and turned in a large, slow circle, watching the NightWings without fighting back. He looked faintly amused.

"Tiny dragons," he boomed. "Listen, I'm impressed, but this *really* isn't necessary."

"We're not going to let you hurt our tribe!" shouted one of the dragonets. It was hard to tell from a distance, but Turtle thought that was Mightyclaws.

"By the shining moons, I'm not planning to hurt the tribe," said Darkstalker. "It's my tribe, too, isn't it? I'm a loyal NightWing. Don't the stories ever mention that? Come on now, NightWings are usually so clever; you must have noticed this isn't working." He caught Mightyclaws gently in his talons and set him on a ledge.

The other NightWing darted in and wrapped herself around Darkstalker's neck, trying to plunge her claws in between the scales of his underbelly.

"I don't mean the attack itself," Darkstalker went on, as if he barely noticed his new violent scarf. "Although that's not working either. I mean the distraction. It's not actually possible to distract me, because, guess what, mind reading! Plus also visions of the future. But good try." He whipped around, dove toward the forest, and emerged a moment later with a third NightWing dragonet struggling between his talons.

"No, no." Darkstalker shook his head at her. "Listen, I understand; if I were you, I'd want to sneak off and warn the rest of the tribe, too. But you know what they'll do then? I do; I saw it in a vision. They'll run away and try to hide from me again! Without even giving me a chance to introduce myself."

"We know all about you!" Mightyclaws yelled. "We know you've been trying to break free for two thousand years so you can get revenge on our tribe!"

"That makes no sense," Darkstalker said reasonably. "I did just escape a two-thousand-year trap, but the *tribe* didn't deceive me and stick me underground. That was two foolish dragons, using magic — it was nothing to do with the other NightWings. I adore my tribe. I'm wildly excited to rejoin you and let everyone see the real me."

He set down the NightWing next to Mightyclaws and unwrapped the other one from his neck as though she were a harmless sloth. "So we're not going to ruin the surprise, all right? We can all go together to tell the tribe I'm back. Trust me, it'll be great! Much less bloody and horrifying than what you all have in your minds. More . . . feasting and rainbows! Hang on, where did that come from? Ah, I know."

Darkstalker turned toward the landing area that led to the main school entrance. Clay and Sunny stood there, both of them breathing heavily, as though they'd been running.

"Feasting," Darkstalker said, pointing at Clay. "And rainbows." He pointed at Sunny and grinned.

"Step. Away. From my students," Sunny hissed.

"Sunny!" Darkstalker cried with enormous delight. He swooped down to land facing her. "You're so tiny for such a shaker of worlds! Don't you know who I am?"

"I do. You're the Darkstalker," she said.

"It's just Darkstalker," he corrected her. "Not sure where this 'the' came from. That makes me sound like some kind of lurking kraken-type monster."

Clay cleared his throat. "Isn't that, um . . . kind of what you are?"

"Not at all," Darkstalker said with a laugh. "Sunny! Get this. I'm your great-great-great-great-great-okay-I'm-losing-count-many-greats-great-uncle!" He bowed. "Surprise! More funny-looking family for you." He spread his wings and Turtle realized he had a line of silvery scales against the black, along the curve under his wings where they met his body. *Those must be from his IceWing father.*

Sunny hesitated, glancing around at all the listening dragons lit by the pink-orange sunrise sky. The three NightWings stood close together on the ledge where Darkstalker had put them, shivering but unharmed. Overhead, the sunlight glinted off the scales of Turtle's companions: Winter's bright white, Qibli's pale yellow, and Peril's fiery copper.

Moon landed beside Sunny, and they brushed wings for a moment, each reassuring the other silently.

Turtle wished he could read minds like Moon did. What did Sunny think of Darkstalker? She'd obviously prepared to defend her students from a monster, only to find a charming relative instead. Beside him in the library window, Tsunami was lashing her tail as though she couldn't decide whether to go out and attack him or not.

"Uncle?" Sunny asked Darkstalker. "Really?"

"Great-Uncle Darkstalker." The huge NightWing shook his head, chuckling. "That sounds SO weird. Like I'm a thousand years old — I mean, I know I'm technically ancient, but I sure don't feel that way. Did Whiteout end up marrying that glassblowing dragon with the spectacles? I'll have to ask Starflight; I bet he knows. Sunny, you have my sister's eyes. Hers were bluer, of course, not so green, but the same shape. You would have loved her."

"How can you say that?" Sunny asked. "You don't know me."

"Of course I do," said Darkstalker. "I can read your mind and see your futures, remember? I woke up several months ago to find myself under a mountain and twenty centuries older than I was when my friends betrayed me. Since then I've had nothing to do except read all your minds and dream of freedom."

"All our minds?" Clay asked. "That's kind of . . . nosy, isn't it?"

"Literally nothing else to do," Darkstalker said apologetically. "But don't worry, Clay, your thoughts are all very sweet. Especially when it comes to *certain* dragons." He winked, and Clay managed to look embarrassed, alarmed, and confused all at the same time.

"But wait, what makes you think we're related?" Sunny asked.

"Your father's a NightWing animus," Darkstalker pointed out. "So he must be descended from me or Whiteout, and I know *I* didn't have any dragonets . . . although I was supposed to." He caught a fragment of cloud between his talons and watched it fade into empty air.

"So . . . your sister, Whiteout, was my great-great-great-something-greats-grandmother?" Sunny asked.

"She must have been," Darkstalker said, shaking himself. "But there's so much I don't know. All my friends and family are gone, Sunny. I miss them, and I have no idea what happened to them. So I've asked Starflight to find some scrolls for me — just to fill in the gaps and answer my questions. I hope that's all right." He smiled, but his eyes were sad.

Turtle glanced over his shoulder. Starflight was hurrying around the library, pulling out scrolls and putting them back, checking their titles with his claws. He kept slipping on the loose scrolls and catching himself. Every once in a while he paused and gave a scroll to Fatespeaker, who wrote the title down on a slate.

Maybe this really is all Darkstalker wants, Turtle thought. *A few answers about what happened all those hundreds of years ago. Maybe he's as friendly and harmless as he seems.*

And yet . . . and yet . . . the way he'd looked at Turtle and Winter. That flash of darkness deep inside him, peering out.

Not to mention the ominous prophecy, of course.

Turtle touched the pouch that rested against his heart. *Don't be noticed.* He would stay hidden until he was absolutely, positively sure it was safe.

"Darkstalker!" a voice called from above. A peal of thunder boomed off the clouds like an echo.

Turtle looked outside again, and up, just like everyone else, including Darkstalker.

Lightning flashed, illuminating the outline of a dragon against a sky that was suddenly and rapidly getting darker. She spread her front talons, and wind rushed up behind her with a howling force that made even the giant NightWing stagger back a few paces. Her wings twitched, and the thunder rolled again, louder and closer and more menacing than before.

Darkstalker gathered his wings and planted his feet, watching the dragon overhead. A slow smile spread across his face.

"Anemone," he said. "Just the dragon I was looking for."

CHAPTER 4

"Oh no," Turtle breathed.

"Me?" Anemone echoed, sounding as young as she was and heartbreakingly delighted. She flicked her claws to make the lightning flash again, now illuminating her face. "You were looking for *me*?"

And you made it more than easy for him to find you, Turtle thought. *Not to mention announcing your power to everyone else who didn't know the SeaWings have an animus.* Now every tribe in Pyrrhia would know about Anemone's magic. Apart from all the dragons outside, he could see faces watching from nearly every window in the school — students roused from their beds either by the commotion outside or by the panicked IceWings.

Oh, Anemone. Why would anyone ever draw so much attention to themselves?

Tsunami snapped her tail, hissing. "What is she *doing*?" she cried.

Before Turtle could answer — not that he had any sort of

answer, unless maybe *losing her mind* counted — Tsunami was out the window and flying up toward Anemone.

"One moment, big sister," Anemone said, holding out her talons. The wind spiraled up and around, spinning Tsunami away from her. Below them, Clay and Sunny both started forward with a gasp, but Tsunami caught herself on the second spin and hovered where she was.

"Why were you looking for me?" Anemone asked Darkstalker.

"Because I sensed a kindred spirit," he said, gesturing at the storm rising around her. "I've been listening to your mind since you arrived at Jade Mountain and I saw instantly how special you are. A dragon as smart and practical as I am. And, of course, a fellow animus."

Did he know about me before I hid myself? Turtle wondered. Only Winter, Qibli, Peril, and Moon knew about his animus power . . . but neither Peril nor Moon wore skyfire to protect their thoughts. Darkstalker could have lifted that information from either of their minds. Or he could have seen it in a vision of the future, if there was a crazy future where Turtle used magic in front of him.

"That's me," Anemone said, lifting her front claws into the air. Lightning sizzled down from the clouds and gathered in her webbed talons like deadly trapped moons. The light gave her face an eerie glow, shining over her scales like an Aquatic birthmark, making sure everyone could see how different she was. "Finally. Someone who understands me."

"Anemone," Tsunami said, her voice cracking.

"Oh, I know you *love* me," Anemone said to her. "Plenty of dragons *love* me. But understanding me . . . see, that takes another animus."

I'm not sure it does, Turtle thought. He'd never felt further from understanding her than he did right this moment.

I did this all wrong. Like I always do. I should have told her the truth about me, or I should have lied about Darkstalker. I should have come up with something *that could have stopped this from happening.*

"I'm very impressed, Anemone," Darkstalker said, spreading his wings at the churning, stone-colored sky. "You know, I've never tried controlling the weather. What a clever idea. What did you enchant?" Dark clouds now blotted out the sunrise, bloated with rain that was forbidden to fall. Small flickers of lightning curled in the depths of the clouds like the breath of newly hatched SkyWings. The air smelled like the sea was hiding overhead, ready to drown everyone.

"These," Anemone said, displaying two beaten copper armbands on her wrists, the metal rippling like waves of fire. "I wanted you to see what I could do," she said proudly.

"But Anemone," Tsunami choked out. "Your soul —"

"I feel *fine*, Tsunami," Anemone said, flicking her tail. "I mean, we are supposed to use our powers *sometimes*, right?" she asked Darkstalker. "Like when it's really important? And couldn't these be totally useful?" She reached up again and opened a small hole in the clouds for the sun to pour through.

"Absolutely," Darkstalker agreed. "They're brilliant. Don't worry, Tsunami; Anemone is many spells away from massacring anyone. And now I'm here to help her with that soul problem. Come on down, Princess, and let's talk."

Anemone soared down to him with no hesitation. Turtle watched her go with the same sick, sinking feeling that had hit him the day he heard his father had been captured by Queen Scarlet's troops.

There's nothing I can do.

He could feel Peril watching him, but he couldn't meet her eyes.

Don't wait for me to fix this. I can't. I don't know where to start and I don't have any good ideas and whatever I tried, I'd do it wrong anyway.

As Anemone and Darkstalker stepped into the main entrance cave, Anemone looked back up at her sister and the other dragons still outside.

She smiled, and the rain began to fall.

Heavy droplets pelted Turtle's wings as he flew up to where his friends were gathered in the sky.

"I'm sorry," he said as soon as he was close enough to speak. "I did try to warn the school, but I guess it didn't make any difference."

"Warn the school about what?" Winter asked.

"The . . . giant two-thousand-year-old superdragon that just climbed out of a mountain?" Turtle answered.

"Oh, he's not here to hurt anyone," said Winter. "I know, I was worried at first, too, but Darkstalker's not a monster. He just wants to make friends and start over."

"See, I *feel* like that's true," said Qibli, "but then Winter, of all dragons, says something like that, and I get nervous."

"Call off the exploding-guts plan, Turtle!" Peril called cheerfully, swooping around them with her wings carving paths of steam through the pelting rain. "He's not evil after all!"

"Wait, really?" Turtle tried to blink away the rain that kept pooling on his snout. "Are we sure? What happened to change your mind so fast?"

"Well, he's been super nice to me," said Peril. "Which kind of never happens, so he's obviously more awesome than the average dragon. And he pointed out that animus powers and firescales are the same, because other dragons are always scared of us, but they shouldn't be. Totally true, right? I mean, I wouldn't want MY insides exploded by magic just because someone thinks I'M scary."

"You are scary," Qibli said to her. "But I'm also in favor of you staying in one piece."

"Why, thank you," she said, pleased. "So it makes sense, right, Turtle? If *we* deserve a chance to prove ourselves good, then why doesn't Darkstalker?"

"That's right," said Qibli. "That's a good point."

"But didn't he already have that chance?" Turtle asked. "And didn't it end with killing his own father?"

"Oh, that's a good point, too." Qibli scrunched his eyes

shut as though his head hurt. "My brain feels like it's trying to swim through honey."

"That father business is ancient history," said Winter. "We don't know exactly what happened. I'm sure he has a good explanation."

"Me too," said Peril.

"So we're all . . . we're not worried anymore?" said Turtle. "Welcome back, Darkstalker, carry on, do all the magic you'd like?"

"You just need to spend a little time with him and you'll see," Winter said. "Are we done with this boring conversation? I'd like to go get dry, if you please." He shook off his wings and dove toward the caves without waiting for an answer.

"Never tell him I said this," said Peril, "but I agree with the chilly prince. Off with your hiding spell, Turtle, and onward with your face!"

She gestured toward Turtle's pouch and he shied away from her, covering it with his talons.

"Or you can keep skulking around," she said with a shrug. "Whatever you want. I'm going to go say hi to Clay! I mean, to uh, him and his friends. So I can tell him what I did to Scarlet! I mean, tell all of them. What Ruby did, technically. But with my help! He's going to be so excited. Don't you think? So excited? I mean, not that it's any big deal. Well, I guess it's kind of a big deal that I stopped his, like, super worst enemy from coming after him. He'll be happy about that. Right? Not that it matters. Why am I nervous?

I'm not! STOP BEING NERVOUS, PERIL. Ha ha! That'll work."

"Three moons, just go talk to him, you unexpected flutterhead," Qibli said with a laugh.

"I will! I'm going!" Peril said. "Don't wish me luck because I don't even need it because why would I because who cares!" She shook herself from horns to tail, wiped raindrops off her snout, and spiraled down to the school.

"Wow," said Qibli. "Am I like that around Moon?"

"Are you?" Turtle asked, only half-listening. Peril did seem like the kind of dragon who could change her mind about someone at a moment's notice. So maybe this was normal, and maybe Darkstalker was as great as they all thought and Turtle was wrong to be so anxious. But something didn't feel right.

"Just kidding," Qibli said quickly. "Forget I said that. Um, Turtle . . . I think, actually, don't unhide yourself yet."

"Really?" Turtle twisted toward him in the air. Raindrops kept splashing in his eyes and making it hard to see. It felt as if the clouds were gathering lower and lower, as though they might all pile on top of his wings at any moment.

"My instincts tell me I can trust Darkstalker," Qibli said, tilting his claws to watch the raindrops slide in different directions. "But my head says to be more careful. So maybe it's smart to have one dragon who can watch him without being seen for a little while. Can you do that? Watch him and then tell me what you see?"

"I guess." Turtle tugged the webs between his talons

nervously. "But like what? What if I miss something? What am I looking for?"

"I don't know," Qibli admitted. "But whatever you see, come talk to me about it, all right? We'll figure it out together."

"All right," Turtle said uncomfortably.

He stayed in the air for a moment as Qibli flew away. *At least I'm not the only one who's worried.*

But he couldn't shake the dread that crept along his wings. It was a lot of pressure, being the one who had to keep an eye on Darkstalker. Being the only one who *could*, really. He didn't like the feeling that Qibli was relying on him.

I don't want to be the spy. In all the stories, spies are competent and quick-thinking and clever, and I'm none of those things. Or else they're incompetent, and then they get caught, and their part of the story ends in a dungeon or a quick death.

Not exactly the character arc I was hoping for.

I'm not the right dragon for this.

He followed his friends slowly, listening to the thunder roll overhead, and wondering where the lightning would strike.

CHAPTER 5

Inside the main entrance cave, Turtle crept around the small groups of gathered dragons until he was huddled behind the bronze gong. Nobody noticed him. He'd perfected the art of moving slowly, of being boring and forgettable and ordinary.

And it certainly helped that everyone had a much bigger, flashier dragon on their minds at the moment.

"It's such a vague threat," Darkstalker was saying to Anemone as Turtle curled into his hiding spot. "I mean, what is a soul? How do you really know if someone's losing theirs or it's going bad or whatever the big danger is supposed to be?"

"Right!" Anemone said, as though she were pouncing on a scuttling crab. "I mean, there haven't been that many animus dragons in history, have there? What if Albatross was already bad and it had nothing to do with his magic at all?"

Turtle shivered. He'd had these thoughts himself, many times, but it was unsettling to hear them spoken aloud. He wanted to believe that his soul would be fine no matter what he did. He would still be the one making all the choices, good or bad, wouldn't he? And he was a good dragon — a perfectly nice, harmless dragon with no reason to hurt anyone.

A plume of blood flickered through his memory. Was it only two days ago? Or three? He remembered the clammy feeling of mud between his talons as they confronted that dragon, Peril's father — Soar or Chameleon or Shapeshifter, the one with many names. He'd been holding Darkstalker's scroll, and Turtle had used animus magic to take it from him.

The truth was, he hadn't just taken the scroll; he'd attacked Chameleon with it, bashing him in the face and probably breaking his nose. It was the only violent spell he'd ever cast.

Once more, he noticed his talons were clenched against his will, and he had to force them straight. Deep breaths. *I am in control of my own self. I am not a bad dragon.*

He'd never done anything like that before in his life. He certainly wouldn't be able to do it with his own claws. But with magic it was different. It didn't feel like he was really hurting someone else. Except for now, in his memories, where the screaming dragon kept appearing over and over again.

But he hurt Kinkajou, Turtle reminded himself. *He put her in a coma. He also tricked Peril and put a spell on her to make her work for Scarlet again.*

He deserved it.

He brushed his front talons together as though he were wiping off wet sand. Was this what it felt like to lose part of his soul? Was this the first step toward darkness? He still felt like himself . . . but maybe a slightly more powerful version of himself. Was that bad?

"I know what you did," Darkstalker rumbled softly, and for a moment Turtle's heart stopped. "I know what you worry about."

"You do?" Anemone whispered.

Turtle peeked out and saw that the cave was almost empty now. Only Darkstalker, Anemone, Tsunami, and Moon remained.

"She was protecting us," Tsunami said quickly. "She was *saving* us."

Turtle felt a flash of panic. *What did Anemone do? Something terrible? When? How did he miss it?*

"I agree," said Darkstalker. "You shouldn't feel guilty, Princess."

"I don't," Anemone said, lifting her chin. "He deserved it."

Turtle heard the echo of his own thought and winced. Who was she talking about?

"But did it change you?" Tsunami asked. "Do you feel . . ."

"Soulless?" Anemone laughed a little too brightly. "No way. I think I have a pretty normal soul for a dragon."

"But you won't ever have to worry again if we protect that soul, like I protected mine." Darkstalker flicked his tail. "With a different spell this time, though. We're going to need something to enchant. None of my talismans survived the two thousand years underground with me."

"I can find us something!" Anemone said, jumping to her feet. "I have some great treasure! Mother always gives me the best jewels."

"It doesn't have to be fancy," Darkstalker said. "It just has to be sturdy, so our souls will be safe forever." He smiled at Moon. "I know that would make certain dragons here a lot happier."

"I don't know," said Moon, studying him with a wary expression. "Your soul was 'protected' before and you still killed your father."

"Oh, by all the moons," Darkstalker said crossly. He reared up, filling the cavern with his giant wings. "Listen, Arctic was about to betray the whole tribe. He was trying to sell my sister to the IceWings in exchange for his own safety. He would have made her marry an IceWing and live in their kingdom forever, *and* he was mind-controlling her. If I hadn't stopped him, Sunny wouldn't even exist! And maybe the NightWings wouldn't either, because Arctic was going to help the IceWings wipe us out. He was a traitor who had to die." Darkstalker pointed at Moon. "I was protecting *you* and all the tribe's future descendants. I'm shocked that everyone has completely forgotten about that."

"Well," said Moon, "watching a dragon *disembowel himself* probably has kind of a traumatizing effect on one's memory."

"Wait, WHAT?" said Tsunami. "Disem-what now?"

"Did you really do that?" Anemone said, looking up at Darkstalker. But Turtle didn't like her expression. There wasn't nearly enough disgust or horror there. He didn't like it at all.

"Did I say disembowel?" Darkstalker waved one talon. "I was exaggerating. It was a simple honor suicide. Even he knew he deserved it."

Moon crossed her front talons, arching her brows at him skeptically.

"Wow," said Darkstalker. "Are we sure Clearsight didn't have dragonets after I was gone? Because you do an uncanny impression of my true love's disapproving face."

"I'm only trying to make sure you don't overuse your power, go crazy, and hurt someone," Moon said.

"Moon," Darkstalker said reproachfully. "I can see the future, remember? I know how to stop myself from doing that. Do you want me to show you where our paths are going?" He held out one of his talons to her. "I can take you along the whole timeline for the next hundred years, if you like." His tail nudged her mischievously. "Want to see which one of them you should choose? I can show you what the future looks like with both options. Although, frankly, I think neither of them are good enough for you."

"No, no, no, thank you," Moon said quickly, covering her ears. "I don't want to hear it. I have no idea who you're talking about — I mean, what you're talking about — stop thinking about them! LA LA LA ignoring you."

"Hey, what about me?" Anemone interjected. "I want to see the future! Will you show me what's going to happen to me?"

Tsunami looked from her sister to Darkstalker, her expression wavering between concern and curiosity.

A vision could show us that Anemone turns out all right, Turtle thought. *We wouldn't have to worry about her soul anymore if we saw a peaceful future ahead for her.*

"Anything you want," Darkstalker said, expanding his wings to their full width. "You both have so many possible amazing futures. And now that I'm here, if you trust me, we can make sure you get exactly the right future for you."

Anemone's eyes were shining like the skyfire comet. Even Turtle couldn't help thinking *It would be nice to know my future . . . to have someone who could tell me the right steps to follow to make sure my life turns out all right. Which spells are safe to cast, how to protect myself and my soul. What I'm here for.*

Darkstalker raised one of his talons and Turtle nearly ducked behind the gong again, out of sight. But he managed to stay put, sinking into a crouch, and so he was watching as Darkstalker lifted a claw to gently touch the earring in his ear, pale against the black scales.

An earring . . .

Had that been there before? Turtle tried to think back, to remember what Darkstalker had looked like when he rose from the earth. He thought he remembered no jewelry . . .

and didn't Darkstalker just say that nothing had survived the two thousand years underground with him?

But now he was wearing an earring — a plain white half-loop stabbed through his earlobe.

Turtle squinted at it. It looked as though it was made of bone.

Like a bone one might get from one's prey after hunting.

Could Darkstalker have made the bone earring and enchanted it today, while Turtle was flying to Jade Mountain to warn the school?

And more important: If it was animus-touched . . . what was the spell?

A short while later, Tsunami and Moon went off to separate parts of the school. Turtle crouched in the shadows, watching them leave. He felt like stalagmites were growing through his talons, pinning him to the floor. He didn't want to be left alone here, the only one keeping an eye on Darkstalker.

Who would ever think that was a good idea? He couldn't be trusted to do anything right.

Maybe I need to enchant someone else to be hidden with me. Someone who could be a better observer, a better spy. A real hero.

He thought about that while Anemone brought Darkstalker several pieces of treasure from her travel chest. Turtle remembered that chest, because he'd had to help carry it here from the Kingdom of the Sea, and it was ridiculously heavy. Now, seeing the ropes of pearls, bulky silver neck-bands, and sapphire-laden tiaras she laid out on the cave floor, Turtle could understand why.

Although he still wasn't entirely clear on why she needed *any* of this for history lessons and math classes.

Together, Darkstalker and Anemone picked through the jewels, discussing the merits of each. It was difficult to find anything that fit Darkstalker's enormous size, but they eventually settled on a piece that was supposed to be a metal breastplate for Anemone, fitting around her entire chest to protect her from attacks. It clicked neatly around one of Darkstalker's wrists.

"Mother is always giving me ridiculous things like that," Anemone said. "As if I need armor to protect me when I have magic like ours."

"She has no idea what it's like to be an animus," Darkstalker said sympathetically. He passed Anemone a necklace. "Maybe this one for you? If you think you'd be happy wearing it all the time."

"Oh . . . sure," said Anemone, taking the heavy silver band in her talons. "I mean, I never liked it before, but if you think it would work, then I like it, too."

"It's up to you," said Darkstalker. "It should be something you love."

"I love this," Anemone said emphatically. She snapped it around her neck with a sound like eggs cracking. Turtle's stomach twisted as though it were full of rotten shrimp.

"Now the enchantment," Darkstalker said. He touched his wristband with one claw, gazing thoughtfully up at the vines draped between the stalactites. In a slightly deeper voice, he intoned, "I enchant this bracelet to protect my soul from the effects of animus magic forever."

There was a pause.

"Is that it?" Anemone asked. "Seriously? It's that simple?"

Surely not, thought Turtle. *It can't be.*

"I don't know." Darkstalker twitched his wings back and held out his arm to study the bracelet. "I guess we'll have to see if it works." He squinted. "My visions of the future seem to indicate that it does. Yup. Yup. I'm still a pretty awesome dragon fifty years from now."

"All right," said Anemone with a giggle. "Well, three moons, I can do that! I could have done that months ago. Why hasn't every animus done something like this?"

"They haven't always known to worry about these things," Darkstalker observed. "Or perhaps they did have objects like this, and we just don't know about them."

"Hmm." Anemone touched her necklace with one claw, mirroring Darkstalker's movement.

"Wait," said Darkstalker. "My soul is safe now. Let me use my magic to enchant yours, so you don't have to waste any more of your soul."

No! Turtle thought. *Don't let him! Anemone, don't trust him!*

"Great idea!" Anemone said happily.

Should he stop this? Could he stop this? *What can I do? I*

have to do something, don't I? Like what? I need more time to think!

But Turtle couldn't think of anything he could do without Darkstalker noticing, and it was already too late.

"I enchant this necklace to protect Anemone's soul from the effects of animus magic forever," said Darkstalker, tapping the silver collar lightly with his claws.

It sounded safe. It sounded exactly like the spell on Darkstalker's own talisman. But Turtle knew all too well that spells could be cast without speaking. Had Darkstalker added anything to the spell with his mind?

Oh, Anemone. I'm sorry, I'm sorry, I'm sorry.

"This is so cool," said Anemone. "Now we can do anything we want!"

"That," said Darkstalker with a grin, "is the whole idea."

CHAPTER 6

Darkstalker spent the rest of the day in the main entrance cave, reading through scrolls and talking to any students who were brave enough to approach him. By the middle of the day, it began to feel quietly normal to have him there. He didn't do anything sinister. He didn't use any magic. He acted like a friendly visitor who just needed to use the library on his way through the mountains.

Anemone sat beside him with her chin lifted, looking as royal as she did when she sat beside Mother at council meetings. Every once in a while Darkstalker would pass her a scroll and ask her to read it out loud to him, or to check it for references to Fathom, and she would do so, beaming.

The school gradually returned to its usual activities. From his spot, hidden behind the bronze gong, Turtle saw MudWings pass through on the way to the art room; he saw SandWings carrying musical instruments; he saw RainWings with baskets heading out to pick berries.

There was no sign of the IceWings. Turtle wondered if they were hiding somewhere.

He also wondered why nobody came to make Anemone go to whichever class she was supposed to be in. Pike stalked through a few times, eyeing Darkstalker suspiciously, but didn't try talking to him.

At one point, around midday, Turtle watched Clay gather the SkyWings to hear Peril's story of the duel between Queen Scarlet and Queen Ruby. Soon they came back through the cave, all of them with relieved expressions, knowing that Scarlet was dead and Ruby was safely their queen for certain now.

One of them paused not far from Darkstalker and gazed enviously at the treasure Anemone had swept into a messy pile. He was the one with the badly scarred face, from the Gold Winglet. He had a black leather pouch around his neck, like most of the students, but no other accessories — nothing like Anemone's confections of sparkles from the sea. Turtle couldn't remember speaking to him; the SkyWing always looked as if he was in a murderous mood.

"Hello, Flame," Darkstalker said politely. He put a rock down on the scroll he'd been reading to hold his place.

"Stay out of my head," Flame snarled at him.

"With pleasure," said Darkstalker.

"I know you were poking around in my mind before." Flame lashed his tail and glared up at the NightWing. "I felt it. I hated it."

"Yes," Darkstalker said thoughtfully. "Indeed. It's quite dark in there."

"What's that supposed to mean?" Flame demanded.

"Like, evil-dark?" Anemone asked curiously. "Or there's-nothing-going-on-inside dark?"

Flame hissed at her and Darkstalker gently stepped between them.

"You know, I have an idea, Flame," he said. "I could fix your face."

The SkyWing dragonet started back and touched his venom-slashed snout, scowling. "Don't lie to me," he said. "I already asked an animus to do that, and he said he wouldn't. Or couldn't. Slithering toadstool worm."

"You mean Stonemover?" Darkstalker said with a surprised expression. "I wonder why he said no. It wouldn't be that hard, or take very much out of him."

"Really?" Flame looked even more furious. "He moaned and griped and acted like it would kill him. He said he couldn't cure all the wounded dragons in Pyrrhia, so why even start. Festering rotted lungfish!"

"Oh, dear," said Darkstalker, shaking his head. "Well, I'm sure he has his reasons. But I could certainly do it . . . if you want."

Flame hesitated. Turtle could see his talons trembling slightly, although his face was fixed in a state of permanent rage. Finally he said, "Why would you do that for me? What do you want in return?"

"Nothing at all." Darkstalker caught a deep indigo flower that was drifting down from one of the banners overhead and cupped it in his claws. He took a step toward Flame, who held his ground. "I am currently trying to prove to certain dragons that I'm not the villain they think I am. I can be trusted. I'm here to help others. So why shouldn't you be one of the ones I help?"

"No strings attached?" Flame said. "Ha. I don't buy it."

"I have a lot to make up for," Darkstalker said. "What's that word . . . oh, I'm *atoning*. I need M — everyone to see that."

"I don't need your pity and I don't want to be your experiment," Flame growled.

"It's a simple good deed, Flame. There's no need to be so suspicious." Darkstalker stopped in front of him, his head nearly brushing the fire globes on the ceiling. Flame stared up at him as though he was frozen in place, paralyzed by wanting something and not believing he could truly have it. "I've seen in your mind how badly you need this. Just accept it."

Darkstalker reached out and brushed the flower across Flame's face, tracing the scar from one end to the other. "I enchant this flower to heal Flame the SkyWing, without pain, erasing his scars and returning his face to the way it was before the accident with the SandWing."

He lifted the flower away and Flame jerked back. Turtle watched, awestruck, as Flame's scales writhed and rippled over his snout like snakes suddenly rising up and shaking off their skins. Flame let out a yell, clapped his talons over his eyes, and wrapped his wings around his head.

In the ensuing silence, Darkstalker quietly plucked the petals off the flower and let them drift down to the stone floor.

Finally Flame folded back his wings and lifted his face toward the light.

Turtle stifled a gasp. He'd expected it to work, but it was shocking to see the smooth, unblemished ruby scales and the perfect shape of Flame's face. The SkyWing dragonet looked years younger and infinitely more innocent. Turtle wondered with a stab of shame whether he had judged Flame by his damaged looks, assuming he was a scarier dragonet than he truly was.

Flame's claws touched his snout, brushing over the new scales with disbelieving care, as though they were made of the thinnest ice and might shatter at any moment.

"Wow!" Anemone blurted. "You look totally different! Darkstalker, that's amazing!"

Flame glanced up at Darkstalker, then turned and bolted from the cave.

"Oh, right, don't bother saying thank you!" Anemone called after him. "Some dragons," she said to Darkstalker, shaking her head. "You know, I offered to cure Starflight's blindness once, but Tsunami said no, my soul was too valuable, whatever whatever." She touched her neckband. "But now I can! Or you can! One of us can. Won't Starflight be excited?"

"I'm not sure," Darkstalker said kindly. "It's a generous idea, but in my visions, he's reluctant to accept a magic cure from us. Maybe if we give him a little time to get used to the idea."

"Reluctant? Why?" Anemone demanded. "We can fix *everybody* now!"

Darkstalker didn't respond. His eyes were on a tunnel across the cave, where, a moment later, Moon emerged, leading the other three NightWing students.

"Well, this is exciting," said Darkstalker with a smile.

"I thought a better introduction might be in order," Moon said. She glanced at the other NightWings anxiously. "All right? Everyone, this is Darkstalker. He promises he's not as bad as all the stories say he is. Darkstalker, this is Mightyclaws, Mindreader, and Fearless."

"I know," Darkstalker said. "I've been looking forward to meeting you all face-to-face. It seems like the NightWing tribe has changed a lot since I was around."

Fearless was the first to speak. Turtle peeked out and saw her claws nervously picking at the rock below her. "What was it like in your day?" she asked.

"Amazing," said Darkstalker. "We were without question the most powerful and sophisticated tribe. Our kingdom had a remarkable library, a huge training arena where we hosted all the tribes for tournaments, a museum with the most beautiful art in Pyrrhia, and a new music festival every full moon. It was glorious."

"It was?" said Mindreader wistfully.

"I can't believe it's all gone," Darkstalker said, shaking his head. He touched the scroll beside him as though all his memories had vanished into it.

"Do you know where we've been living all these years?" Mightyclaws asked. Turtle noticed that he was the only one with a note of hostility in his voice.

"I can see it in your memories," said Darkstalker. "The island, the volcano — it looks terrible."

"It was terrible," Mightyclaws said accusingly.

"In a place of such darkness and danger," Darkstalker mused, "the NightWings who are left must have been very strong to survive."

The dragonets hesitated, glancing at one another. The sound of the rain pouring down outside filled in the silence. It sounded like claws running overhead, like the waterfalls in the Summer Palace, like hurricanes closing in as the waters rise.

"I guess," Mightyclaws said thoughtfully. "But we live in the rainforest now."

"That's much better," Mindreader interjected. "Now we're not starving or sick anymore, and we can breathe."

"I'm sure," said Darkstalker, "although . . . now you don't have a queen."

"We do!" said Moon. "We have Queen Glory."

The other three nodded — Mindreader first, Turtle noticed, and the other two more slowly.

Darkstalker's eyebrows twitched, but he didn't say anything for a moment. "And I understand no one in the tribe has powers anymore," he observed.

"Were those really real?" Fearless asked. "Could NightWings really do all those things, once?"

"Some of them could," he said. "If they hatched at the right time. We had mind reading and prophecy classes for the gifted in my school."

"Oh, wow," Mindreader breathed. "Not just classes on *pretending* to read minds and how to make up believable prophecies?"

Darkstalker chuckled. "No, it was all real."

"I wish I could really read minds," she said sadly.

"Do you have any jewelry on you?" Darkstalker asked.

"Um . . . this?" Mindreader held out her arm to display a bracelet of green and silver glass beads strung along a twisted black wire. Turtle guessed she had made it here, in art class.

"Heads up, Moon," Darkstalker said, sliding the bracelet off Mindreader's arm. "Exciting things about to happen!"

"Is this a good idea?" Moon said anxiously.

"We can't leave this poor dragonet with a name that's a lie, can we?" he asked. Darkstalker held the bracelet between his claws for a moment, with something glimmering in his dark eyes. Finally he passed it back to Mindreader.

"Wish granted," he said, smiling again.

"What — oh!" She gasped as the bracelet touched her scales. She looked up at him, eyes wide with wonder. "I can — I can hear what everyone's thinking! I really can! Is this real? Three moons! Let's see — the SeaWing princess is thinking I don't deserve a gift like this. Moon is worried about whether it'll be too much for me, hearing everything all at once. Mightyclaws and Fearless are both super jealous. Ha! This is amazing!" She did a little jump into the air, fluttering her wings.

"Moon's right," said Darkstalker. "It's a lot to handle at first. But Moon can help you if you feel overwhelmed."

"Moon can?" said Mightyclaws. "Why?"

"Darkstalker —" Moon started.

"Have a little faith in your fellow NightWings, Moon," Darkstalker said. "Don't you think it's fair for them to know that you have mind reading and prophecy powers?"

"WHAT?" Fearless cried. They all looked at Moon as though she had suddenly sprouted six extra heads.

"But *I* was going to tell them," Moon protested. "I mean, eventually. Soon. When I figured out how."

"Well, now we're even for you telling your friends about skyfire," Darkstalker said cheerfully. "Besides, I promise nobody's going to hate you, the way you were so worried everyone would. Right, my friends?"

"*I* don't hate her," Mindreader said with a touch of smugness, admiring her bracelet.

"How could you keep something like that a secret?" Fearless demanded.

"That's not *fair*!" Mightyclaws cried. "She got to grow up in the rainforest, safe and fed and happy, *and* she gets all our lost powers?"

"Ooooo, he's thinking, *why couldn't it be ME*?" Mindreader announced gleefully.

"All right, genius, anyone could guess that," Fearless snapped at her. "Does your mother know?" she asked Moon. "I'm assuming yes, since lying apparently runs in your family."

"How could I tell anyone when I knew you'd react this way?" Moon confronted her. "Exactly the way I expected?"

"Hey now, hey now," Darkstalker said. He reached out with one massive talon and nudged Fearless back a few paces, away from Moon. "That's right, I forgot one little step. Sorry, Moon." He turned to Mightyclaws and tapped the miniature diamond stud embedded in the dragonet's earlobe. It was so small that for a long time Turtle had thought it was a tiny silver scale, but now he could see that it was an earring.

"Tell me, Mightyclaws, if you could have any power, what would you choose?" Darkstalker asked.

"Darkstalker," Moon said warily. "Shouldn't you be thinking about your soul?"

"All taken care of," Darkstalker said, waving one of his wings at her. "Right, little princess?"

"That's right." Anemone flared her wings and looked imperious. "So you can quit acting like you know everything, *Moon*. Darkstalker and I are just fine."

Moon gave her a puzzled sideways look.

"So, Mightyclaws." Darkstalker's eyes glittered at the young NightWing. "What do you think? Any power at all."

"I guess . . . prophecy?" he said. "I mean . . . to be different from Mindreader."

"You're thinking too small." Darkstalker grinned with all his teeth. "Don't limit yourself to traditional NightWing powers. What if you could do anything? Any power you can imagine!"

"Oh, Darkstalker," Moon said, starting to pace up and down the cave. "I'm really not sure about this."

"Oooo, she's imagining all *sorts* of terrible things!" Mindreader reported enthusiastically.

"Shouldn't we check with Sunny or Tsunami or Queen Glory, at least?" Moon asked.

"Do you think they'd really stop me from improving these dragons' lives?" Darkstalker asked. "Look how happy Mindreader is now."

"Yes . . . but . . ." Moon trailed off.

"But you want all the power for yourself, is that it?" Mightyclaws asked, lashing his tail. "You don't like the idea of other dragons being special, too?"

"Powers like these can be hard to live with," Moon said fiercely. "I'm just worried for you all."

"I'll take yours if you want to give them up," Mightyclaws suggested.

"Me too!" Anemone said. "Ooo, then I'd be just like Darkstalker!"

"Moon is sensible to worry," Darkstalker said soothingly, "but luckily I am here to make sure everything turns out fine. Mightyclaws, what have you decided?"

"And me?" Fearless interjected. "Am I getting a power, too?"

"Do you have anything to enchant?" Darkstalker asked, looking her up and down.

"I will!" Fearless whirled and ran out of the cave.

"I have one idea," Mightyclaws said hesitantly. "But it might be stupid."

"It's not," said Darkstalker. "I can see what you're thinking. It's very creative."

"What?" Anemone demanded. "What is it?"

"I don't get it," said Mindreader. "He wants to draw things and then make them real?"

"Like, if I draw a sword, then I could touch it and it would become a real sword," Mightyclaws said, glowing a little with excitement. "And if I drew a pond, I could touch it and it would become a real pond. Or if I drew a banana, then I could touch it and, and, um . . . have a real banana to eat."

"Oh, that's what he really wants," Mindreader giggled. "An endless supply of food."

"Would have been pretty useful back on the volcano," Mightyclaws bristled. "You wouldn't be making fun of me then! You'd be kissing my claws for a banana!"

"We don't *live* on the *volcano* anymore," Mindreader pointed out. "We live in basically the banana capital of the universe. We don't *need* a magic banana-maker."

"It's not just for bananas!" Mightyclaws cried.

"Well, *I* think it's extremely clever," Darkstalker said, and Mindreader subsided at once. "Let me think for a moment about how exactly to word the spell." He tapped his chin pensively for a few long, silent seconds, and then he touched Mightyclaws' earring again, whispering under his breath.

"There we go," he said.

"Did it work?" Mightyclaws asked.

"Run to the art cave and see," Darkstalker suggested.

"Bring me back a banaaaaaaana!" Mindreader called after him as Mightyclaws darted away.

"Darkstalker, why are you doing this?" Moon asked. She stopped pacing and sat down with her tail around her talons. Turtle wished he were brave enough to stand next to her, taking strength from her strength. He wished she could tell him what to think about any of this. The more he watched Darkstalker, the more confused he felt.

Because this was a good thing Darkstalker was doing, wasn't it? Giving other dragons powers?

That's what you want to think, his conscience whispered.

"Our tribe needs help, Moon," Darkstalker said earnestly. "They've fallen so far. I want to restore them to the powerful tribe I remember, and if I can do that by sharing my gift, why shouldn't I?"

"Because . . . are you sure you won't turn evil?" Moon asked. "And these are huge decisions — shouldn't you think about them a little more?"

"I have been thinking about them," Darkstalker assured her. "I've been thinking nonstop since I woke up, and I've checked all the possible futures. This is the best path, believe me. A happy NightWing tribe. Talons of power for everyone!"

"Talons of power?" Moon echoed, her eyes wide. "Like the prophecy? The whole 'beware' part?"

"I'm just joking," said Darkstalker. "Try not to worry so much."

"I'm back!" Fearless ran into the room, panting. "I'm here! I have something!" She thrust out her arm. A pair of silver and black wires had been hastily twisted into a rough bracelet, barely visible on her wrist. She smiled up at Darkstalker in a frighteningly worshipful way.

"Superstrength, please," she said breathlessly.

Darkstalker smiled back at her. "Anything you wish."

He touched her wrist and muttered something. When he finished, she turned her talon over, then spun around and slammed her tail into a stalagmite. It instantly crumbled into a cascade of tiny rocks.

Fearless let out a shriek of delight. "Did you SEE that?" she cried.

Mindreader toyed with her own bracelet, frowning. "Well," she said. "It's cool, I suppose, if you like that kind of thing. I mean, a bit obvious, but all right."

Darkstalker suddenly sat up, lifting his head as though he could see monsters crawling out of the stalactites. He stared into space for a moment with faraway eyes. The other dragons all held their breath and watched in silence.

"Did you sense something?" he said finally, looking down at Moon.

She shook her head. "What was it? A vision?"

"More of a premonition," he said. His expression was troubled — and if this was an act, Turtle thought, then Darkstalker was really good at it. Even Turtle felt his anxiety jump a few notches higher. "Someone's in danger. Can you feel it?"

Moon closed her eyes. Mindreader saw her do it and immediately closed her eyes, too, putting on a deeply pensive look.

"Hmm, yes," said Mindreader, nodding. "The princess who smells like fish is thinking maybe she should give herself some cool powers like ours. Ha ha, copycat. Oh, and there's Sunny's mind — coming this way with a squirrel for Darkstalker, wondering what he's found out about Clearsight."

Turtle felt a flash of worry that she'd hear his mind, hiding nearby, and give him away. But then he remembered the skyfire, which shielded him from all mind readers. He felt for his armband with a sigh of relief. Only three stones left; the other three holes marked the stones he'd given to Winter, Qibli, and Kinkajou. Would Moon want a stone for herself, now that there were two other mind readers around? Maybe not; he wasn't sure she'd still be able to read other minds if she was holding a skyfire rock.

"It's Stonemover!" Moon cried suddenly, her eyes flying open. She leaped to her feet, wings spread wide, and turned toward Sunny as she entered the cave. "Sunny, your father — someone's trying to kill him!"

CHAPTER 7

There was a sudden rush of wings, like a million seagulls taking flight at once. Sunny, Darkstalker, and Moon dove out into the storm; Anemone pivoted in a circle, as though startled that they'd left without her, then flew after them. Mindreader and Fearless exchanged a glance and finally followed as well.

Turtle hurried out from behind the gong and stood in the cave entrance for a moment, dithering. It would be hard to sneak along behind them; but then, he wanted to know what was happening; on the other talon, it was raining quite a lot; but then again, Qibli had asked him to keep an eye on Darkstalker, so that was really what he had to do, wasn't it?

"Rrrgh," he growled softly, and then he was out in the rain, instantly drenched, flying through flashes of lightning. He chased the dragons around the mountain to the cave Stonemover had chosen to live in for the rest of his life, like a petrified hermit crab.

Turtle had never visited the old NightWing animus during his time at Jade Mountain. He had a weird, irrational fear that the dragon would somehow recognize him as a fellow animus and reveal his secret. Although if he searched deeper, he'd also have to admit that he was afraid of seeing what an animus could become when he used his magic too much.

He heard Darkstalker roar, angry and earthshaking, sending a slide of rocks clattering down the mountainside. Turtle wobbled down to the ledge outside the cave and slid himself into the very edge of the shadows inside.

He sucked in a sharp breath as he suddenly realized how close he was to Darkstalker's scales. The enormous dragon filled the mouth of the cave, leaning in toward the others. His smooth ebony side rose and fell only a thin slice of air away from Turtle's nose.

If I touch him, will he notice me then? Or will he wonder why he can touch something that he cannot see?

Turtle held himself tensely frozen, wings pinned to the wall behind him like stingrays caught on a SeaWing's sharp claws. From his position, he could just see a sliver of the cave beyond: Stonemover's gray, fossilized arm; a tangle of NightWing tails; a pool of blood slowly creeping across the stone floor.

"Father!" Sunny cried, was crying, had cried several times over, the word echoing around the cave.

"Who did this?" Moon's voice, then a glimpse of her teardrop scales as she turned to Darkstalker. "You must know."

"He went into the tunnels," Darkstalker said, pointing, his wings shifting warm, fire-smelling breath past Turtle's face. "Otherwise I'd chase him down myself."

"I'll do it!" Anemone yelped from her spot at Darkstalker's talons. She seized a loose prey bone on the floor. "Lead me to Stonemover's killer."

"Anemone, no!" But Sunny was too late; Anemone's pale blue tail flashed a trail through the blood, and she was gone.

"Why didn't you see this coming?" Moon asked Darkstalker. "I thought you could see everything, all the futures."

"There are billions upon billions of futures," Darkstalker answered. "I'm sorry; even I can't study all of them, especially when something small can set off a sharp turn. Sunny, is he still alive? It seems like I can still hear a glimmer of life in his mind."

"Oh — so can I!" Moon gasped.

"Um, yeah, ME TOO," Mindreader declared quickly.

Darkstalker squeezed forward another few steps, and as he ducked his head, Turtle could see a slash of dark red beads dripping across Stonemover's neck.

If Stonemover was still alive — Turtle's healing rock could save him. This was a wound like Winter's, on the surface, where the enchantment Turtle had crafted so thoughtlessly could actually help.

But to bring it out now would be suicidal. Not only would everyone discover that Turtle was an animus, but Darkstalker would want to know where the rock came from — who'd enchanted it, and how he didn't know about it.

No, there was no way to help. Once again, Turtle had to sit on his claws and do nothing. He had to stay useless if he wanted to stay safe.

"He's alive," Darkstalker said firmly. "I can save him." He reached up and snapped a stalactite off the roof with casual, terrifying strength.

"But — you shouldn't — should you?" Sunny asked.

"He's my family, too." Darkstalker wrapped his front talons around the spear of rock. "Enchant this stalactite to heal the wounds of any dragon it touches," he said in a deep voice.

A little deeper than necessary, Turtle thought. *A little theatrical, let's be honest.*

But it seemed to have the intended effect on the dragons watching. All their eyes followed Darkstalker's movements as he reached down and tapped Stonemover lightly on the chest.

A hushed moment passed, and then Stonemover let out a sigh. The slash of red on his neck knitted together and vanished. He rolled his head back with a groan of pain, opened his eyes, and saw Darkstalker.

"Hello," Darkstalker said. "You're all right now."

"Who are you?" Stonemover croaked in his dust-covered voice.

"An ancestor of yours," said Darkstalker. "Returned from the dead. So we have that in common! My name is Darkstalker."

"No," whispered Stonemover, his eyes widening.

"Don't be scared," Moon said quickly. "He's not here to hurt us."

"He saved your life," Sunny added. She rested one of her small talons on Stonemover's petrified shoulder, a tiny island of gold among all the black scales in the cave.

"With magic?" Stonemover said, sounding half-panicked. "No. You can't. It's wrong, it's wrong — my claws! They're not mine!" His eyes rolled wildly toward his talons and Turtle saw the stone cracking all along his arms, crumbling back to release the scales underneath.

"What do you mean?" Sunny asked. "What's wrong?"

"These aren't *my claws*!" Stonemover shrieked. "What are they doing? Stop them! Somebody stop them!"

Bewildered, Sunny pounced on one of his front talons. Darkstalker dropped the stalactite and gently pinned the other.

"Don't panic," he said. "You've had a shock. Someone tried to kill you, but you're safe now. Your petrified scales are healing, that's all — you're not used to being able to feel your limbs anymore. In a moment all the rock will be gone and you'll be back to normal."

"They're not mine," Stonemover said again, in a low, desperate voice. Tension radiated through his muscles, down his arms to the claws that twitched and twitched, breaking free. "No. No, I gave mine up. My talons are gone. These are monsters crawling out of the earth and they will rend the sky and crush the wings of small dragons and I *can't let them I won't I won't I won't let them be used again!*"

His voice rose and rose to an agonized roar. The head-splitting sound pounded images of blood and death and slashing claws through Turtle's brain: *Do you trust YOUR talons do you trust them do you?*

"Stop him!" Moon shouted to Darkstalker. "He's trying to use his magic to hurt himself!" Mindreader had her talons over her ears and was huddled in a ball on the cave floor.

Darkstalker took Stonemover's head in his claws and forced the roaring dragon to meet his gaze. "CALM DOWN," he said in a voice that shook the mountain.

Stonemover's voice dropped away. He stared back at Darkstalker.

"I'm healing you," Darkstalker said. "That's all."

"Don't," Stonemover whispered. "It's not safe."

"You don't have to punish yourself for being an animus." Darkstalker flicked his tail, frowning. "You're allowed to be whole, to be happy."

I agree with Darkstalker, Turtle thought. *Is that a bad sign?*

I don't want to spend my life in terror of my powers. I want to be happy, too.

Does that mean I'm in danger of turning out like Darkstalker? Would I rather end up like him or Stonemover?

He couldn't imagine willingly fossilizing himself . . . but he looked down at his clenched talons and wondered what he would do to stop them from hurting anyone. Did Stonemover have flashes of blood and screaming in his head, too, before he cast his spell?

Stonemover rolled his eyes toward his tail, where more rock was crumbling away. "I can't be free," he said. "I don't know what I might do. Cage me again. Leave me in stone. It's the only way to be safe."

"He means it," Moon said to Darkstalker. She edged around the pool of blood to catch some of the falling pebbles from the old dragon's wings. "He's terrified of his power, of his own claws, of any dark magic. His mind is shredding itself to pieces."

"Yeah, and it's giving me the worst headache," Mindreader complained.

"All this fear," Darkstalker said with a sigh. "I've seen it before." He brightened. "Maybe I can fix it! The right spell could take away all his worry —"

"No!" Sunny and Stonemover said at the same time, looking equally alarmed.

"No spells on my brain," Stonemover said, his voice rising toward panic again.

"Why not?" Darkstalker asked with genuine bewilderment. "If it would make you happier?" He turned to Moon. "Isn't it all right to make other dragons happier, if you can?"

"Not if they don't want you to," she said gently.

"But they *should* want me to," he said. "It makes no sense." He lifted his wings in a shrug that nearly whacked Turtle in the nose. "Fine, all right, I'll leave him in his misery."

"And put me back the way I was," Stonemover asked, leaning against the wall and closing his eyes.

"Dragons who wallow in their own tragedy," Darkstalker muttered. "So pointless." He scooped up a talonful of rocks and crushed it in his claws, then blew the stone dust all over Stonemover's wings, tail, and arms. A moment later, the cold gray of the cave began creeping over Stonemover's scales again, embedding him into the walls and floor once more.

"There you go," Darkstalker said. "May you always be as thoroughly unhappy as you want to be."

"Thank you," Stonemover whispered, relief printed all over his face.

Darkstalker wrinkled his snout at Moon and she shook her head at him. Turtle wondered if they were communicating telepathically. Did Moon really like Darkstalker?

If she did . . . did that mean Turtle was wrong about him?

Healing Flame, saving Stonemover, protecting Anemone's soul, giving powers to the NightWings. Darkstalker hadn't exactly spent his day spreading evil and doom.

Am I worrying about nothing?

Sunny wrapped her arms around her father's neck and hugged him. Blood from the healed wound smeared her scales, but she didn't seem to notice.

A few minutes passed in silence, and then they all heard footsteps coming up through the tunnels. Sunny sat up and arranged her wings as though she was trying to match an image of a queen in her head.

"I found him," Anemone announced, coming into the

cave. A dragon edged into the space behind her. The sharp edge of the broken prey bone pressed into the crevice below his jaw, enchanted to threaten him forward.

It was Flame, guilt and shame written all over his new, perfect face.

Sunny stared down at him without comprehension for a long moment, not understanding who he was.

"Flame?" Darkstalker said at last. "Why would you do this?"

"Especially when Darkstalker just healed your face!" said Anemone. "I thought you'd be dancing and flying around. It's not exactly normal to celebrate by killing some random old dragon." She noticed Stonemover's eyes open and jumped back. "Yikes! And you didn't even do it right! You guys, the fossil is still alive!"

"We know," Fearless said. "Darkstalker saved him."

"Flame, why would you do something like this?" Sunny asked.

"He lied to me," Flame said through clenched teeth. "He could have healed me, but he chose not to."

"Oh, wow," said Mindreader, squinting at Flame. "Moon, are you hearing this, too? This dragon seriously hates *everyone*."

"Stay out of my mind!" Flame shouted at her.

Mindreader jerked back with a yelp.

"But you *are* healed," Sunny said to him wonderingly. "So why would it matter who did it? Enough to kill someone for it?"

"He *lied* to me," Flame growled, sinking closer to the floor.

"That's an interesting complaint coming from a dragon with his own secrets," said Darkstalker. He beckoned with one claw, and Flame's leather pouch ripped free and floated into Darkstalker's talons.

"Give that back!" Flame roared, but when he tried to leap forward, Anemone stood in his way, glittering with self-righteousness. The bone pressed itself harder into his neck, conjuring a jeweled drop of blood, and Flame stopped with a gasp of pain.

"Wow, he is so angry," Mindreader reported. "Oooo, he wants to horribly kill all of us!"

Darkstalker shook the pouch and caught two objects as they tumbled out:

Flame's library card, and . . .

. . . a blue sapphire, shaped like a long, elegant star.

"The third dreamvisitor!" Sunny gasped.

"That's right," said Darkstalker, holding it up to catch the light. "This is what I've suspected since I first heard Moon's prophecy. Flame is the darkness of dragons . . . and *he's* the stalker of dreams."

CHAPTER 8

Beware the darkness of dragons . . . beware the stalker of dreams.

A breath of cold air shivered along Turtle's wings. Was Darkstalker right? Was one of the dangers of the prophecy seething under their noses this whole time?

"I'm not any of that!" Flame snarled. "What does that tripe even mean?"

"You must have stolen this from Starflight on the NightWing island," Sunny said, pointing to the dreamvisitor. "But how did you hide it all this time? While you were injured and everything?"

"I had help," spat Flame. "Idiot help, but that's all I had to work with."

"He's thinking about a dragon with a weird name. Ogre? Okra?" mused Mindreader. "Who he also hates, by the way."

"Stop sticking your snout in my brain," Flame hissed. "Or I'll slice it off."

"I wish I could," flared Mindreader. "You're a miserable dragon and your thoughts are like nasty boiling tar."

"What are we going to do with you?" Sunny asked Flame. "I'll have to tell Queen Ruby what you did . . . but until she sends someone for you, it's not like we have somewhere to lock you up."

"Really? What kind of respectable school doesn't have a dungeon?" Darkstalker asked. Fearless and Mindreader turned toward him with wide eyes, and he chuckled. "I'm just kidding. Sunny, I can take care of this for you."

"How, exactly?" she asked warily.

Darkstalker took Flame's library card and touched it to one of Flame's front talons. Instantly it flipped over and outward, transforming into an iron band that clamped around Flame's forearm. A thick metal chain sprouted from the band like a coiling snake. It plunged into the rock, trapping Flame in place.

Flame roared his fury, but he couldn't move, couldn't reach any of the throats he was clawing for.

"There," Darkstalker said. "He's not going anywhere now."

He backed out of the cave. Turtle pressed himself tightly against the wall, closing his eyes, as the mass of ebony scales rippled by. Giant claws scraped the stone perilously close to his own pitifully small webbed talons.

Sunny circled Flame, her expression uncertain, until she noticed that she was leaving tracks of Stonemover's blood across the floor. With a sigh, she bowed her head and slipped away into the tunnels.

"That was awesome!" Anemone danced out of the cave and spread her wings, looking up at Darkstalker where he stood in the rain. If she noticed Turtle as she went by him, she didn't acknowledge his presence. "Let's solve some more mysteries! Catch some more bad guys! Be even more awesome!"

"You should have an early night," Darkstalker said to her. He swept his wings toward Mindreader and Fearless, who were huddled under the cave overhang looking severely displeased about the weather. "You all should, because tomorrow we're going to the rainforest, and it's a long flight. Moon!" he called as she slipped out of the cave. "Come flying with me!"

She hesitated. "Qibli and I told Starflight we'd help him clean up the library and look for more scrolls for you. Maybe later?"

"Of course," Darkstalker said. "No problem." He watched her fly away, raindrops slithering down his sides. His expression reminded Turtle of someone, but he couldn't think who.

"I'll go flying with you!" Anemone chirped. "I'm way more interesting than Moon and I'm not tired!"

"You will be tomorrow," Darkstalker said. "And we're not stopping on the way to the rainforest. Thank you, Princess, but I'll be fine by myself tonight." He spread his wings, and Turtle realized who Darkstalker had reminded him of: the soldiers in the garden of the wounded. The ones who couldn't swim anymore, who'd lost a tail or a limb or a wing and didn't quite know yet how to go on living without them.

That was the expression he'd glimpsed, very briefly, on Darkstalker's face.

The enormous NightWing turned and flew away, higher and higher into the gray, glowering clouds until the storm seemed to melt into his scales and swallow him whole.

Turtle thought about following him, but his wings felt coated in thick sand. He hadn't slept all night, and he'd spent the entire day before flying across the continent as fast as he could. His fear of Darkstalker had kept him awake for most of the day, but now his eyes were desperate for sleep.

He hasn't done anything terrible yet, he told himself as he flew back to the entrance hall. *And I have to sleep sometime.* He dragged his tail through the tunnels. *I can't watch him every second of his life forever.*

He paused in the doorway to his own sleeping cave.

It was so empty. Like a giant, hollowed-out oyster shell, the walls rose around him, bare and scraped of all life.

In the Kingdom of the Sea, the sons of Queen Coral were almost always together — they shared rooms, classes, prey. They filled the palaces with their wrestling matches and shouting games.

So when one of them did something wrong — and if someone was paying attention to them long enough to notice — their punishment was almost always isolation.

Sometimes it was imposed from above, by someone like their uncle Shark or cousin Moray. Sometimes it came from within, when the brothers banded together to exile one of their own.

Turtle's punishment for failing his father was chosen and carried out by his own brothers. The older ones caught wind of the news that Gill was furious about something, and they finally pried the whole story out of Octopus and Cerulean. Turtle was shut out completely for a month. Nobody spoke to him. He was left to sleep in an empty room, and his brothers all behaved as though he didn't exist.

Turtle had felt his sense of dragonhood drifting away, dissolving into the ocean like a mist of ink. If no one could see you, were you real? If no one spoke to you, how long could you go on existing before disappearing completely?

Which was why he'd finally used his magic on them. An enchanted seagull egg, cracked into their fish stew one night, and forgiveness was suddenly his.

But it left him with an unshakeable sense of doubt. Would they ever have forgiven him on their own? Or would he have been alone forever?

He knew he hadn't earned it, this beguiled friendliness, this false tide of mercy that had washed away his sins.

Empty caves always reminded him of that feeling — first the loneliness, and then the guilt. He'd had trouble sleeping in his school cave ever since his clawmate Umber had run away with Sora. Umber had all the warmth and energy that Turtle didn't have, and as a MudWing, he needed brothers and sisters around him, too. From the first night, they had dragged their reed mats together and slept back to back, feeling as if the world was really still there as long as there were other scales close by.

Umber had felt like a new brother right away. Turtle missed him.

He glanced along the hall, then slipped quietly down to Qibli and Winter's room.

It looked a lot bigger without Winter's scavenger cage taking up half the space. Winter was tinkering with a new wire construction, muttering, while Qibli sat curled on a ledge, surrounded by scrolls, a pensive look in his black eyes.

"Hey," Turtle said, poking his head inside. "Can I sleep in here tonight?"

Qibli snapped back to the world immediately. "Of course!" He jumped off the ledge and hurried over to Turtle.

"Oh, hello, yes, there is another dragon in here," Winter observed. "I wonder if HE has an opinion about extra snoring in his sleeping cave."

"What's happened?" Qibli asked Turtle, ignoring his clawmate. "What have you seen?"

"Not much," Turtle said. "Darkstalker's been really quiet all day. He read a bunch of scrolls, fixed Flame's face, made talismans to protect his soul and Anemone's, and then gave powers to the NightWing students. And then Flame tried to kill Stonemover and —"

"Wait, whoa," said Qibli. "That doesn't sound like not much. Start from the beginning."

So Turtle told him and Winter as much as he could about Darkstalker's activities that day. Both dragons looked horrified when they heard what happened to Stonemover, but Winter seemed even more horrified by the news that Darkstalker was handing out superpowers to the NightWings.

Winter threw his silver-blue wings up in the air. "We only just found out that those powers were fake — and now they're real again?"

"You don't have to worry, though," Turtle reminded him. "You still have the skyfire, so no one can read your mind."

"I can be a little worried about superstrength," Winter growled. "And whatever that other one can do."

"Make bananas," Qibli filled in. "Absolutely terrifying. Run for your life."

Winter narrowed his eyes at his clawmate.

"So what is Darkstalker up to?" Qibli said thoughtfully. "What does he want?

"Seems obvious to those of us whose brains work," Winter snapped at him. "He wants to make friends and help dragons."

"That is what it looks like," said Turtle. "It's really confusing . . . he's only done good things all day."

"As far as we can see," Qibli pointed out. "We don't know what he might be doing in secret. That being the entire point of secrecy."

"Why do you have to be so suspicious?" Winter flared. "Darkstalker is the one who saved Stonemover! He's a good dragon with a good heart!"

"Also that," said Qibli. "Does that sound like our Winter at all? Remember yesterday when he was yelling at Moon about how you could never trust Darkstalker? Wouldn't he normally be more suspicious than anyone else?"

"I've changed and grown!" Winter protested. "I'm a much more open-minded dragon since my parents decided to sacrifice my life in exchange for my brother's place on a wall."

"I'm sure you are, Winter, but still . . ." Qibli spread his front talons. "Listen, I'm just picturing myself as Darkstalker, right? So I pop out of a mountain, and yikes, here's a fierce, smart, excessively shiny IceWing prince with an ego the size of an iceberg and a million potential great futures. I'm pretty sure I'd think, *hmm, that dragon could be a serious threat.* And then I'd think, *first thing I'd better do is neutralize you.* I'm just wondering if that's what he did."

Winter fluffed his wings as though he wasn't sure whether to be flattered or offended. "Well, stop wondering. I would *know* if I was under a spell."

"Right. Of course," said Qibli. "With your . . . magic IceWing brain? How exactly would you know, Lord Genius?"

"I don't have to stay and listen to this," Winter said, flouncing out of the cave.

Qibli poked his head out the door to watch until Winter was gone, then came back inside and sat down in front of Turtle with a rueful expression. "I have a really bad feeling that he's gone to tell Darkstalker about this conversation."

"He can't tell him about me, though," said Turtle. "Or if he does, Darkstalker won't hear it. My enchantment hides me completely from him." *I hope. I hope I hope I hope. If I did it right. Which seems unlikely, knowing me. Ack.*

"That's clever," said Qibli. "How did you think of that?"

"I used this brainstorming method called pure terror," Turtle admitted. "It wasn't so much clever as deeply cowardly."

"How does your soul feel?"

"Like it's still there," Turtle said with a shrug. He wasn't going to talk about the flashes of screaming Chameleon in his head. Or the way his heart sped up when he thought about how he'd do the same thing again to anyone else who hurt Kinkajou.

"Would you be willing to do a couple more spells?" Qibli asked. "If I had any powers of my own, I wouldn't ask . . ."

"Oh," said Turtle. "I mean, yes, I suppose so. The problem is I don't know what. I've been thinking about it all day. I should be able to do something useful, shouldn't I? If I can just figure out the exact right thing. Peril wanted me to kill Darkstalker, but I don't think that's possible, and I'm just . . . not the kind of dragon who kills other dragons. I don't want to be."

The flashes again; the enchanted scroll case smashing into Chameleon's face, the blood flying. The power tingling in Turtle's claws. The power to punish those who deserved punishing. The power to cause violence with a twitch of one talon.

No. No, no, no, that's not me.

"Plus what if he actually is good?" he hurried on, pushing the images away. "Winter's not the only one who thinks so — Peril does and I think Moon does, too. Then it would be really wrong to kill him. So then I wondered if I should do something to protect Anemone from him, right? Just in case? But I don't want to do anything he might notice. You know? That's the most important thing. I don't want him to suspect there's another animus out here. Just in case he's evil. I don't want him to have any clues that I exist."

He shifted his tail, thinking of all the heroes his mother had ever written about, and how none of them would have ever said anything like that.

"I understand," said Qibli. He took a deep breath. "This is something small. I was hoping you could tell me if there's a spell on me."

"On you?" Turtle said, startled.

"Remember that little fight I just had with Winter?" Qibli said wryly. "Applies to me, too. The thing that bothers me is, I like Darkstalker. He's funny and charming and he *does* seem helpful and he acts like I'm an important, valuable dragon. Why aren't *I* more suspicious? I can think logically of all these doubts and worries, but none of them seem to change the way I feel. And that makes me crazy, because I've always trusted my mind to figure things out for me when my gut is wrong."

"All right," said Turtle. "But the spell might not be on you. It might be on something else, like the earring Darkstalker is wearing, and it might apply to everyone around him."

Qibli frowned. "I hadn't thought of that." He tapped his

claws. "Then what else can we do? Could you —" He hesitated. "You probably wouldn't want to do this."

"What?"

Qibli traced a crack in the cave wall with one of his claws. "Could . . . could you turn me into an animus dragon, too?"

Turtle's stomach gave a guilty lurch. "I shouldn't," he said. "You wouldn't want that. You think you do, but you really don't."

"I'd be careful," Qibli insisted. "I'd protect my soul first thing, I promise. For my very first spell, I'd enchant something to make sure my soul was always good, or that I always made the kind and right choice that helped the most dragons. Doesn't that make sense?" He looked down at his claws. "That's what I would have done with Darkstalker's scroll, too. In case you were wondering."

Turtle remembered the fight Winter and Qibli had had, over who could keep Darkstalker's scroll and use it for themselves. It had scared him — but not as much as Darkstalker did. What would the world look like if either Winter or Qibli now had all this power instead?

"I believe you," he said, "but I still don't think it's a good idea." Making him an animus would put Qibli in danger in too many ways. Turtle would always feel responsible for whatever happened to him.

"Sure, that's all right," Qibli said quickly. "Sorry I asked. I'd probably feel weird about making more animus dragons if I were one, too."

"It's not —" Turtle started. "I mean, it's not *you*. I'm not trying to —"

"Don't worry about it," Qibli said, fiddling with his earring. "Maybe something else would make more sense anyway. Can you make me immune to animus spells?"

It was strange to be discussing his power openly with another dragon. Strange to be taking someone's advice, and to know that the other dragon would never be able to stop wanting things from him, even if it was a friend like Qibli.

"*All* animus spells?" asked Turtle. "Are you sure? I mean, some spells are good, aren't they? Like my healing rock, or the dreamvisitors — being immune means those wouldn't work on you anymore. And if you're completely immune, then an animus couldn't even change you back if you changed your mind."

"That's true," said Qibli. "What if you just made me immune to Darkstalker's spells, then?"

"Don't you think he'd notice?" Turtle fretted. "If he suddenly couldn't control you, or he tried to cast a spell and you didn't react . . . he'd get really suspicious, wouldn't he?"

"I'll take that risk," Qibli said. He tapped his claws against the floor in a nervous drumbeat rhythm. "As long as he can't use magic against me, I can handle anything else he does."

"Oh," Turtle said, feeling like even more of an inchworm. "I meant — yes, of course, suspicious of you, too, but then he'd know it's a spell, and that could lead him to me.

Which . . . I guess *I'm* not sure I can handle anything else he does."

Qibli picked up a scroll that had rolled across the cavern and tucked it back into one of the racks by the door. "You are some kind of worrying expert, aren't you?"

"Yes," Turtle said, his wings drooping. "I'm sorry. I like to think through everything as much as possible before making any big decisions."

"That's all right," Qibli reassured him. "It's smart. As long as you can also make decisions even when there's not enough time to think about them."

Turtle didn't like that idea. It gave him a scrunching feeling in his chest.

"Listen, Turtle, it's your magic. You're the boss of whether you want to use it. But I look at Winter and I think, *that is NOT the normal behavior of Her Majesty Queen Glacier's nephew.* And then I think, what about me? What if I'm acting like a hallucinating sunbaked lizard and I have no idea?"

"You seem normal to me," Turtle said. "Does that help?"

Qibli shrugged and turned away, rolling up another scroll. "I need to know my mind is my own. That's all. It's all I have. No superpowers, no firescales, no royal family. Just me and my brain, if it's working."

I am the lowest of cowards. How can I say no to the one dragon who's still willing to think twice about Darkstalker? To my friend, who needs protection?

"I'll do it," Turtle said. "Of course I will. Immune to Darkstalker's spells — that's what you want?"

"Really?" Qibli said, his face alight. "Yes! That would be amazing. Here, enchant my earring." He took it off and dropped the small gold and amber earring into Turtle's palm. "Do you know what you're going to say? Want me to write down some ideas?" He seized a scroll and a pot of ink before Turtle could answer and started scribbling on a blank corner.

"If this works," he went on, "we could do a spell like this for Winter, too, couldn't we?"

"Sure," Turtle said uncomfortably. *Here I go again. Helping my friends, which could mean getting noticed, which will surely lead to getting caught and slowly dismembered by a giant nightmare dragon from the past.*

There weren't any stories in the scrolls like this. He didn't know quite what role Qibli saw Turtle playing. Helpful wizard? Those often died by the end, too. Or maybe in Qibli's story, Turtle was the enchanted fish who granted three wishes if you caught him. *You've got two left, Qibli,* Turtle thought wryly. *Then I think I turn your nose into a sausage and escape back into the sea.*

"Wait," Qibli said, lifting his ink-stained claw from the scroll. "Have you made something to protect your soul yet?"

"Um . . . no," Turtle said. "I mean, I think it's fine."

"You should do that first," Qibli said. He started absent-mindedly drawing a series of concentric circles around the words he'd written on the scroll. "Something like what Darkstalker and Anemone have. That's more important than this."

"Let's do this first," Turtle said, reaching for the scroll. "Since it's all ready to go. It could take me all night to decide how to do the soul spell." He tried to return Qibli's grin.

"If you're sure . . ." Qibli said. "And you're feeling totally nonviolent . . ."

Turtle read the words carefully a few times, then focused on the small amber teardrop in his palm, glowing like sunlight against the dark green. "*Enchant this earring to make the wearer immune to any spell Darkstalker has cast or will cast, whether past, present or future.*"

Qibli inspected the earring like a poorly drawn map, then picked it up between two claws to squint at it. "I thought it would get all sparkly or something," he said.

"See if it makes you feel any different," Turtle suggested.

The SandWing slipped it back through the hole in his ear and blinked a few times. "Huh," he said. "I think so."

"You think so?" Turtle echoed, somewhat disappointed. If he was going to use his magic, he wanted it to make a big obvious cool helpful difference.

Qibli started pacing, tipping his head from side to side as though he was resettling everything inside his skull. "Let's see. I still think Darkstalker is funny and charming. But I definitely feel more anxious about that. There was this calm trusting feeling I had before, and that's vanished."

"Could be a coincidence," Turtle observed. "Like, all psychological."

"No." Qibli stopped in front of him and met Turtle's eyes. "I feel like my mind and my instincts are linked up again. Which is really important to me. Thank you."

"Hmm," Turtle said. This didn't seem like a particularly useful use of his magic, honestly. He guessed Qibli hadn't been under a spell at all. Darkstalker was charming and convincing enough to win everyone over without magic.

"I can help you figure out your soul spell!" Qibli offered. "I know how I'd phrase mine, if I could protect my soul with magic."

"You've thought about it that much?" asked Turtle. "When have you ever had to worry about your soul? Aren't you one of those naturally heroic dragons?"

Qibli let out a startled laugh. "No way," he said. "I grew up in the Scorpion Den, remember? I was stealing before I could fly. My mother was an assassin who tried to teach me garroting and poisons instead of reading and writing. I've done lots of bad things, and the problem is, I know I'd do more if it was for — for, um, Queen Thorn."

"I guess I could make you a soul spell, too," Turtle offered, trying to hide his reluctance. What was wrong with him? Darkstalker was giving out powers all over the place, helping other dragons he barely knew. Why couldn't Turtle be equally willing to share with his closest friends?

Was it just that he was afraid of being exposed? Or was he worried about how the magic might affect his friends?

"Thanks," Qibli said, pinning down the scroll he'd been writing on. "But let's make sure yours is safe first."

Maybe that's it, Turtle thought anxiously. *Maybe my soul isn't as fine as I think it is. Maybe using my magic has made me selfish and a terrible friend.*

Qibli blew a small flame on the corner where he'd written the first spell. As it burned away, he checked the other side of the scroll and made a face.

"I probably shouldn't have used my history reading for this," he said. "Well, too late now! It was really boring anyway. All right, one soul spell, coming right —"

A sudden thud from above shook the caves. Qibli and Turtle looked up, then at each other as more thuds followed, and then the scraping of scales and claws against rock echoed down the tunnels.

"What is —" Qibli started toward the door, but before he could get there, black scales blotted out the fire globes and Darkstalker was squeezing his head and shoulders through the narrow space to peer into Qibli's room.

Turtle scrambled to the back wall, as far away as he could get. *Why is he here? WHY IS HE HERE?* It took all his willpower not to close his eyes and curl up completely. He stood perfectly still as Darkstalker's sharp gaze scoured the cave.

"That looks uncomfortable," Qibli said to Darkstalker in a friendly voice. "I can't believe you squashed yourself into our tunnels."

"Not a problem," Darkstalker said, a bit breathlessly. "I'm surprisingly squishy." He grinned at Qibli, but there was something a little forced about his smile. "This is your cave?

I thought it might be Anemone's. What were you just doing in here?"

"Looking at scrolls," Qibli said, waving at the ripples of paper that covered his sleeping ledge. "Trying to figure out if I should bother studying. Accidentally setting history on fire. The usual." He waved at the thin trail of smoke that was still rising from the scroll on the floor.

Darkstalker studied each outcropping, each shadow with such slicing intensity that Turtle was sure he'd be seen, and not just seen, but peeled and flayed from horns to tail by those searching eyes.

"Is something wrong?" Qibli asked.

"Was Anemone in here a moment ago?" Darkstalker asked.

"No," Qibli said cautiously. "I haven't seen her."

"Are you sure?" Darkstalker demanded. "Or maybe passing by? She might have been talking to herself or doing something unusual?"

A lightning bolt of fear scorched through Turtle's body.

The spell on Qibli's earring. Darkstalker showing up only moments later, asking about Anemone.

He was looking for the source of a spell. Somehow he knew magic had happened here, and he came immediately to find out what Anemone was up to.

Darkstalker's given himself the power to sense animus magic.

— CHAPTER 9 —

If Darkstalker can tell when an animus casts a spell, Turtle realized, his heart floundering wildly around in his chest, *then I can never use my magic again.*

Turtle couldn't tell from Qibli's expression whether he'd figured it out as well. But then Qibli said, "Oh, Anemone — yeah, she might have gone by a little while ago. I'm not totally sure," and Turtle knew that he must have made the same connections.

"Interesting," Darkstalker mused. "If you see her, please tell her I wish to speak with her as soon as possible."

"Sure," said Qibli. "You bet. I'll do that."

Darkstalker gave him another appraising look. "Qibli," he said, "please order that scroll to roll itself up."

Qibli laughed. "Don't you think I've spent my whole life hoping magic would suddenly pop out of my claws?" he said. "Hey, scroll, roll yourself up." The scroll lay there, inert and uninteresting. Qibli shrugged at Darkstalker. "Disappointed again."

"I think that's for the best," Darkstalker said, smiling at him a bit more genuinely. "With your mind, you'd be a very formidable animus." He backed out of the cave. "See you in the morning."

"You too," Qibli answered. Darkstalker disappeared down the hall, with the sound of scraping scales jittering through the walls behind him.

"He *knew*," Turtle whispered — not because Darkstalker might hear him, but because his voice didn't quite seem to be working the way it should. "He knows when someone is using animus magic. He must have enchanted something to warn him."

Qibli waited until the vibrations of Darkstalker's passage had faded away. "Lucky you cast your hiding spell before he did that."

"Yes," Turtle said fervently.

"You're also lucky he didn't cast the enchantment to tell him exactly what the spell was," Qibli mused. "That's what I would have done. But he didn't act like he knew what we did."

Turtle couldn't speak for a moment, he was so appalled. He'd come so close to getting caught! In a way he hadn't even *imagined* worrying about! What other spells did Darkstalker have in place that might tangle him up?

"Now I can't use my magic anymore!" he finally managed to say. "Or else he'll figure out I'm out here, hiding from him."

"His spell seems to be location-based," Qibli pointed out. "Maybe if you were standing near Anemone or Stonemover when you cast it, he'd think it came from one of them."

"Maybe, but then wouldn't he ask them what spell they just cast? And if they say they didn't use their magic, what then? Would he think they're lying? I don't want him to think Anemone is secretly using her magic, maybe against him." He worried the edge of a wing between his claws. "I don't want to get her in trouble. I don't want him to blame her for what I'm doing."

"That's true," said Qibli. "Yeah, that could be bad."

"Arrrrrrrrrrrrrrrgh," Turtle groaned, lying down and covering his head with his wings.

"Look, I know it's terrible, but it's smart, too," said Qibli. "If you got trapped underground by an animus spell, wouldn't you want to keep a pretty close eye on any new spells after you got out? He's not going to let himself be fooled again. I'm sorry you didn't get to cast a spell to protect your soul, though."

"I'm going home," Turtle said, leaping up and whirling toward the door. "I'm going back to the Kingdom of the Sea to hide in the Deep Palace. He can't follow me there. Unless he can! He could enchant something to let him breathe underwater. Or something to make the entire ocean evaporate! HE COULD DO ANYTHING."

"Moons above, stop panicking!" Qibli jumped in Turtle's way. "It's not the end of the world. This doesn't prove he's evil. All we know for sure is he's protecting himself. So we keep watching him like you have been."

"I can't," Turtle said. "He's going to the rainforest tomorrow with the other NightWings."

"All the NightWings?" Qibli asked. "Including Moon?"

"I don't know," Turtle answered. "I think so."

Qibli thought for a moment, drumming his claws again. "I don't have a good excuse to go along with them," he said. "It'll have to be you."

"Me?" Turtle said, startled. "You mean follow him to the rainforest?"

"So we can see what he does next," Qibli said. "I can watch things here — you know, keep an eye out for any thunder and ice coming to destroy the school. Then we'll report back to each other and see what we think. If only we had a dreamvisitor, too, so we can send each other messages . . . maybe Sunny would let me use hers . . ."

Oh, Turtle realized. *I'm not his enchanted fish. He thinks we're in some kind of detective team story. Solving crimes together; investigating strange behavior. Or maybe I'm his sidekick. But the sidekick doesn't get sent on the crazy dangerous mission alone, does he?*

He was dangerously tempted by this vision. In detective stories, it was all right for one of the partners to be incompetent and unreliable, because the other one would make up for it. In that kind of story, Turtle's character wouldn't have to make all the decisions. No one would be waiting for him to save the day.

That was the kind of story he might actually survive.

"I might have something we could use," he said hesitantly.

He checked and triple-checked that Darkstalker was long gone from the hallways, then led Qibli back to his own lonely cave. Tucked under his woven-reed sleeping mat was the small satchel of belongings he'd brought to the school — a significantly lighter burden than Anemone's sparkle extravaganza.

Turtle tugged it out and shook the contents onto the floor.

A broken piece of coral. A pair of small, cracked writing slates with a slate pencil. Three pieces of curved wood that slotted together to form a weathered, food-stained bowl.

Qibli regarded the tiny pile with an extremely polite expression. "Well," he said. "Honestly, I've seen weirder treasure in the Scorpion Den."

Turtle checked the corridor again. "These are the things I've animus-touched," he whispered.

"Oh," Qibli said, his eyes alight. "What do they do? Protect your loved ones from harm? Smite your enemies? Make everybody love you?"

"Er . . . no," Turtle said awkwardly. He touched the coral. "This one helps me find things I've lost." He assembled the bowl and tipped it toward Qibli. "This doubles the amount of food you put in it — I just drop it in and say 'twice as much, please!' Then instead of two mussels, I'd have four, or instead of a ladleful of clam soup, I'd have twice that amount — that kind of thing."

Qibli tipped his head to the side. "Aren't you a prince? I thought that meant you'd have plenty of food."

"Well . . . yes," Turtle admitted. "But I was still competing with all my brothers for it. And I'd get hungry between meals and wouldn't feel like hunting. You know?"

"All right," said Qibli. "What about those?"

The slates clattered like falling seashells as Turtle picked them up and passed one to Qibli. "With these, if you write a note on one, it'll appear on the other."

He took the pencil and wrote "Hi Qibli" on the smaller slate. The message appeared simultaneously in his looping, scraggly handwriting on the other slate. When Turtle erased his slate, the message stayed in place on Qibli's.

Qibli turned his slate over in his talons, as though he were hoping to discover a better spell on the other side. "Huh," he said.

"So we can use these to communicate, I think," Turtle said. "I've never used it across a really big distance before. Oh, and it only works one way. But at least I can send *you* panicked 'help, he's got maaaaarggghh' messages."

"It only works one way?" Qibli echoed. His face seemed to be struggling with the concept of a world in which amazing magic could be given to a dragon like Turtle instead of him.

"Well," said Turtle, "yeah. I mean, I never thought I'd use it *with* anyone else."

Qibli, to his credit, managed to restrain his reaction to a slow blink. "Then . . . what in the world did you use this for?"

"It's a little embarrassing," Turtle admitted.

More embarrassing than a bowl that doubles your royal meals? said Qibli's expression.

"I used to think I wanted to be a writer," Turtle said. "So sometimes when I was out hunting or training or whatever, I'd have a great idea or think of how I wanted to phrase something, but I'd always forget it by the time I got home. With these, I could take notes on the slate I carried with me, then erase it quick before my brothers saw it — but the notes would be there waiting on the other slate once I got home."

"I see," Qibli said, finally looking sympathetic. "I had siblings who picked on me, too. A writer! So fancyscales."

"Oh, I gave that up a long time ago." Turtle shook his head. "I wasn't any good anyway." He nudged the other items. "I keep these kind of for sentimental value. I don't use them very much, since I don't want anyone to notice me using them."

"Sure," Qibli said. He tipped his slate up to the light. "But this is a great idea. I'll hang on to this one, and you can send me notes on what Darkstalker is doing. Or anytime you need me. Or if Moon needs me. Or anyone, I mean, hypothetically Moon, but anyone. I'll come flying, all right?"

Turtle nodded. It made him a little nervous to let half of one of his animus-touched objects out of his sight — what if it fell into the wrong claws? On the other talon, it was reassuring to have someone he could call for help.

I guess I just agreed to follow Darkstalker to the rainforest, he realized.

A clatter of talons came from the hallway, followed by a *whoosh*ing sound, a yelp of fury, and the distinct smell of something burning.

"Think I can guess who that is," Qibli said with a grin.

Turtle peeked out the door and found Peril jumping around trying to stomp out a small fire, except every time she touched it the flames got higher. A few sleepy faces peered out from their caves and immediately withdrew when they saw her.

"Ack!" she yelped. "Stop! Buckets of gizzards! Go OUT already!"

"Back back back," Qibli said, hurrying over and flapping her away with his wings. "I got it." He pulled one of the message chalkboards off the wall and smothered the fire, then trampled out the last few glowing sparks as they tried to scuttle away.

"WHAT KIND OF JERK leaves scrolls lying around in the HALLWAY where ANYONE COULD SET THEM ON FIRE?" Peril demanded. "Someone is TRYING to pick a fight with me, is that it?"

"Um . . . that was my homework," mumbled a RainWing nervously from the nearest doorway.

"Oh," Peril said. She drew her wings back in, eyeing the hapless dragonet, who was half her size and a nervous fizzy green color. "Um." She shot a glance at Turtle, of the "there's a right thing to say here, isn't there?" variety. "Well, next time, keep your mess in your own cave, all right?" she said, with what Turtle knew was about as much gentleness as she could muster.

"S-s-sorry," stammered the RainWing.

Turtle cleared his throat. "I'm sure Peril is sorry, too," he offered.

She tilted her head at him.

"For burning up this dragon's homework. Which he probably worked very hard on." Turtle tipped *his* head at the dragonet.

"Ah, okay, sure," Peril said, nodding vigorously. "I'm sorry your scroll got under my claws and met a fiery end," she said to the RainWing. "On the plus side, at least it was a scroll and not, say, your tail."

He turned an even paler shade of green and vanished into his cave.

"Good idea!" she called after him. "You shouldn't leave tails lying around the hallways either!"

"That's our Peril," Turtle said to Qibli. "Spreading a little terror before bedtime."

"Was I?" she said. "Hrmph. I thought that was a very nice apology myself."

Turtle liked the dragon he was when he was with Peril, although he hadn't quite figured out how their stories fit together. He might be *her* sidekick, although she wasn't exactly a normal hero. Or he might be her voice of reason, like the dragon assigned to take care of a mad prophet or something.

The closest parallel he could think of, though, was this scroll he'd once read about a dragonet who'd been lost and raised by a pack of orcas. So when she returned to her tribe, she had to be taught everything about language and relationships and how to interact with other dragons, and occasionally she would have furious fits and bite someone. With Peril, he sometimes felt like that wild dragon's foster brother — a minor character, but one of the few willing to risk hanging out with her.

He was pretty sure they were friends, though. Which was crazy; never in a million years would he have guessed that he might end up friends with the SkyWing queen's deadliest weapon.

She followed him and Qibli back into his sleeping cave, where he hurriedly scooted his sleeping mat to the far end of the room, away from Peril. He could move it to Qibli and Winter's cave later. He packed the smaller slate, the slate pencil, and the coral into his pouch to take with him to the rainforest. The pieces of the bowl were too big to fit, so he repacked them in his satchel and hid it under Umber's sleeping mat.

"How was your meeting with Clay?" Qibli asked Peril.

"Fine!" she blurted. "Fine, normal, great, weird, totally fine, why, what did you hear?"

"Nothing at all," he assured her. "Just wondering."

"Right," she said. "He was very pleased to hear about

Quee — about Scarlet." She paused, looking like she'd swallowed an exploding cactus for a moment. "There was hugging!" she finally burst out. "I mean, he gave me a hug. No big deal. Normal stuff, I'm sure. Dragons probably hug you guys all the time."

Oh, Peril. Turtle kind of wished he *could* hug her, to let her know he understood.

"Clay likes you, too," Qibli said to Peril.

"Really?" Peril glowed like molten glass. "He does? How do you know?"

"I can tell. He just doesn't know quite what to do about it yet," Qibli said. "Give him some time to figure it out. Like, lots and lots and lots of time."

"I have lots and lots of time," Peril said, exhaling. "That's totally all right with me." She beamed at Turtle. "Qibli thinks Clay likes me," she said in a loud whisper.

"I heard." Turtle smiled back at her.

"I was a little worried he'd hate me after I burned the magic scroll and released a giant bad guy," Peril admitted, "but I guess Darkstalker's not bad, so everything's all right?" She squinted at the items Turtle was packing. "What are you doing?"

"I'm going to follow Darkstalker to the rainforest tomorrow," Turtle said. "Just . . . to see what happens."

"Oh," Peril said, her wings drooping. One of them nearly caught on one of the scroll racks by the door, and Qibli quietly dragged it out of her reach. "You're leaving?"

"Only for a little while. I hope," Turtle said. "I wish you could come with me."

Peril held out her front talons. "I wish I could, too. But no firescales in the rainforest, by order of the queen," she said haughtily. "I'll miss your boring face, though," she said to Turtle. "Not, like, a LOT. But I'll miss it a little bit."

"You won't miss me at all," he said. "You'll have Clay to hang out with."

"True," she said. "True true." She tried to squash back her smile, but it kept sneaking out.

I really do wish she could come with me, Turtle thought. Her unpredictable, hilarious company was the only thing that had made him able to leave Jade Mountain in the first place. He'd been able to think of their adventure as *her* quest to find Scarlet. No pressure on him. Nothing enormously major he could mess up. Nobody expecting anything of him.

Not like tomorrow, when he'd be following Darkstalker to the rainforest alone.

Without the option of using his magic.

Alone, powerless, useless . . . this story couldn't possibly end well.

Ice Kingdom

Sky Kingdom

Queen Thorn's
Stronghold

Claws of the
Clouds Mountains

Kingdom of
Sand

Scorpion Den

Jade Mountain

PART TWO

RISE TO POWER

CHAPTER 10

The rainforest was an ocean of leaves below Turtle, tossing and rippling in the wind like a dark green sea. A spray of bright yellow birds flew out of it, squawking and diving and looping back down again to sink beneath the surface. But the smell here was nothing like the ocean: wild fruit and monkey droppings, heat and rich dirt, and roots growing in thick tangles in place of fish, salt, wide open air.

"I have no idea why *you* decided to come," Anemone said, sweeping up on Turtle's left. He started, then glanced around at Darkstalker, but the large dragon was far in the lead, scanning the forest below. Anemone had been so close to him all morning that Turtle hadn't had a chance to speak to her — or try to convince her not to come.

"I could say the same about you," he pointed out. "Shouldn't you be in school? Mother wouldn't want you wandering around Pyrrhia like this."

"I can learn far more from Darkstalker than from a crusty old shipwreck like Webs," Anemone snorted. "And

Mother doesn't have me on a leash anymore. I can go wherever I like."

"Wasn't Pike worried about you leaving?" Turtle tried. His pouch thumped lightly against his chest as he twisted in the air to keep Anemone in sight. "I'm surprised he didn't insist on coming with you, at least."

"Oh, I didn't tell him," she said, tossing her head. "He was sleeping outside my cave, which he often does, because he's *such* a weirdo, and I snuck right past him. Not much of a guard, if that's what he was trying to do! Ha ha!"

Poor Pike, waking up to find the princess had disappeared on his watch. He'd feel like such a failure. Turtle knew what that was like.

"But what's your excuse?" Anemone demanded. "I thought you were terrified of Darkstalker. You said he doesn't like you, but he never even looks at you."

"I just . . . want to see what he does," said Turtle. His claws itched to reach for his pouch, to make sure the stick was still there, but he fought back the urge.

"In case he does something SUPER EVIL?" Anemone teased, pouncing at him. Turtle flinched away. "You jellyfish. He's going to rescue his tribe, that's all."

"Queen Glory already rescued his tribe," Turtle pointed out. "They're not on the volcano anymore. They're perfectly safe."

"Right, safe to be the crushed seashells under the talons of the RainWings." Anemone rolled her eyes. "Think about it, big brother. Imagine if Mother died and I was too spineless to take the throne, so all the SeaWings decided to go live in the Mud Kingdom and let Queen Moorhen boss us around. Is that any way for a self-respecting tribe to live?"

Turtle noticed Fearless listening to them with a scowl on her face. He decided it might be a good idea to change the subject.

"Did you get in trouble with Darkstalker last night?" he asked. "I mean, I heard he was looking for you." He needed to know what was going on in Darkstalker's head. Did he suspect there was another animus around?

"Oh, that was the most ridiculous thing," Anemone said with a laugh. "He asked me if I cast a spell without his permission. I said, 'oh, PERMISSION, is that how this is?' and he said, 'without my *brilliant advice*, then.' I said I didn't think so, but sometimes I've used my power accidentally without noticing. Like, you'd think an animus would learn not to yell at her stuff, but sometimes I forget and do it anyway. I made a pearl necklace explode that way once. Anyway, no, of course I'm not in trouble! He knows I'm a princess and can do whatever I want."

Oh, does he? Turtle thought. But he didn't have a chance to respond. Up ahead, Darkstalker shot a burst of flame into the sky and beckoned to Anemone and the NightWings. They darted over to him as though he was the sun and they all wanted to fall into it.

"Time for our grand entrance!" Darkstalker announced. He dove into the canopy and the others followed, one by one.

Turtle sighed and flapped along behind them. He wondered what would happen if Anemone figured out that Darkstalker couldn't see or hear Turtle. She tended to accept that the world revolved around her, so it would probably be a while before she noticed.

And then . . . will I tell her the truth?

He dropped from the hot-sun sky down and down into dappled green light that reminded him of the Summer Palace, before it was destroyed. Long-limbed creatures of fur flurried out along the branches as he maneuvered carefully between the thick vines and grasping spider webs. The trees were interwoven like living nets, lying in wait for their prey.

Far below them, on the rainforest floor, the entire NightWing tribe was gathered in a clearing, looking up. All around them were grass huts and ramshackle wooden structures, many of them only half built. The scent of crispy boar meat rose from a fire pit that glowed in the center of the village, carefully lined with rocks.

Queen Glory stood on a mahogany platform, facing the tribe. She was the only RainWing present, or at least visible, and her scales were set in an intricate overlapping leaf pattern of bright green, gold, and black. Beside her, as close as her shadow, was a NightWing with a worried expression. Turtle guessed that was Deathbringer, from the stories he'd heard about the young RainWing queen and her loyal, self-appointed bodyguard.

Glory watched Darkstalker descend without a hint of

emotion on her face, nor even the slightest color change in her scales. Turtle wondered if she'd ever been afraid of anything in her life.

He perched on a branch overhead, where the tooth-shaped leaves matched the dark green of his scales. Below, Darkstalker soared down to land next to Glory, instantly dwarfing her and Deathbringer. A muffled gasp rustled through the crowd of NightWings. Deathbringer sidled a step closer to Glory, but the queen herself neither flinched nor moved.

Anemone hovered for a moment at Darkstalker's shoulder, but there was no room on the platform for anyone else. Huffing grumpily, she landed on the ground close by, then spent several minutes pointedly scraping all the muddy leaves out of her little patch of dirt.

"Darkstalker, I presume," said Glory. She nodded to Moon and the other three NightWing dragonets as they slipped into the tribe. Turtle saw each of them find their parents; he saw Moon's mother wrap her wings around her daughter. He saw Mindreader whispering excitedly to a tall male NightWing, holding out her bracelet.

"I see Sunny used the dreamvisitor to tell you we were coming," Darkstalker said. "Even though I asked her very nicely not to. Interesting."

"The tribe prefers not to be surprised," Glory said, indicating the sea of black dragons below them. "But as you can see, despite your prediction, no one has run away. They chose to be brave, to stand together and face you."

That wasn't entirely accurate; Turtle had seen a few dragons bolt into the forest as Darkstalker flew down. But he didn't blame them, considering Darkstalker had been the tribe's worst nightmare for the last two thousand years. He was amazed so many of them were able to hold their ground. He wondered what Queen Glory had said to them to give them that strength.

Darkstalker smiled his dazzling smile. "There's no need to be brave," he said. "I'm no monster. The history you've been fed is all a pack of lies." He opened his talons palm up toward the tribe, as if revealing all his secrets to them. "They told you I was evil, that I was about to do terrible things, and that I was locked away to protect you. None of that is *true*, my fellow NightWings.

"I had a majestic future planned for our tribe. Power and security and wealth and peace for every dragon. No running, no hiding, no lying or starving or living in fear. But there were dragons who didn't trust my vision for us. They feared what our tribe could become."

He swept one wing open in an arc as though he were flinging diamond dust over the entire crowd. Turtle wondered how much Darkstalker had rehearsed this speech, alone in the dark, deep under layers of rock.

"I was betrayed on the brink of changing everything." Darkstalker took a breath, as if he could feel daggers stabbing into his back. "Dragons I thought I could trust trapped me underground, where I've been asleep against my will for the last two thousand years. Meanwhile, our tribe fell apart — lost its power, its home, its position in Pyrrhia. And history scrolls were written about me by deceitful dragons who feared my powers.

"Am I evil? No. Murderous? Not even remotely. Dangerous? Not to my own tribe, or to my friends."

His eyes went to Moon, and a few other NightWings turned to look at her as well.

"Here's the real truth. I love our tribe." Darkstalker looked alive in a way Turtle hadn't seen yet. He looked . . . happy. "The NightWings were once the most powerful, most respected and creative tribe in Pyrrhia. And I can show you the way to become that tribe again."

He paused, perhaps expecting applause, but the only sound was the wind in the trees and a jaguar roar in the distance.

"These dragons have been working hard to build their new home," Glory said, her calm voice carrying across the clearing. "They have security and peace here. They are smart, fierce, determined, and full of surprising ideas. They don't need any help to become a great tribe — they already are one."

Now there was a reaction — a rustling as several NightWings stood up straighter, tipped their wings back, lifted their chins.

"I'm sure they are," said Darkstalker. "But I know what they could be. I can see the shining future ahead, if everyone follows me."

"Follows you?" Deathbringer jumped in. Glory gave him a quelling look, but he barreled on. "Follows you where?"

"Back to our old kingdom, of course," said Darkstalker. He gazed down at Glory, a slow smile spreading across his face.

"Queen Glory," he said, and there was a lilt to his voice that hinted at how amusing he found that phrase. "I'm here to challenge you for the throne of the NightWing tribe."

CHAPTER 11

Turtle wasn't sure why he was so shocked — after all, wanting to become king of the NightWings certainly fit in with everything else Darkstalker had done so far. But it still hadn't occurred to him. No tribe had ever had a king in the history of Pyrrhia, as far as Turtle knew. He never could have imagined this scene, or how Queen Glory could suddenly look as though she were made of spun glass.

If he *could be king, then* I *could be a king, too.*

Where did that thought come from? Turtle would never want to be king in a million years — and he would never be able to do what it took to become one.

Even after what I did to Chameleon?

He frowned down at his twitching talons. That was not the real him. These thoughts were not the real him, either.

Moon broke away from her mother and started pushing forward through the crowd.

"You can't do that," Deathbringer spat at Darkstalker. Glory didn't stop him; she was staring at Darkstalker as though he'd upended eighty million words on her head and she was trying to put them in the right order to make a scroll.

"Why not?" Darkstalker asked.

"For one thing, you're male," said Deathbringer. "And for another, you're not royalty, so you have no right to the throne."

"In case you hadn't noticed, she's not exactly of royal NightWing blood either," Darkstalker said, flicking his tail at Glory. "And just because we've never had a king before doesn't mean we shouldn't have one now."

"Pyrrhia has only had queens for the entirety of dragon history," said Deathbringer. "Male dragons cannot rule their tribes. That's just the way it is."

"Things can change," Darkstalker said airily. "We're dragons, not ants. We can do things differently if we choose to."

Turtle had a flash of déjà vu and touched his claws to his head. Where had he heard that before? From one of the teachers at Jade Mountain?

"Darkstalker!" Moon hissed from the front of the crowd, and he looked down at her. "What are you doing? You promised not to hurt my friends!"

"Feel free to check on your friends," said Darkstalker in an unsettlingly gentle voice. "I'm sure you'll find that they're all safe and perfectly unharmed."

"But Glory's my friend, too," Moon said, her voice wobbling. "I don't want you to kill her."

Was that real sympathy in Darkstalker's eyes? "Oh, Moon," he said. "The truth is you don't want me to kill anybody. And neither do I . . . but we are *dragons*. There's a way these things have to be done."

"I cannot accept your challenge," Glory said, and Darkstalker turned back to her, leaving Moon with her talons helplessly outstretched. "The RainWings need me, too. If I fought you, I'd be putting their tribe and throne at risk."

"Maybe I could be king of both tribes!" Darkstalker said. "Ha ha, just a joke. I have no interest in ruling a bunch of snoozy colorful vegetarians."

Turtle wasn't sure if he was imagining it, but he thought a few of the NightWings actually looked a bit offended by that comment.

"There's another alternative," Darkstalker went on. "You could just *give* me the NightWing throne." He shot a glance at Moon, as if to say, *Look, I'm making an effort! Now do you approve?*

"That would not be fair to the dragons here who swore loyalty to me," said Glory.

"Well," said Darkstalker, "let's all remember that they had a volcano pointed at their heads at the time. You're certainly more appealing than death by lava, but if there were a charming, handsome, superpowered NightWing as an option instead . . ."

Queen Glory looked out at the gathered NightWings.

What are they thinking? Turtle wondered. *Would they rather be ruled by a RainWing or by a legendary monster?*

He remembered the stories he'd read about Albatross, the SeaWing animus who massacred most of his family. If Albatross somehow came back to life, and he acted like a sane, friendly dragon, and Turtle had to choose between him or, say, Queen Glacier to rule the Kingdom of the Sea . . . who would he pick?

"Oh," said Darkstalker, nodding at Glory. "Very interesting idea, Your Majesty."

Glory looked at him sharply.

"Let the NightWings choose for themselves," he said.

"Indeed. I could agree to that."

"I haven't offered it to you yet," said Glory. "In this time period, it's considered bad manners to read another dragon's thoughts."

"My apologies. But you had such a good idea. A peaceful transition of power — maybe dragons have evolved in the last two thousand years after all! What do you think?" Darkstalker said to the assembled NightWings. "Shall we put it to a vote, like some enormous sprawling mess of a council? King Darkstalker or Queen RainWing?"

"No," Queen Glory said, stepping forward into a bar of sunlight that lit up every brilliant scale. "Not a vote. I don't want my tr — any NightWing to be forced to live somewhere or under someone they are unhappy with." She studied the ebony dragons below her. "Those who wish to stay in the rainforest with me, in the village you've built with your own talons, are welcome here forever. Those who would rather follow Darkstalker to the old kingdom are free to go."

Darkstalker looked down at the crowd, too, from a considerably greater distance, and he did not look pleased with what he saw — or what he was hearing in their minds, Turtle realized.

"But you don't have to decide right now," Darkstalker said quickly, slippery-smooth. "You should get to know me first! I presume Queen Glory won't mind if I spend a day or two in the rainforest, reacquainting myself with my tribe."

"Be our guest." Glory rested her quiet gaze on him for a moment — just a moment, while something puzzled flickered behind her eyes. Then she turned to Deathbringer, and the two of them hopped down from the stage to walk among the NightWings.

A hubbub of voices rose, hushed and panicked at the same time. Who would stay? Who would go? What would become of them?

Darkstalker's eyes went to Moon. "See?" he said softly. "I knew I wouldn't really have to kill Glory. But I had to present myself as a strong leader, Moon. That's what dragons understand."

Moon gave him a wounded look and turned away, back toward her mother's wings.

Turtle watched Darkstalker watching her go.

I think I've found one true thing about Darkstalker, he thought. *He actually cares about Moon.*

But how does she feel? She's the one who's been helping him so far — will she follow him to the Night Kingdom? Or will she choose Queen Glory . . . and if she does, how is he going to react?

Queen Glory stayed in the NightWing village until midafternoon, answering questions and talking with any dragon who approached her. Darkstalker installed himself on a flat boulder by the river and did the same, while Anemone splashed and swam in the fish-flickering water.

It all seemed very peaceful. Entirely open. Nothing suspicious or underhanded. Turtle wrote a quick note on his slate to Qibli:

DARKSTALKER WANTS TO BE NIGHTWING KING.
NIGHTWINGS DECIDING WHAT THEY WANT.

Then he wiped it clean and tried not to fall asleep while Darkstalker droned on about parliamentary procedures in the ancient Night Kingdom.

But then Glory left, flying back to check on her RainWings. Darkstalker saw her go. He waited a few minutes, swirling his tail in the river as he listened to a sly-looking dragon named Obsidian complain about rainforest insects.

Finally Darkstalker said, "That does sound dreadful. You know, the Night Kingdom doesn't have *any* mosquitoes." He sat up and called "Mindreader!" touching his head as though summoning her by telepathy as well.

A few moments later, the dragonet came scampering through the village with an older, significantly more reluctant-looking NightWing limping behind her.

"Here!" she said breathlessly, skidding to a stop below Darkstalker. "Come *on*, Father, you have to meet him. He's got *amazing* powers."

"So I hear," Mindreader's father said gruffly.

"But don't you understand that he's sharing them?" she said. "If you could have any power in the world, what would you want, Father?"

He snorted. "To be an animus, of course. Is there anything more powerful?"

Mindreader turned to Darkstalker with shining eyes, but Darkstalker was shaking his head with a regretful expression. "I'm sorry," he said. "That is the one gift which is beyond my abilities to grant. An animus dragon cannot make other animus dragons."

Huh, thought Turtle. He knew that was a lie. *Does Darkstalker know he's lying, or does he believe that?*

"That's not the only thing Father wants," Mindreader said quickly. "I can hear it in his head! He wants the ability to heal instantly from any wound. Not just new wounds, but all the old aches and weak bones and clouded lungs he got from living on the volcano. Aw, Father, I'm sorry. I didn't know you were always in pain like that." She twined her tail around his, and Turtle found himself liking her for the first time.

"You're not supposed to know these things," her father said with a wince. "I'm not sure it's going to be good for you, little one, hearing everyone's thoughts this way. Dragons like to keep their secrets."

"I know, it's incredible how many secrets there are," Mindreader said, her eyes widening. "If I were a blackmailing sort of dragon, I could get so much treasure! But I'm not, of course; of course I'm not, and I wouldn't." She let out a little laugh. "Enough about me! Darkstalker?"

"I'm not sure about this," said her father, edging away as Darkstalker reached toward him. "I don't trust anyone to put a spell on me."

"So we'll use something temporary," Darkstalker said winningly. He sliced a vine off the tree branch overhead and wove it into a simple loop, which he dropped over the other dragon's neck. "I'll enchant this to heal you, and when it rots away, come back and let me know if you liked it and want something more permanent." He hooked one claw in the vine necklace and muttered something under his breath.

Mindreader's father let out a startled gasp. He stretched his wings and tail; he turned his head from side to side. He looked forty years younger just from the way he was suddenly standing and the way his eyes were shining.

"Oh," he said. "Three moons! I couldn't even remember what it was like to feel this way!"

"I'm here to help," said Darkstalker with his charming grin. "Now . . . go tell all your friends."

Uh-oh, thought Turtle.

Uh-oh was right. The first trickle of curious NightWings became a waterfall once word spread that Darkstalker was handing out superpowers.

The ability to catch any prey — done.

Flight speed faster than any SkyWing, or indeed, any other dragon on Pyrrhia — done.

Camouflage scales like the RainWings — Darkstalker chuckled and talked that dragon out of his choice. "Why would you want to blur the lines of what you really are? Be a NightWing and proud of it. If I give you advanced warrior skills, you'll never need to hide again anyway."

Advanced warrior skills — done.

The ability to go for days without sleep — done.

And then Darkstalker announced that powering up five dragons per day was his limit. "But this way you can think about it overnight," he said. "What do you each really want? What would be the best possible power for you? I promise you, I'll share my gift with five more dragons tomorrow — on the way to the old Night Kingdom."

Wow, Turtle thought. *He's not messing around. Follow me, and I'll make you special. Or stay here . . . and remain your own ordinary self.*

What dragon could resist an offer like that?

What chance does Glory have, when that's the alternative?

He pulled out his slate and thought for a moment, then wrote to Qibli:

THE NIGHTWINGS ARE GETTING A KING.

CHAPTER 12

Turtle could feel the tides shifting in the village: dragons whispering about another side to Darkstalker, about how the history scrolls could have been wrong, about how NightWings should stick with their own and stop mingling with lazy vegetarians.

I should tell Glory. Shouldn't I? She has no idea who I am. But she'd want to know what Darkstalker is doing. Wouldn't she?

He worried for a while, watching Darkstalker tell stories of the old days to a rapt audience of dragons. Finally he scooted back along his branch and set off in the direction Glory had gone.

A short distance beyond the NightWing village, all the trees began to look the same.

Not long after that, Turtle realized he didn't exactly know where he was going. He stopped, hovering in midair, and glanced around at the dense, never-ending greenery. Lost in the rainforest — that sounded exactly like what would happen to the Turtle character in a story. While the heroic heroes battled onward, wondering vaguely where he'd gone.

Except in this case, there were no heroic heroes battling, because they were all too busy making friends with the potential supervillain.

Turtle sighed. *So I can't be lost in the rainforest,* he thought. *I can't be the inept best friend right now. I have to be someone else — the messenger, perhaps, who warns the heroes of the danger and then fades back into the background.*

What would a successful, determined messenger do about being lost in the rainforest?

He found a very fat tree with comfortable wide branches to sit on. All around him the bright red flowers danced, the leaves twitched, the shadows and sunlight darted and glimmered as wind pushed the treetops around.

"Hello?" he said. "Any chance I'm being followed?"

If he was, no one answered.

He tried again. "I have an urgent message for Queen Glory. She'll want to hear it, I promise. But . . . I don't know how to find her."

More silence. More trees flapping their leaves at him dismissively.

So. That didn't work. He wasn't quite lucky enough to have any camouflaged RainWings spying on him right now.

His immediate instinct was to use his magic. That would be the easiest solution. That was always the easiest solution. Whenever he felt a little sick or too tired for anatomy class or needed help finding something, he'd reach for a magical solution — as long as it was small enough for no one to notice.

But he couldn't do that now, because Darkstalker would notice *any* spell, no matter how small.

His talons went to his pouch. Wait . . . maybe he already had what he needed.

He slipped the pouch open with careful claws, tipping it so his animus-touched treasures clicked and tumbled together.

Near the bottom, wrapped in leaves to protect it, was the piece of coral. It was shaped like a small, lacy red tree with little bubbles all along its branches. Turtle remembered the night he'd enchanted it — the night he'd realized he was an animus.

Queen Coral's sons were rarely invited to royal functions, as there were simply too many of them. But when Turtle, Octopus, and Cerulean were all one year old, their father managed to get them invited to their first grand ball. Turtle's brothers were excited; Turtle was mostly nervous. Would he say the right things? Would he remember all the rules about when to eat (and more important, when *not* to eat)?

Gill had sent matching earrings for all the princes to wear: each one a heavy gold ring with a pearl hanging from it. Octopus and Cerulean clipped theirs on easily, but Turtle could not figure his out. He'd never worn an earring before. His claws felt too big and awkward to work the catch open far enough and the earrings kept slipping out of his grasp and floating slowly down to the seaweed-carpeted floor of his room.

Octopus and Cerulean laughed at him as he scrabbled in the seaweed, which had swallowed one of the earrings completely. *It's not that hard!* Octopus teased, his phosphorescent scales flashing. *By all the whales, Turtle, do you have tentacles for talons?*

They turned to swim out of the room. *See you there!* Cerulean called mockingly.

If you ever make it! Octopus agreed, and they cackled their way down the hall.

Grimly, Turtle glared at the remaining earring, pinched between his claws.

"AAAAAARRRRRGH! Earring," he snarled, shaking it, "get on my ear right now and *stay there.*"

The earring moved, shimmying in Turtle's grasp.

Startled, he let go, and the earring confidently made a beeline straight for Turtle's ear. A moment later, he felt a nudging pinch, and when he looked in the mirror — there it was, hanging from his ear exactly where it was supposed to be.

Did I do that?

He felt terrified and elated at the same time. If he did that, there was only one explanation.

He'd heard the stories about Albatross, the ancient animus SeaWing — although that particular story didn't end very well. There were fewer stories about other animus

SeaWings, like Fathom, who were much more cautious with their powers.

Despite the horror stories, a part of Turtle had always wondered what it would be like to be an animus, with all that power in his claws.

He had to test it out — to find out if it was real. One of the walls of their room was made of coral, and he'd noticed a small piece that was nearly broken off. He swam over and carefully snapped it free, then clasped it between his talons.

I enchant this piece of coral to help me find whatever I'm looking for.

He peeked at the coral, but it looked exactly the same. Hmmm. *My other earring,* he flashed at it in Aquatic. He caught himself wondering whether coral could speak Aquatic just as the little red tree twitched and twisted in his claws. It tugged him down to the seaweed carpet, where it poked through the flapping overlapping strands until it bumped against his missing earring.

That might have been the most glorious moment of Turtle's life. (It was certainly all downhill from there, if you asked him.)

He was an *animus*! His brothers couldn't laugh at him now! His mother and father would have to pay attention to him! He'd be the star of the whole palace!

That was kind of a frightening thought, actually. Everyone looking at him? Everyone wanting him to perform? Everyone waiting for him to mess up?

But the truth was, only one thing stopped him from swimming straight into the ball and announcing his discovery to everyone.

Stories. Turtle knew how stories worked. He knew that a dragon with strange powers could be a hero or a villain, and a lot depended on how everyone found out what he or she could do. The best heroes were the ones who took everyone by surprise in their hour of need. Just when all hope was lost, the unexpected hero would swoop in and save the day! And if Turtle revealed his power that way, when it was really needed, then no one would be scared of him. He'd clearly be a hero.

Drama, excitement, and the chance to do something wonderful when no one saw it coming — that's what Turtle wanted in his story.

So he hid his power, waiting for the perfect moment of revelation. The tribes were all at war; surely it would come soon.

But then it came, when his father needed him, and he didn't recognize it, and then it was gone.

In the rainforest, far from home, Turtle sighed and turned the coral over in his claws. The last time he'd used it was the day Gill sent him searching for Snapper. Turtle had had to be very surreptitious, since Octopus and Cerulean insisted on following him around and giggling over how incompetent he was. At first he thought he'd been very clever to think of using the coral — but it hadn't worked. Something was wrong with it. It kept trying to lead him out of the Deep

Palace, which was why he was uselessly prowling the gardens when Gill found him.

He should have enchanted something else, even with Octopus and Cerulean watching. He should have realized that finding Snapper was the great thing he was meant to do; he should have revealed his secret right then and saved the day.

In fact, he should have used his magic to find the assassin who was killing off the princesses. It was embarrassing and awful that he'd never even thought of that until years later, when Tsunami showed up and figured out who it was.

But after Turtle's failure, he didn't know how to tell anyone he was an animus. He'd lost the plot of his story. He kept imagining his father saying, "But if you had magic the whole time, why didn't you find Snapper? Why didn't you save your sisters? What kind of dragon has this power and doesn't use it to help his family? I'm more disappointed in you than ever."

And the longer he hid it, the worse it got. Why didn't he use his magic to rescue his father from the SkyWings? Why didn't he use his magic to stop the attack on the Summer Palace?

Why was he such a useless, wretched excuse for a dragon?

Turtle realized he was gripping the coral so tightly that it was leaving an imprint in his palm. He unclenched his fist and looked at it. He wasn't even sure why he'd kept the thing after it failed him. Maybe because it was the first real enchantment he'd ever cast. It reminded him of that brief moment when he'd been so happy and excited about his future.

Most likely it wouldn't work now either. But he couldn't enchant anything new, he didn't have many other options, and it was worth a try.

"Queen Glory," he whispered.

The coral twitched and hummed softly, then tugged him northward. He spread his wings and flew, paying attention to the signals it gave, turning him this way and that and upward through the forest toward the canopy.

I could have used this to help Peril find Scarlet, he realized. *Or to find my friends in Possibility.* Instead he had left it behind at school with his other animus-touched objects. It hadn't even occurred to him to try using it. He wouldn't have expected it to work, and he wouldn't have wanted Peril to notice it.

But it certainly would have been useful, he thought ruefully. *Add that to the list of ways I could have helpfully used my magic and didn't.*

Soon enough, there was Glory — there, in fact, was the entire RainWing village, tucked into the treetops. As Turtle flew closer, he saw more and more shapes emerge from the leaves: hammocks and walkways, pavilions and dwellings, silver-furred sloths and beautiful dragons of all colors everywhere.

Queen Glory was on one of the highest pavilions, bathed in sunlight, with her wings spread wide. She was asleep, but

Deathbringer sat watchfully beside her, scanning the undergrowth for any threats.

Threats seemed hard to imagine here, in this peaceful place — but Turtle thought of Darkstalker and his five new superpowered NightWings, only a short flight away, and he shivered.

The coral tugged him stubbornly toward the platform. Deathbringer saw him coming and sat up with a sharply curious, but not unfriendly, expression.

"Halt!" he called when Turtle was only a short distance away. "What business do you have with the queen?"

The animus-touched coral did not like it at all when Turtle stopped and hovered in midair. It jabbed painfully at his palm, trying to move him forward.

A bit late, Turtle remembered the coral's weird habit: It would not stop searching for the thing he wanted to find until he actually touched the object with the coral. It wouldn't fly away on its own, but every time he picked it up, it would squirm and poke him until it reached its goal. This had been confirmed rather gruesomely when it dragged him through the palace the night after his failure, just so it could bump itself against the side of Snapper's corpse, in a way that Turtle thought was entirely too smug for a malfunctioning scrap of coral.

"Um," Turtle said, clapping his other talon around the one that held the coral. "I've been watching Darkstalker since you left the NightWing village, and I thought the queen should know what he's been up to."

"What's a SeaWing doing in the rainforest in the first place?" Deathbringer asked doubtfully. "Are you here with Darkstalker, like the princess?"

"No, no," Turtle said. "I mean — I'm just watching him. Anemone is my sister," he fumbled, but apparently that was enough of an explanation for Deathbringer.

"I see," he said. "Well . . . I'm reluctant to wake the queen during her suntime. Is it urgent?"

"Um," said Turtle. Probably not? If Darkstalker wasn't going to enchant any more dragons today, did it make any difference?

"Deathbringer," Queen Glory said with a sigh, opening her eyes. "I'm not sure if you're familiar with the concept of ears and how they work. But most normal dragons would find it very difficult to sleep through your loud interrogations."

"I was giving you the opportunity to *pretend* to sleep through them," Deathbringer objected. "You're usually much better at it."

"I nearly gave myself away by laughing when you said 'halt,' though," Glory said, stretching and sitting up. "I mean, who says 'halt,' seriously?"

"I thought it sounded dignified and commanding," said Deathbringer.

"Indeed. Or like a pretentious NightWing," Glory observed.

"I AM a pretentious NightWing. It's part of my appeal."

"All right, hush, you," said Glory, patting Deathbringer's talons with her tail. "Come here, SeaWing. What's your name?"

"Turtle, Your Majesty," he said. The coral was kind of

going berserk as he landed beside her, and she shot a curious look at his squirming talons. "I'm Tsunami's brother — one of them. I'm nobody, really." *The messenger. Here to tell someone who can actually save the world.* "I just thought you should know that Darkstalker has given a few NightWings special powers."

"Special powers?" Deathbringer echoed. "Like what?"

"Mindreading," Turtle listed off. "Superstrength. Fighting skills, the power to catch any prey, instant healing — that kind of thing."

"Wow," said Glory. "It's going to be hard to compete with that."

"I wouldn't leave you, even for a superpower," Deathbringer said loyally.

"I think that is your superpower," Glory said to him. "Extreme heroic idiocy." She arranged her face to look serious again and turned to Turtle. "Well, if that means all the NightWings decide to go with Darkstalker, I suppose my job around here will get a lot easier." She looked wistfully out at the rest of the village, where many of the RainWings were asleep in their leaf hammocks and sunlit nests.

"That's true," said Deathbringer. "Much less grumbling and complaining to deal with."

"They were kind of growing on me, though," Glory admitted. "They're impressively . . . resilient."

"Not to mention obsessed with scrolls and learning and stuff," said Deathbringer. "All your favorite things."

"I did think the NightWings and the RainWings could be

good for each other, once they had some mutual respect and trust in place." Glory lifted her wings up and down in a soft sigh. "Ah, well."

"Wait," said Turtle. "You're not going to do anything? To stop him?"

"We have an agreement," Glory said, surprised. "Why would I stop him?"

"Um . . . maybe because he's turning his tribe into kind of a super army? Doesn't that worry either of you?"

"Huh," said Deathbringer. "I guess you could look at it that way."

Isn't it your job to look at it that way? Turtle thought, frustrated.

"Maybe if it was anyone else," Queen Glory agreed. "But I mean, Darkstalker's such a great dragon. I just trust him — don't you?"

"I do," Deathbringer said, nodding. "I like him."

Turtle couldn't speak. His head felt as if it was full of squirming, flashing electric eels. All his suspicions coalesced into one diamond-bright conviction.

This was not a normal reaction. Not to Darkstalker, nor to any dragon who came in to steal the tribe you were ruling. None of the dragons who'd spoken to Darkstalker were reacting to him in a normal way.

Qibli was right, after all. He *had* been under a spell. That "calm trusting feeling" he'd had about Darkstalker — that was the work of magic. This was why everyone was behaving so *weird* and unworried.

Darkstalker had crafted some kind of spell — something that affected every dragon who met him. It made dragons like him and trust him, and perhaps worse. What if it made everyone obey him? Or willing to sacrifice their lives for him?

If Darkstalker wanted to, he could turn all the dragons of Pyrrhia, one by one, into his own personal puppets . . . and nobody would be able to stop him, because nobody would even know anything was wrong.

CHAPTER 13

So . . . maybe now *it's time to run and hide,* Turtle thought. Back to the Kingdom of the Sea; back to the anonymity of his pack of brothers. Back to a world so distant that Darkstalker might never come there; back to the only place that might be safe, at least for a little while.

This was too big for him to handle. He sort of had Qibli — but what if something happened to Qibli, or Darkstalker figured out how to ensnare him again? Turtle could end up as the only dragon in Pyrrhia who saw Darkstalker the way he really was — and then what? Spend the rest of his life as the unbalanced invisible dragon, trying to convince his friends they were bewitched by a sinister magician?

The mad prophet of doom . . . not exactly the role I ever saw myself in.

But the alternative was "coward who sits and waits for the inevitable apocalypse." If he scurried off back to the ocean, would anyone ever notice what Darkstalker was doing? Would anyone ever be able to stop him?

So if he couldn't run away and he couldn't change anyone's mind and he couldn't fight Darkstalker himself . . . what could he do?

I need help.

He touched the cord of his pouch, tied around his neck. Should he write to Qibli? Ask him to come here?

He could feel his worrying reflex kicking into action. His scales felt hot and clammy at the same time.

Was he sure that Qibli was free of any Darkstalker spells? What if Darkstalker had enchanted his spell to be irreversible, even by other magic?

Or what if he'd enchanted Qibli to stay at Jade Mountain, so seeing him in the rainforest would make him suspicious? Everything Qibli did might give Darkstalker a clue that his spell wasn't working on him anymore. Turtle's safety would be in danger if Qibli and Darkstalker spent too much time near each other.

I wish I could get his advice, though. Turtle dropped his talons, frustrated. *Too bad the slates don't work both ways. Thanks to me being a short-sighted idiot again.*

Who else could help him?

I need someone who hasn't met Darkstalker yet.

Someone who'll believe me. Someone who can actually be the hero.

His mother? Would Queen Coral believe him if he went to her with this story? Would she be able — or willing — to fight Darkstalker?

He couldn't really imagine her trusting him that much.

And if she did and brought the SeaWings out to fight Darkstalker, wouldn't that put Turtle's entire tribe in danger?

So perhaps one of the other queens. Glacier, Ruby, Moorhen, or Thorn . . . would any of them listen to a SeaWing? And wouldn't they fall under Darkstalker's spell the moment they met him?

Not to mention, in order to convince them his story was true, he'd have to tell them everything.

As in, *oh, yes, and I'm an animus* everything.

He shuddered, and his hold on the coral loosened, and it darted forward in a flash and bopped Queen Glory on the side of her tail.

She turned to stare at him. "What was that?"

"Nothing! Nothing," he said. "My talons slipped. Sorry."

She raised one eyebrow. "You're an odd dragon, Turtle."

"That's what my friends tell me," he said, and his friends rose up in his mind, and a possibility shot through him, shining with hope.

"Your Majesty," he said. "May I ask — how is Kinkajou?"

"I don't know," Glory said, her wings drooping. "The healers can't understand why she hasn't woken up yet. They don't know what to do for her. We all thought that once she was back in the rainforest, around the smells and sounds and sun that she grew up with, she'd —"

"Back in the rainforest?" Turtle interrupted. "She's *here*?"

"Of course." Queen Glory flicked her tail, knocking loose a shower of yellow blossoms. "I wasn't going to leave her alone on the other side of the continent. The healers got back with her yesterday."

"Can I see her?" Turtle asked. His claws were tingling. Kinkajou hadn't met Darkstalker. Kinkajou would believe him. He could trust her with his secret.

And Kinkajou was much more cut out for heroism than he was.

Glory gave him directions to the healers' pavilion, not far away, tucked into a little alcove of the rainforest that seemed even more peaceful than the rest of the village. Turtle could smell healing herbs and oranges as he flew to the opening.

Inside, sunlight poured through the rooms from skylights that had been opened in the roofs. A pair of pale blue healers were asleep in one corner; another was neatly folding cobwebs and moss into bundles on one of the shelves. She looked up as Turtle came in, but seemed only mildly surprised to see a SeaWing in her pavilion. She swept one wing toward the bed where Kinkajou slept, and Turtle nodded, unconsciously flashing his scales in Aquatic, *yes, that's who I'm looking for.*

Kinkajou lay in a sunbeam that outlined every scale with gold. She was still as white as an IceWing — white being the color of pain or shock to the RainWings — but in this sun it was the white of opals, jeweled and glinting with hints of hidden colors, pearl-pinks and sparks of green.

It wasn't the color of her scales that made her look so unlike Kinkajou. It was her complete stillness. Turtle had never seen Kinkajou sit still for a moment. Even in class, her wings always twitched or her claws fidgeted or her face would make sideways expressions at him or Moon: *WHAT did he say? I knew that answer! Is it time to eat yet are you starving I'm starving! Isn't school AMAZING?*

Turtle sat down beside her bed and curled his tail in, missing her in a way that filled him with heavy seaweed from nose to tail. He knew this was ridiculous; he didn't even know her that well. They'd had barely four days at Jade Mountain before everything went wrong. Before Kinkajou left to find Winter's brother, defeat Scarlet, and save the world from Moon's prophecy . . . while Turtle chose to slink back to the safety of the school instead.

That was exactly why he needed her. "Kinkajou," he whispered. "Can you hear me? I need you to wake up."

Knowing Kinkajou, he half expected her to open her eyes and joke, "Oh, well, if you *need* me to, then sure! I was just taking a really long nap, but let's go fight some bad guys!"

She didn't, though.

He'd already tried this, back in Possibility, but now he fumbled his healing river stone out of his pouch again. His stupid, shortsighted enchantment that only healed surface wounds. Still, he brushed it lightly along Kinkajou's bruised spine, over the bandages on her broken ribs, and gently around her fractured skull.

In Possibility, they'd watched the bruises fade and all the scrapes and cuts disappear. But it didn't work any deeper, and Kinkajou did not wake up. This time wasn't any different. Kinkajou still lay quietly, quietly breathing, eyes closed.

Turtle had wanted to enchant something right then that could wake her, but he was afraid that one of the Possibility doctors would notice. And Moon had been worried for his soul. She'd suggested waiting two more days, at least, to see if Kinkajou woke up on her own. But then they'd flown off to find Peril, which had led them to the scroll, and then the release of Darkstalker, and now here they were, and now he *couldn't* use magic to help her.

He crushed a bright orange flower between his claws, frustrated. If only he'd been brave and stubborn enough to heal her earlier!

But then she would have met Darkstalker along with everyone else. She'd be under his spell, too.

"Kinkajou," he said sternly. "Enough sleeping. Time to get up and save the world."

No reaction.

"You know you've always wanted to," he wheedled. "Think how impressed Queen Glory will be! All you have to do is wake up. And figure out how to stop the most powerful dragon in the history of Pyrrhia. No problem, right?"

No reaction from Kinkajou, but he got a very odd look from the healer at the other end of the pavilion.

All right, he couldn't talk her awake, and he couldn't use his magic . . .

Wait.

He couldn't use *his* magic.

Turtle thought for a long time, his brow furrowed into serious wrinkles. Five iridescent purple butterflies settled on his tail and fluttered serene butterfly thoughts at one another without him even noticing they were there.

Finally Turtle blinked and sat up, scattering indigo wings in all directions. He had a plan. Possibly a terrible plan, but the only one he could think of.

He flew out of the pavilion and used his coral again to navigate the rainforest and find his way back to Anemone. The SeaWing princess was swimming in a pool several lengths upstream from Darkstalker's gathering. Her pale shape flickered like a dolphin below the water, in and out of the shadows.

Turtle landed with a squelch in the mud, let the coolness sink into his claws, and waited for her to surface.

"Oh, hi!" she said cheerfully when she finally saw him. "I was wondering where you went! Darkstalker's stories are great, but I'm kind of not so interested in ancient NightWing history. Blah blah eight million years ago they had a cool library YAWN. I was like, so what were the SeaWings up to back then? and he was all, 'getting massacred.' So THAT was cheerful. I would say come on in, but I should warn you there are all kinds of weird sticky plants under the surface here."

"Thanks anyway," Turtle said. "Hey, Anemone . . . is it true you can do as many spells as you want now?"

"Yup!" His sister ducked under the water and surfaced again, shooting a spray of water at a grumpy-looking frog on the riverbank. "Thanks to my cool enchanted silver necklace." She tapped the collar with one claw. "I'm going to cast so many spells, it'll be like the sea is full of magic! I could rebuild the Summer Palace! Or make us a new palace, maybe. I can stop hurricanes! I could make Uncle Shark's scales turn bright pink and all his teeth fall out, ha ha. I could enchant every pearl in the ocean to come rolling up to our door!"

"Oh," Turtle said, bewildered by this rush of ideas. "But . . . the pearl divers like their jobs."

"It's just an *example*, Turtle," Anemone said scornfully. "I'm just saying, when we get home, things are going to be pretty different in the Kingdom of the Sea."

"You're not . . . you're not going to try to take the throne, are you?" Turtle asked. He hadn't quite thought ahead to what might happen if Anemone decided to use her magic against their mother in a challenge duel. It didn't seem fair; although Queen Coral had somehow defeated Orca, who had turned out to be an animus, too, but a secret one. *Like me.*

"Not yet," Anemone said with a laugh. "I want to have a lot more fun before I get stuck in a boring old palace making decisions all day. And I want to learn everything Darkstalker can teach me about being an animus. Isn't he cool? Don't you feel like an idiot for being so worried?"

"Right." Turtle glanced downstream, realizing that Darkstalker might come looking for Anemone any moment now. "So — since you're so superpowerful now — could you do something for me?"

An irritated look briefly flitted across Anemone's face, and Turtle winced, knowing exactly how she felt. Other dragons wanting to use your magic . . . it was like they were asking to wear your scales.

"Like what?" Anemone asked.

"It's Kinkajou," Turtle said. "I wouldn't ask for me, but — she's really hurt, and she won't wake up, and I'm afraid only magic can save her."

"Oh," Anemone said, her frown clearing like the tide pulling away from the beach. "Awww. You want me to save the cute little RainWing you're in love with!"

"I'm not in love with her!" Turtle protested. "But she's — you know, she's awesome — and I just want her to get better."

"I can totally do that," Anemone said gleefully, splashing out of the pool toward him. He bopped her lightly with the wriggling coral as she went by, but she didn't notice. "But I *am* going to tease you about it forever. You think she's cuuuuuuuuuuuuuuute, you totally looooooooooooooove her."

"ANEMONE." Turtle swatted at her with his tail and she danced away, giggling.

In the palace, Anemone had been a distant figure. Always attached to the queen by a harness, she was never allowed to wander freely or associate with her rough-and-tumble brothers. Turtle had only known her as the beloved princess who got all their mother's love. He'd seen her at royal gatherings or at Queen Coral's scroll readings, sitting quietly beside her, soaking up all that attention.

But then Tsunami came and caught the assassin, and a new princess finally hatched, and Anemone was released from the harness at last. She began visiting her brothers out of curiosity, and Turtle watched her closely, wondering what her life was like as a known animus. She seemed funny and happy much of the time — but there was a dark streak to some of her jokes, along with an imperious certainty that she deserved all of her princess privileges.

It worried him, and it worried him more the more he found he liked her.

"All right, take me to your sleeping beauty," Anemone said dramatically.

"Oh, brother," Turtle said, rolling his eyes.

He tucked the coral back into its pouch and lifted off into the trees. Anemone followed him, singing, *"Turtle and Kinkajou, flying in the sky, Getting all K-I-S-S-Y —"*

He clapped his talons over his ears and kept them there the rest of the way to the RainWing village.

Anemone fell silent as they crossed the threshold into the healers' pavilion. She gazed around at the other patients: a RainWing with a head wound and a NightWing with a jagged tear in one of his wings. Both of them were unconscious, probably tranquilized. Turtle wondered if their injuries made Anemone think of all the wounded SeaWings who'd survived the war and the bombing of the Summer Palace. Maybe instead of collecting pearls and turning their unfriendly uncle shades of fuchsia, Anemone might think about healing some of her fellow dragons instead.

Not that I'm one to judge. How many dragons have I ever helped with my magic?

Turtle stopped next to Kinkajou, and Anemone went around to her other side, studying the pale little RainWing. Kinkajou was older than Anemone, but they were not very different in size. Anemone lifted one of Kinkajou's drooping talons.

"Wow," she said softly. "She does look terrible. I'm sorry for teasing you, Turtle."

"Oh, good," he said.

"I mean, I'm going to keep doing it," she added. "But not until she's well again. OK, let me think for a minute." Anemone scrunched up her snout. "Oops! I was supposed to tell Darkstalker if I decided to do any more spells. He doesn't really want me trying new things on my own yet."

"Seriously?" said Turtle. "Haven't you been doing spells on your own pretty much your whole life?"

"That's TRUE," said Anemone. "And I mean, what does he care if I heal some random RainWing, right?"

"Exactly," said Turtle. He held his breath.

"I'll tell him about it when we get back," Anemone said, flicking one of her wings and startling a cluster of dragonflies in the leaf roof.

"What are you going to enchant?" Turtle asked, exhaling with relief.

Anemone glanced around dubiously at the flowery vines, the leaves, the wooden bowls of herbs; all the biodegradable rainforest things that wouldn't last very long. Her eyes fell on the black leather pouch that was tied to Kinkajou's ankle.

"Maybe something in here?" she said, poking it open.

"Wait —" Turtle started to say, but already Kinkajou's library card was tumbling into Anemone's palm, along with one of the skyfire rocks from Turtle's armband. A gift to protect her thoughts from Moon — or any mind reader — although Anemone had no way of knowing that.

His sister peered at the rock for a moment, then looked up at him with wide eyes, apparently noticing the holes in his armband for the first time.

"Ha! You gave her one of your rocks from the sky!" she crowed. "You love her SO MUCH!"

"Can we please get on with this?" he demanded. It was going to be a hilarious day whenever she discovered that he'd also given matching rocks to Winter and Qibli.

"Well, this should work," she said, curling her claws around the star-speckled rock. She closed her eyes.

This is it, Turtle. One chance. Perfect timing. Right . . . NOW.

"I enchant this rock to heal Kinkajou of all her injuries so she can wake up, as happy and healthy as she's ever been," said Anemone.

And at the same moment, Turtle thought with all his might, *Enchant this skyfire to make Kinkajou immune to any spell Darkstalker has ever or will ever cast, and enchant it to make her completely insignificant in his eyes — not worth thinking about, not visible in his futures, not in any way a threat to him.*

He wasn't sure how many times over you could enchant an object, or if one animus touch might cancel out another, so he added hurriedly, *and enchant it to heal all her injuries as well.*

This was the key; casting his spell in the same moment as Anemone's. He didn't know the details of Darkstalker's warning system, but he hoped one spell would obscure the other, like Qibli thought. He'd considered the phrasing of his spell as carefully as he could, borrowing Qibli's words and adding more of his own. He hoped Darkstalker would forgive Anemone for using her spell to help Kinkajou — that was why he couldn't hide Kinkajou the way he'd hidden himself — and he hoped Darkstalker wouldn't think too hard about what else might have happened here.

Anemone opened her eyes and gave Turtle a sly smile. "And while we're at it," she said, her voice playful, "I also enchant this rock to make Kinkajou love Turtle just as much as he loves her."

CHAPTER 14

"What?" Turtle cried, horrorstruck. "Anemone! You can't do that!"

"I so absolutely can," she said triumphantly, already sliding the skyfire back into Kinkajou's pouch. "My magic can do anything!"

"But that's awful! You can't enchant someone's feelings! Anemone, *please* take that spell off."

"I don't think I can," Anemone said with a shrug. "Squids and sea monsters, you should be *thanking* me. I just did such an awesome nice thing for you." She reached over Kinkajou and patted one of his talons, grinning. "I'm the best sister ever."

"But I don't want her to like me because of a spell!" Turtle felt as if he was caught in one of the rainforest's enormous, spider-laden cobwebs. He couldn't undo the enchantment himself — if that was even possible — or else Darkstalker would notice. But he couldn't take the skyfire away from Kinkajou either. She needed it to be safe from Darkstalker.

"You'll thank me later," Anemone said confidently. "When you're maaaaaaaaaarried and have lots of little pink dragonets with webbed talons!"

Turtle buried his face in his claws. Poor Kinkajou. This was so wrong, so *wrong*.

"Who's getting married?" said a soft, hoarse voice.

He looked up and saw colors rising slowly into the scales all across Kinkajou's back, like the time he'd spilled five different ink bottles over his blank scroll, back when he still dreamed of being a writer. Sunrises drifted into her wings, pale peaches and yellows strengthening into glorious bands of orange and gold.

Her green eyes were open, and her head was turned, pillowed on her arms. She was looking at him.

"Hey, Turtle," she said sleepily. "We missed you on our heroic quest."

"I missed you, too," he said, a lump rising in his throat.

"At least, I think it was a heroic quest," she said. "I'm a little bit fuzzy on whether we actually succeeded."

"You did!" he said. "You saved Winter's brother and stopped Queen Scarlet."

"I did?" she said. "Really? Like, how? In my sleep? Am I so amazing that I can save the world and nap at the same time?" She laughed and her gaze drifted up to the ceiling. She sat up, startled. "Whoa! This place looks exactly like the rainforest!"

"It is the rainforest," Turtle said. "You're home. There's . . . a lot to explain."

"Hiiiii," Anemone said, elbowing Turtle out of the way. "I'm Princess Anemone. I don't think we officially met at school. I'm the one who totally just saved your life." She fluffed her wings and stretched her neck a little longer.

"Oh, wow. Thank you," Kinkajou said earnestly. "Um — saved my life from what?"

"You got clobbered by a bad guy," Anemone said. "You've been unconscious for, like, *days*. You might never have woken up except that Turtle begged me to heal you." She poked Turtle's backside meaningfully with her tail.

"What bad guy?" Kinkajou cried. "Did we clobber her back? Three moons, did I miss all the excitement AGAIN?" She flared her wings, then did a double take at one of them and jumped. "Hey! My venom splash scars are gone!"

Turtle remembered the triangle of black spots that had dotted Kinkajou's wing. He shifted uncomfortably on his talons. "I guess Anemone's spell healed those along with your other injuries," he said.

"SPELL?" Kinkajou yelped. "You healed me with *magic*? That is AMAZING!"

"I know, it really is," said Anemone, preening.

"I did like those scars, though," Kinkajou said a little wistfully. "They made me seem all battle-hardened and tough."

Turtle bit back a laugh. As much as he adored her, it would never in a million years have occurred to him to use those adjectives to describe Kinkajou.

"Ah, well," she said with a shrug. "Thanks again, Anemone. Oooo, I'd love to be an animus. Is it fun?"

"It is now," Anemone said. "Now that I'm the one in charge of my spells and nobody's telling me what to do all the time."

There was a crash outside, like a tree falling not too far away. Anemone's face brightened and she darted to the doorway.

"Don't be scared," Turtle said to Kinkajou quickly in a low voice. "A very big, scary-looking dragon is about to show up, but he can't hurt you. And he can't see me or hear me, so don't be confused by that. I'll explain everything when he's gone."

Kinkajou's eyes were shining with excitement. "I feel like I fell asleep in one adventure and woke up in a totally different one! What is happening! This is amazing!"

"Anemone," rumbled Darkstalker's voice outside the pavilion. "Have you been doing more magic?"

"Just a little healing spell," Anemone said cheerfully. "Kinkajou, come here."

"I don't know if you should be walking yet —" Turtle said, but Kinkajou was already bouncing off the bed.

"Whoo," she said, wobbling on her talons for a moment. "Guess I haven't stood up in a few days! Here we go." She flared her wings for balance and hopped over to the opening, where Anemone was holding the flower curtain aside.

Kinkajou stuck her head outside. "YIKES!" she yelped. "Who are you? You are SO BIG!"

"Oh," said Darkstalker, his voice immediately softening. "Moon's friend. That's all right. I was planning to heal her myself, in fact. But Anemone, please remember to run your spells by me first."

The three healers had all disappeared somewhere, perhaps scattering at the sight of Darkstalker. Turtle crept to the window and peeked out. The great NightWing had landed on a pavilion outside, and all around him were flurries of leaves-that-weren't-leaves and branches-that-weren't-branches as alarmed RainWings tried to hide and spy and sidle away at the same time.

"I don't like being bossed around," Anemone said, lifting her chin. "I know what I'm doing."

"Of course you do," he said. "But a second eye on your spells can be helpful. I wish I'd had someone to give me advice about my scroll, for instance — so I could enchant it to be used only by me, or to return to me if it was stolen. Wouldn't that have been smart? I can give you advice like that, because I've already made my mistakes."

"Oh," Anemone said, considering. "Sure, that makes sense."

Turtle breathed a sigh of relief. Darkstalker wasn't angry, and he didn't seem to have noticed Turtle's spell underneath Anemone's. Apart from the horrible fact that Kinkajou was now bewitched into loving him, the plan had worked.

"Your Majesty," Darkstalker called. Turtle saw Glory and Deathbringer gliding through the treetops toward them. They landed on a branch nearby and Glory studied Darkstalker thoughtfully.

"How did you find our village?" she asked.

"I followed the sounds of RainWings thinking," he said, tapping his head. "Or at least, what passes for thinking in a RainWing these days. This tribe has really gone soft."

"Hey!" Kinkajou objected. "We defeated YOUR stupid tribe, didn't we?"

Darkstalker didn't bother to respond; he didn't even bother to look at her. "I came to deliver a warning, Your Majesty." He glanced around at the whispering trees. "There are five dragons on their way here to kill you. They will most likely attack tonight, and unless I stop them, they will succeed."

The trees gasped.

"*I'll* stop them," Deathbringer said, lashing his tail. "I've stopped assassins before."

"I have bad news for you," said Darkstalker. "I'm the one who can see the future. I've seen the part where you get stabbed by a SandWing tail."

"SandWings?" Glory asked. "Why would SandWings want to attack me?"

"They're working with a pair of NightWings you misplaced," Darkstalker said. "Does that ring a bell?" Glory exchanged a glance with Deathbringer, and Turtle remembered the missing prisoners he'd heard about while eavesdropping — the ones who'd escaped from the SandWing stronghold.

"You know what you need?" Darkstalker went on. "A nice strong prison of your own. Wouldn't that solve a lot of problems?"

"RainWings are not really a prison kind of tribe," Glory started to say, but Darkstalker was already snapping a branch off one of the trees overhead.

"Branch," he commanded, "grow into a fine, strong, indestructible prison, with room for at least ten prisoners, that no dragon could ever break out of."

He flung the branch down toward the ground, and as it fell it began to grow, snapping outward and up, smashing through everything it hit as it plummeted. When it finally crashed to earth, far below them, it was a massive, dense cube of some unfamiliar material, with no windows. The last few blocks slammed into place, and then it fell silent, apparently finished.

The RainWings all stared down at it. Turtle could see Kinkajou leaning over the edge of the walkway outside the healers' hut, her face a picture of outrage.

The prison was gray and solid, large and forbidding. It hulked on the rainforest floor like a sinister cloud that had been dragged to earth and chained down. Everything about it exuded wrongness.

"Perfect," said Darkstalker. A ring of metal keys had appeared in his talons, and he tossed them to Queen Glory. "You're welcome."

Glory caught the keys and held them at arm's length like a talonful of slugs. "I don't see any windows on that . . . thing," she said. "It would be cruel to put any RainWings in there, shut off from the sun. And ten seems like far more prisoners than we'll ever have."

Darkstalker shrugged. "You never know," he said. "But use it however you like. At least you can get Mastermind out of the quicksand now. Or give him to me and I'll take him far away; it's up to you."

Glory lifted her chin. "He still has to answer for his crimes against RainWings."

"Oh yes?" said Darkstalker. "Does this tribe have a terribly complex justice system, or what's taking so long?"

"It's . . . a work in progress," Glory said.

"Let's visit your new prison, which should be a safe place to wait for the assassins," Darkstalker suggested, spreading his wings, "and meanwhile I can tell you all about the courts and trials and laws we had in the old Night Kingdom. It was a fascinating process, really, beginning and ending with the queen's judgement, of course . . ." He spiraled down to the rainforest floor, his voice fading as he dropped. Queen Glory, Deathbringer, and Anemone all flew after him.

Turtle took a step back into the pavilion. His heart was beating anxiously. What if his spell didn't work, and Kinkajou was as bewitched by Darkstalker as anyone else? Or what if Darkstalker wasn't using a spell after all, and everyone else genuinely liked him, and Turtle was just wrong?

Kinkajou ducked back inside, catching a delicate lavender orchid on one of her frills, and sauntered over to him.

"So, *that* dragon's totally evil," she said.

"You think so? You really do?" said Turtle. He felt as though he could collapse right here and nap for three days. He wasn't imagining things. And he wasn't alone anymore.

"He's acting like the boss of Anemone, he's making creepy unnecessary un-RainWing-y things with his magic, and he's clearly trying to manipulate everyone with stuff like 'I'll save you from assassins!' and 'oh, *I* was going to heal her myself, actually.' The good news is, Queen Glory and Deathbringer will see right through him. They're probably planning some clever way to drive him out of the rainforest right now."

"Um," said Turtle. "Unfortunately, they're not. They like him — or they think they do. See, I think he's using his magic on everyone. I don't know the details of the spell, but it seems like everyone who meets him or talks to him ends up thinking he's perfectly nice, harmless, and trustworthy."

"Everyone?" said Kinkajou.

"Even Winter," said Turtle. "Winter worst of all."

"Holy coconuts." Kinkajou scratched her nose, turning a thoughtful shade of deep blue. "I'm really surprised. That NightWing seems like the kind of dragon who believes he's super charming — like he wouldn't need magic to win dragons over."

"Maybe," said Turtle, "but it's failed him once before, so I think he wants the extra security of the magic." He explained Darkstalker's history to Kinkajou, at least as much as he knew of it. That led him to Darkstalker's animus scroll, so then he had to explain what had happened with Peril and Scarlet, and then as much as he knew of the story with Hailstorm. It was getting dark by the time he finished.

"Bah!" Kinkajou grumbled, flicking her wings as orange starbursts went off across her scales. "I really *did* miss everything. That's so unfair."

"Well, you're not missing this crisis," Turtle pointed out. "You and I are the only dragons here who are safe from Darkstalker. Which means"— he took a deep breath — "you're the only one who can stop him."

"You mean WE'RE the only ones who can stop him, right?" Kinkajou said.

"I was sort of hoping you would do it," Turtle admitted.

"Turtle!" She nudged him so he teetered sideways. "I totally would, but I'd rather do it with you! Saving the world is more fun plus also less terrifying with friends." She gave him a sweet smile that made him extremely nervous about what Anemone's love spell might be doing to her brain.

"I am not a heroic dragon," Turtle protested. "I don't have good ideas, I'm lazy, and I hide when bad things happen."

"Waking me up was a good idea!" Kinkajou said brightly. "And look, you're not hiding. You're right here, where the bad things are. And you left Jade Mountain to find me and Moon and the others — that's not lazy or hiding either."

"I was following Peril," Turtle pointed out. "If I'm anything in the story, I'm maybe the hapless sidekick."

"Awesome!" Kinkajou leaped to her feet, beaming. "I've always wanted a hapless sidekick! OK, I don't know what hapless means! But it sounds like happy, so I bet it's awesome! Let's go take him down!" She made a beeline for the door.

"Wait, now?" Turtle said. "What's the plan? Is there a plan? You know the hapless sidekick is the one who dies, right?"

"Not in our story!" Kinkajou called.

"Kinkajou, WHERE ARE YOU GOING?" Turtle shouted as she barged through the hanging orchids into the dusk.

"I'm going to go study him," Kinkajou explained as he emerged behind her, as though this were all perfectly obvious, "so we can figure out what he's enchanted to hypnotize everybody, and then we're going to steal it or break it, and then everyone will be all, 'AAAAAH THERE'S A MONSTER DRAGON TRYING TO MANIPULATE US!' and they'll rise up and stop him. Done! The day is saved!"

Turtle was beginning to wonder whether his problem-solving approach and Kinkajou's might be completely incompatible.

"I don't think it'll be that easy," he said, rubbing his forehead.

"Why not? You said he can't hurt me," Kinkajou pointed out. "Wait, why can't he hurt me?"

"Because of the spell *I* put on you," said Turtle.

Kinkajou stared at him.

"Oh, right," he said. "There's one more thing I should probably have mentioned."

She bundled him back inside the healers' pavilion. *"You're an animus?"* she hissed softly.

"Kind of a secret one?" he said with a shrug. "Like, please don't tell anybody? I went through this already with Peril and Moon and Winter and Qibli."

"Three moons!" Kinkajou cried. "Why am I always the last to know everything?"

"Well, no," he said. "That would make you fifth. The fifth to know, out of all the dragons in Pyrrhia, or sixth I suppose if you count me."

Kinkajou considered that for a moment with her snout scrunched up. "Cool," she said finally. "All right, that's not too bad. But NEXT time you have a major enormous secret, tell me first, OK?"

"OK," he said. "Maybe I should mention that I've cast a spell to hide myself from Darkstalker?" He pulled out his stick and explained what it did, and how he couldn't cast any more spells because Darkstalker would sense them, except for the one he'd managed to hide under Anemone's.

"So you see," he finished, "I'm not actually 'here in the middle of all the bad things,' because I'm really actually hiding. I'm hiding all the time."

"OOOOOOOO," Kinkajou said, her eyes shining. "Totally invisible to Darkstalker! That is an *excellent* spell. Another great idea, see? We'll be an awesome team. You can be the idea dragon and I can be the WHAM BAM SHOVE A PINEAPPLE UP HIS SNOUT dragon!"

"No, no, that won't work. I think his snout is enchanted," Turtle pointed out.

"To be invulnerable to pineapples?" Kinkajou asked, and burst into giggles.

Oh dear. An image of tiny, rainbow-colored Kinkajou lobbing fruit at Darkstalker popped into Turtle's head. Maybe he hadn't entirely thought through his choice of hero.

"Don't worry so much," Kinkajou said, brushing his wing with hers. "Your forehead will get stuck that way. My plan will totally work, I swear! Or if it doesn't, we'll come up with a new amazing plan. Oooo, I bet this is EXACTLY how Glory felt when she was about to save the world!"

She bounded off to the doorway again, and Turtle found himself thinking that he couldn't imagine Queen Glory bounding, or in fact getting this excited about anything.

Outside, the sky was fading into purple-dark, shadows hurrying into all the gaps between the trees. Turtle felt the brush of soft fur as a sloth clambered by right over his head. He could hear snoring coming from a few hammocks already, and the air hummed with the hungry buzz of dusk-happy insects.

Far below them, a ring of fire smoldered on the forest floor, encircling the shadowy figures of Darkstalker, Queen Glory, and the others. Kinkajou let out a small growl when she saw it.

"Queen Glory doesn't usually allow that much fire in our forest," she whispered. "There are strict rules for the NightWings about how and when and how carefully to use it. She's definitely fallen for that baboon butt's act."

"Spell," Turtle reminded her. "It's a spell."

"Let's get closer." Kinkajou wafted down toward the gathered dragons as softly as a falling leaf, navigating the interlocking branches with ease. Turtle realized that RainWings must have some ability to see in the dark, just as SeaWings did.

He followed her, less gracefully and with a bit more noise, but he knew Darkstalker couldn't hear him.

They settled near the prison, outside the fiery circle but close enough to hear the dragons inside it. Damp leaves flapped in their faces and things scuttled away beneath their claws. Kinkajou shuffled in closer to Turtle. He could feel her wings brushing his, her scales cool and camouflaged to a dark black-blue.

Was she really in love with him now? She was acting exactly the same as she always had. But maybe that's the way she was with everyone, no matter how she felt about them?

Or maybe she already felt this way about you, way back at the school.

Turtle shook off that highly unlikely thought. He was not a dragon anyone would notice or fall for — especially when he was standing next to funny Qibli or handsome Winter or kindhearted Umber.

He felt a pang at the thought of his clawmate. *If this is ever over, maybe I could use my magic to find Umber and make sure he's all right.*

"Did you hear something?" Glory asked, turning to look out at the dark, in the direction of Turtle and Kinkajou.

"Just an orangutan," said Darkstalker with a flick of his tail. "I'll be able to hear the killers' minds approaching."

"I heard a noise," said Deathbringer, sounding disgruntled, "but of course I can't *see* anything because *there's a fire in the way.*"

"Trust me, this will keep your queen safe," said Darkstalker. "They'll have to run through the fire to get to her, which they are not brave enough to do — or fly over it, which will let us hear them coming. Although I'll hear them coming my way first, of course." He lifted his head and stared piercingly into the dark.

"He looks like he's posing for a portrait," Kinkajou whispered to Turtle. *"Pompous Sneerdagard the Magnificent Awaits His Legions of Doomed Enemies."*

Turtle smothered a laugh. He realized that his wings were less tense than they'd been in days and that this, perhaps, was the best part of sharing his burden with someone else. He hadn't thought of Chameleon or seen any flashes of blood in his mind since Kinkajou woke up. His constant, pulsing anxiety had ebbed just a little and cracks of hope were sliding in.

"Shhh," he said anyway. "He could still hear *you.*"

"But he won't care," she answered. "I'm less than nobody to him." She paused. "Yeeeek. I don't know if I like the sound of that — being less than nobody. Being unimportant to the future. I want to be *somebody*. Somebody dragons notice and remember."

Nope, Turtle thought. *Nope nope nope. I gave up on that idea a long time ago. If no one notices you, you can't let anyone down.*

Kinkajou was watching him expectantly.

"Oh!" he said. "Um. You're somebody to me."

She clasped her front talons over her snout to hide her giggles. "Right line," she said, "but you need to work on your timing. And believability."

"You *are*," he protested. "I was thinking about something else."

"Oh, now I feel very fascinating," she joked.

"I'm not sure you're taking this seriously enough," he said sternly.

"Here they come," Darkstalker rumbled suddenly, in a voice like the first breath of a snowstorm. "I will take care of them, Your Majesty."

He stepped over the fire with his towering legs. The flames lapped at his scales but left no marks. Turtle shivered.

The powerful NightWing stalked away into the night, the ground trembling with every footstep.

"Ha!" Anemone said merrily from her spot in the center of the circle, as far away from the flames as she could get. "I feel sorry for those assassins! I wouldn't want to run into *him* in a dark forest."

In a startlingly brief amount of time, Darkstalker came back, accompanied by the noise of clanking chains. As he approached the fire, Turtle realized that he was dragging four dragons behind him, all of them linked by chains around their necks and ankles.

One of them was a young female NightWing, and she was spitting mad.

"Let us go!" she hissed at Darkstalker. "Who do you think you are? Are you a NightWing or not? Whose side are you on?"

"Chains," Glory murmured. "We don't usually do chains in the rainforest."

"They're very effective, though," Deathbringer pointed out. "I much prefer seeing your enemies this way."

"Queen Glory," Darkstalker said. "Here are the dragons who were planning to kill you." He stopped and blew out most of the fire in one long breath, leaving only a small section of flames. Turtle blinked away the dancing orange spots in his vision as his eyes adjusted back to the dark.

"Would you like me to dispose of them?" Darkstalker's voice asked, deep and eerie in the shadows overhead.

"Oh, wonderful," said the female prisoner bitterly. "Fat lot of use *you* were," she hissed at the two SandWing captives. The last was another NightWing, a solidly built male, who shuffled toward her and reached his tail to rest gently on hers.

"Wait," said Glory. "I want to talk to them. You're Fierceteeth, aren't you? And this must be Strongwings."

The female only glared back, but the male nodded.

"Listen," said Glory, "what you did cannot easily be forgiven. You kidnapped Sunny and you planned to betray us to Burn in the hope that my friends and I would die — including your own brother."

Turtle blinked at Kinkajou, then back at the other dragons. Brother? Was this hissing ball of fury related to *Starflight*?

"No," Fierceteeth snapped. "I would have kept him out of it."

Glory regarded her for a moment as though she wasn't sure what to believe. "Well, that's something, at least," she said. "What was your plan here tonight?"

"To take the throne for a *true* NightWing, so our tribe can have its pride back." Fierceteeth tried to lift her shoulders under the weight of the chains.

"Oh, already taken care of," said Darkstalker. He gave a little tug on the chain he held and Strongwings stumbled forward into an accidental bow. "I'm going to rule the NightWings now."

"The ones who choose to go with him," Glory interjected.

"You can't," Fierceteeth said. "You're *male*. And where did you come from? You weren't with us on the volcano, that's for sure. What gives *you* the right to rule us?"

"Size, power, timing, charm, and a whole bunch of

dragons who think it's a great idea," said Darkstalker with a grin. "My name is Darkstalker."

Strongwings let out a whimper and covered his head with his wings. "We're going to die," he said in a muffled voice. "It was all true. It was, I knew it. He's come back to kill us all."

But Fierceteeth held her ground, staring up at Darkstalker. "Really," she said. "From the ghost stories. You."

"In the scales," he said.

"Right," she scoffed. "That's a pretty clever trick. Show up, pretend to be everyone's worst nightmare, and scare them into giving you the crown. Well, it's not going to work on me, you scaly worm. I'm not even a little bit afraid of you."

Darkstalker chuckled, rustling the leaves in the trees.

"Fierceteeth," Strongwings whispered. "Stop. It's him! Don't make him mad!"

"It *is* Darkstalker," Anemone said loudly from behind Glory and Deathbringer. "And he could crush you with one flick of his claw!"

"Maybe he should, given what you were planning to do to the queen," Deathbringer added.

"If you're so powerful, then you can handle a challenge," Fierceteeth said to Darkstalker, ignoring the others. "*I* want the NightWing throne. I think *I* should get to be queen. I'm female and I know my tribe; I'd be better at it than some lying stranger."

"Hey," Turtle whispered to Kinkajou. "Maybe I'm wrong about Darkstalker's spell. She doesn't seem affected by it at all."

"Actually, I think this is how she talks to dragons she likes," Kinkajou said ruefully.

"Brave little Fierceteeth," said Darkstalker.

"Don't call me little!" she interrupted him. "Just because you're overgrown doesn't mean you can patronize me!"

"I was going to say I like your spirit," Darkstalker started.

"Can you make that a bit more condescending?" Fierceteeth snapped back.

He paused, and Turtle got the distinct impression that he was trying not to laugh.

"All right," he said at length. "You're not a dragon who likes compliments, I see. So I'll be blunt. I don't want to begin my reign as king of the NightWings by killing one of my subjects, especially one who could be such a valuable asset in rebuilding our tribe." He turned to Glory. "Given the utter failure of all her schemes so far, and her relationship to Starflight, my proposal is this: Grant her your mercy and give her to me. Tomorrow I'll take her to the Night Kingdom with me, where she'll have no reason to bother you anymore. She can be my problem instead."

"I WILL be your problem!" Fierceteeth growled. "No one gives me to anybody! I'll go to the Night Kingdom only if I WANT to." She paused, narrowed her eyes suspiciously, and added, "What Night Kingdom? Where?"

"The old one," said Darkstalker, "where the tribe should have been for the last two thousand years. You'll love it. We'll find you something important to do."

"Hang on," said Deathbringer. "She tries to assassinate Glory, and her 'punishment' is she gets to be part of your court, ruling the NightWings?"

"Makes sense to me," said Glory thoughtfully. "She wouldn't be a threat to me anymore, once she has what she wants. Right, Fierceteeth? And then I don't have to have Starflight's *entire* family behind bars." She took a step closer to Fierceteeth. "Would you leave my rainforest, my friends, and my tribe alone if we give you this second chance?"

Fierceteeth glared sideways at Darkstalker. "Are you lying?" she demanded. "Would I really be in charge of something?"

"All you want is a little power and a lot of respect," Darkstalker observed. "I can give you those."

"And Strongwings," she interjected. "He stays with me."

Darkstalker gave Strongwings an unimpressed look and shrugged. "If you insist."

Fierceteeth tapped her claws on the ground thoughtfully. Strongwings still had his head covered, looking very much like a dragon who regretted all his life choices so far.

"Think about it overnight," Darkstalker suggested. "In our lovely new accommodations for troublemakers." He swept one wing toward the prison, where, Turtle was sure, even a few minutes would convince any dragon to accept alternate offers.

"Hey! What about us?" grunted one of the SandWings.

"Queen Thorn gets to decide your fate," Glory said, drawing herself up regally. "In the meanwhile, you're going in there, too." She tossed the keys to Darkstalker.

Darkstalker twitched the chain and Strongwings stumbled back to his feet. Wings drooping as they marched inside, all four prisoners disappeared into the forbidding gray block behind Darkstalker.

Glory shuddered. "That was awful," she said. "I always thought I'd like dispensing justice more than that."

"I wouldn't call that justice," Deathbringer grumbled.

"We're looking for what brings peace to our rainforest," Glory pointed out, "and for whatever gives dragons a chance to be their best selves." She hesitated, glancing around at Anemone, who had curled up drowsily under a mammoth fern. "Something does feel weird, though," she added in a lower voice. "Like I'm not entirely sure I trust my decisions right now."

She's feeling what Qibli felt, Turtle guessed. *Torn between Darkstalker's spell and what her own intelligence is telling her.*

Darkstalker emerged from the prison, closing the heavy metal door with a grim *clunk* behind him. Turtle noticed that he didn't return the keys to Glory, but neither did she ask for them.

"Now that's taken care of," he said, "and your life has been saved and everything, I'll return to my tribe and get some sleep. We have a long flight ahead in the morning!"

"Thank you," Glory said — a little reluctantly, Turtle thought, or maybe he just hoped so.

"Cheer up, Your Majesty!" Darkstalker said cheerfully. "We stopped some bad guys tonight! Isn't that fantastic? Just think what kind of teamwork our tribes might have ahead of us."

"Wait," said Deathbringer, tilting his head. "Didn't you say there were *five* dragons coming to attack Glory tonight? Why were there only four prisoners?"

Was that a moment of hesitation from Darkstalker?

"I didn't want to alarm you," he said slowly. "There was a third SandWing . . . but he fought back, and I was forced to kill him."

If that's true, he did it very quickly, Turtle thought. *And silently.*

"Oh," said Deathbringer. "Well. Good."

"That's unfortunate," said Glory at the same time. "We should find out his name from the other two. I'm sure Queen Thorn will want that information."

"Indeed. Very wise," said Darkstalker, nodding. "And I'll take care of the body for you, don't worry."

Kinkajou jabbed Turtle in the side and he nearly jumped out of his scales.

"Lying," she whispered, pointing one claw at Darkstalker. "Lying lying super liar."

He agreed with her, but he couldn't see the point of this lie. What was Darkstalker hiding now?

"Very well. We'll see you in the morning," said Glory, spreading her wings. She and Deathbringer flew off to the treetops, leaving Darkstalker and Anemone alone in the dying glow of the embers.

Darkstalker looked down at the sleeping SeaWing princess. Something glinted in his eyes — something that made Turtle want to throw hiding spells all over his sister, no matter the risk. He crouched closer to the damp earth, wishing he were smarter, braver, bolder — really any other kind of dragon than the kind he was.

"Not much longer, Princess," Darkstalker whispered. "Soon it'll be your turn to change the world."

CHAPTER 15

Turtle and Kinkajou spent the night in the healing pavilion, where the healers were pinkly atwitter with delight when they discovered Kinkajou was awake. While they checked her for any remaining injuries — and freaked out when they found none — Turtle wrote another note to Qibli.

KINKAJOU IS AWAKE AND FINE. PLEASE TELL TAMARIN. DARKSTALKER TAKING THE TRIBE TO THE OLD NIGHT KINGDOM IN THE MORNING.

He thought for a moment, then added,

EVERYONE DEFINITELY UNDER HIS SPELL EXCEPT KINKAJOU.

He hoped that was enough information as he erased it, although he wasn't sure what good it did for Qibli to know all that.

Before he fell asleep, Turtle made Kinkajou promise not to go "deal with Darkstalker" without him, however she might interpret that phrase: no "sneaking, stealing, attacking, thwacking, or pineapples," he begged. He also asked her not to tell Queen Glory anything.

"I have to let her know I'm all right!" Kinkajou insisted.

"That's fine," he said, "but don't say anything about me, or our suspicions about Darkstalker, or how much you know about him, or what we might do next."

"Jumping poison frogs," Kinkajou said, looking exasperated. "Why not?"

"Because he *can* read Glory's mind," Turtle pointed out, "and we don't want him to hear anything that might make him nervous or suspicious."

After much arguing, she agreed, and Turtle fell asleep feeling maybe a tiny iota less nervous than before.

At daybreak, Kinkajou woke him and they flew to the NightWing village. As they soared through the trees, Kinkajou tossed mangoes and bananas to Turtle, chattering busily.

"I visited my close personal friend Queen Glory last night," she said. "Just to let her know I'm totally fine now. She was SO MAD and so happy and SO MAD at the same time. I got a seriously serious lecture about staying away from dangerous dragons from now on. La la la, irony. But she'll forgive me when we save the world, right? Right? Turtle?"

"Oh, yes, sure," he said through a mouthful of banana. He hadn't realized this was a conversation he'd have to take an active part in.

"I told her I want to go back to Jade Mountain," said Kinkajou. "Which is *true*. I do *want* to go back there. I'm just going to take a quick detour to the new Night Kingdom on the way and not mention that part to her until later, like, way much later, like maybe when we're a hundred."

"Do we have to go to the Night Kingdom?" Turtle asked. "Maybe there's another way to stop Darkstalker . . . from here?"

"No, I figured it out!" Kinkajou said. "I was thinking about it last night. This is all about Moon's prophecy! It's right there in the words. He's the thing that shakes the earth and scorches the ground, right? So we have to save Jade Mountain by finding the lost city of night, and that's where Darkstalker is going, so we just follow him there and BOOM, catastrophe averted! Everybody safe! Why are you rubbing your forehead again?"

"No reason," said Turtle. He'd read enough scrolls to know that no heroic quest was ever that easy — but he'd also spent enough time with Kinkajou to realize that it wouldn't do any good to tell her that.

Darkstalker had been busy in the night. When they arrived at the village, they discovered that he'd already packed (or made someone pack) several nets full of food from the rainforest. He stood on Glory's platform, counting the supplies gathered below him, as NightWings gradually filled the clearing in whispering clumps of twos and threes.

"I wonder how many of them are going with him," Kinkajou said, swooping down to land at the back of the crowd. Turtle touched down beside her, folding in his wings and ducking his head to avoid the funny looks he was getting from the rest of the NightWings.

"I bet most of them," he said. "Wouldn't you follow a king who could give you superpowers?"

"No way," Kinkajou said with fierce loyalty. "Queen Glory is perfect. I want her to be my queen forever and always. MOON!" she shrieked suddenly, spotting her clawmate as Moon passed by with her mother.

Moon jumped nearly the height of a small tree and turned around. Her face lit up like a thousand dragons shouting in Aquatic at once. "Kinkajou?" she cried.

They barreled into each other, wings overlapping in a ferocious hug, voices overlapping as they both tried to talk at once.

"You're awake!" Moon yelped through tears. "You're all right! I've been so worried!"

"You did everything cool without me!" Kinkajou said at the same time. "I can't believe all the amazing things you've been doing! Without me!"

"I was going to come check on you today," Moon said, wiping her eyes. "After Darkstalker leaves. I would have come yesterday, but I've been busy trying to convince as many NightWings as I can to stay here in the rainforest." She sighed. "I'm not exactly the best spokesdragon, though. Nobody particularly liked me before, and they don't like me much better now that I've returned with mind reading powers and 'the Darkstalker.'"

"I like you enough to make up for ten thousand grumpy dragons," Kinkajou promised. Moon smiled at her shyly, like that was still hard for her to believe.

"What did you tell them?" Turtle asked. "I thought you liked Darkstalker."

"I do!" Moon said. "He's been great so far. But Queen Glory is the best thing to happen to this tribe in two thousand years. She's fair and generous and she's given them a safe place to live. NightWings have always been afraid of living somewhere the IceWings could find them, in case the old war flares up, but Queen Glory made sure there was a truce with Queen Glacier first thing, to keep the tribe safe." She shook her head. "I think Queen Glory has proven herself to be a just and kind queen. We don't know anything about Darkstalker or what kind of king he would be. I feel like this is all happening too fast."

Turtle noticed that several NightWings had edged closer, pretending not to listen but clearly listening to Moon.

"And plus also," Kinkajou chimed in, "don't forget the part where he's totally evil."

Moon raised her eyebrows. "He's not evil," she said. "Not like Scarlet was. If he were evil, wouldn't I have seen it in his thoughts?"

"You've seen the thoughts he wanted you to see," said Kinkajou. "Right? He can totally shield the rest of them, can't he? The EVIL thoughts?"

Moon lifted her head to look over the crowd at Darkstalker.

He had his head bowed and was absentmindedly shredding a mauve flower that had grown up at the edge of the stage.

"Maybe," she said. "But I think he's really trying to help, even if I wouldn't do it the way he's doing it. I think he just wants his tribe back, the way it was before."

Kinkajou opened her mouth and Turtle stood on her foot to hush her up. If Moon were under a spell, telling her about it wouldn't do any good. It was encouraging, though, that she could choose Glory over Darkstalker, despite whatever spells he was using on her.

"Was Darkstalker upset when you told him?" he asked.

"He said he understands," she said. "And that he expects me to change my mind."

"Ha! Not likely!" Kinkajou gave Moon another hug. "So what are you going to do now?"

"Go back to school," Moon said with a sigh. "It feels a little weird, with everything happening . . . but that's what Queen Glory wants me to do. And that's where Qibli and Winter are — and you guys will be there, too, right?"

"Sure, eventually, but don't you want to see the old Night Kingdom first?" Kinkajou asked. "Maybe just a quick visit before we go back to Jade Mountain?"

"Why would we do that?" Moon asked.

"No reason!" Kinkajou glanced around and whispered loudly. "Except maybe a *prophecy reason*."

Moon flicked a fat green beetle off her tail and tipped her head at Kinkajou. "I kind of do want to see it," she said. "I mean . . . I have been thinking about the prophecy . . . but I don't understand how going there will stop anything from happening."

"You never know until you try!" Kinkajou said brightly. "That's settled, then. We'll all go to the Night Kingdom. Not *with* Darkstalker, though. Definitely not with him. More like . . . right behind him. Yes? Yes. Settled. Whew, I thought it was going to be much weirder to try explaining why *I* was in the Night Kingdom, but if I'm there with you, my gifted and awesome clawmate, then it makes total sense."

"I'm not sure —" Moon began, but the crowd suddenly parted and Darkstalker came striding through, straight toward their little group.

Turtle felt himself shrinking as the NightWing loomed over them. Kinkajou, on the other talon, seemed to be trying to make herself look bigger. She spread her wings and puffed up her chest and fixed Darkstalker with her fiercest stare.

"Moon," Darkstalker said quietly. "Last chance. Come with us." He hesitated, dipped his head toward her, met her eyes. "Please."

"Darkstalker . . ." Moon said. "You're my friend. You are. But Glory is my queen."

"Then come as my friend," he said. "I could use a friend there. And I know you will soon anyway. I've had visions of us flying around the Night Kingdom together."

"Maybe soon," Moon said. "But not this way." She gestured at the dragons around them. "I have to make my loyalty clear."

"All right," he said. "All right, it's up to you. But come soon. I'll be there, waiting for you." He leaned down and bumped noses with her, then turned and strode briskly back to the platform.

Standing behind him, revealed by his exit, was Anemone. She lifted her snout haughtily at Moon. "You don't deserve his friendship. You're not loyal at all. I say *never* come to the Night Kingdom. He'll be better off without you!" She stuck out her tongue and stomped away.

"Sorry about my sister," Turtle said sheepishly. "She doesn't like competing for attention. She's not used to it."

"She can HAVE all HIS attention, if you ask me," Kinkajou said.

Turtle looked sideways at Moon. Her face was somber, but resolved. If Moon were under Darkstalker's control, then Darkstalker wouldn't have had to plead with her to come with him. She wouldn't have been able to say no.

Had she escaped his spell somehow? Or did it work differently on her? Or was this all part of a larger plan of Darkstalker's?

"Hello, my fellow NightWings," Darkstalker boomed out over the crowd. "Is everyone here? Are you ready to follow me to the greatest place in the world?" He beckoned to a black dragon in the front row. She leaped up onto the platform, and Turtle realized that it was Fierceteeth.

"Whoa," he whispered to Kinkajou. "She's out of the jail already? Do you think Glory knows?"

Kinkajou hissed softly.

Fierceteeth positioned herself at Darkstalker's side, nudging Anemone off to a corner of the platform, which earned her a glare from the SeaWing princess.

"My new lieutenant, Fierceteeth, will be organizing volunteers to carry our supplies. We'll have a feast when we get there! Wait until you see our kingdom!"

A murmur of excitement eddied around the tribe.

Darkstalker swept his wings wide to encompass the entire crowd. "Our wonderful kingdom is not too far away. Our glorious future is on the horizon! Come with me, NightWings!" He rose into the air just as Glory and Deathbringer appeared from the trees. They swooped down to the platform and looked up at him as he hovered above them.

"Time for all true NightWings to go, Your Majesty," Darkstalker said to Glory. "Thank you for watching over them for me until I could get here. I wish you luck with your *own* tribe."

He ascended into the sky with powerful wingbeats that shook the treetops. And dragons began to follow him.

One by one, NightWings lifted off, until the sky was full of beating black wings, lashing tails, and flashing silver scales. The sound of the tribe in flight rolled like a thunderstorm across the rainforest.

Turtle watched them in despair. He couldn't believe so many dragons had fallen for Darkstalker already. Barely three days free, Darkstalker now had an army at his claw tips and an entire kingdom to serve him. He became more unstoppable with every passing moment.

"There's nothing we can do," he whispered. "He's too powerful."

"But not *all*-powerful," Kinkajou whispered back, nudging him. "Look." She pointed to the NightWings who were still on the ground. Moon and Deathbringer, of course, but also at least fifty others — including, to Turtle's surprise, Mightyclaws and his mother.

"I guess some of them actually like us," Kinkajou said proudly. "The smart ones can see how awesome it is here."

"Or they're just terrified of Darkstalker," Turtle suggested.

Kinkajou whacked him with her tail.

Still, compared to the mass exodus overhead, what remained was nothing that could be called a tribe. The few NightWings left shuffled closer together, glancing around as though the forest had suddenly grown bigger and darker. They looked like refugees from a disaster. *Which they are,* Turtle realized. *From the disaster of the volcano, first, and now from the disaster of a king stealing their tribe.*

"Maybe we should go back to Jade Mountain after all," Turtle said, a sense of hopelessness creeping over him. "It's probably one of the safer places to be, with Tsunami and Clay there."

"Until it falls beneath thunder and ice!" Kinkajou protested. "Because we were too boring to save the world! No way, not me. You go if you want to. Moon and I can do everything."

"Um — I think a bit more definition of 'everything' might be in order," Moon said, sounding a little alarmed.

"No," Turtle said glumly. "I'm staying with you. I promised."

"Nice to see that you're completely thrilled about that," Kinkajou said with a laugh. "Don't worry, I'm sure it won't take long. We'll be back at school learning math in no time."

How does she do that? Turtle wondered. *How can she look at the same exact thing I'm looking at, but think, "oh, here's a problem I can solve," instead of "everything is hopeless"?*

They waited until later in the morning to leave; Moon and Kinkajou said their good-byes to Glory, and Mightyclaws told them he'd meet them back at school in a few days. Fearless and Mindreader and their families had gone with Darkstalker, and Glory wasn't sure whether they'd be returning to Jade Mountain.

Turtle wrote another note to Qibli.

KINKAJOU, MOON, AND I ARE FOLLOWING DARKSTALKER TO NIGHT KINGDOM. HOPEFULLY BACK AT SCHOOL SOON.

That was some advanced wishful thinking there. But maybe if he wrote it down, it would end up coming true. He brushed his talons over the slate, remembering how he used to write down everything — every passing idea or observation, as though they were pools of genius he had to capture before they evaporated. He liked the feeling of the slate pencil in his claws again.

Maybe if I survive all of this, I could try writing again.

It wasn't hard to follow Darkstalker and the NightWings, even with half a morning's lead; the tribe in flight was like a dark cloud in the sky ahead of them. At one point as they flew through the mountains, Turtle looked down and spotted what appeared to be a small, abandoned scavenger encampment. He imagined being one of those little creatures looking up to see literally hundreds of dragons suddenly thundering by overhead. If he were one of them, he'd find a rock to hide under and stay there for the next month.

Darkstalker led them south of Jade Mountain, over the delta where the Winding Tail River spilled into the southern sea, and westward along the coast. Below them, waves pounded against a rocky shoreline and the ocean was dark gray with hints of brilliant green where the sun slipped through.

Turtle couldn't help thinking how easy it would be to dive into those waves. He could disappear into the watery depths and leave all these dangers behind. But he looked over at Kinkajou's gray-blue-sky scales and determined expression, and he knew he couldn't leave her.

Darkstalker flew without stopping, and so the tribe did, too, although as the day wore on, they became more spread out across the sky, with the weakest fliers dropping farther and farther behind. The landscape along the coast shifted from mountains to scrub-covered hills and then desert as they reached the southern edge of the Kingdom of Sand. The wind up this high was chilly, but the sun beat down mercilessly on their scales.

Turtle tried to remember the map of Pyrrhia in his head, so he could figure out where they were going. There wasn't anything in this direction except more sand, as far as he knew, and then the western ocean. Another island?

The sun was slipping down the sky ahead of them, shining right into Turtle's eyes, when Darkstalker suddenly dove toward the land. Like a flock of hungry crows, the NightWings swept after him.

Turtle sensed Moon hesitating beside him. "I don't want to join them," she explained when she caught him looking at her. "I don't want them to think I've chosen Darkstalker. This is just a visit."

"I don't want to hang out with those dragons either!" Kinkajou said firmly. "Or listen to another endless windbag speech. Let's find a spot to sleep where they can't see us."

"But where are they going?" Turtle asked, screening his eyes and squinting west. "Why stop now? How much farther can it be?"

"I have no idea," Moon answered. They both hovered in the air for a moment, watching the faraway cloud of NightWings settle across the dunes and pebbled beach, like a black carpet flung over the ground.

Kinkajou found a small cave facing the ocean that the three of them could just barely squeeze into, and Moon caught them a few crabs to eat. It was a relief to stop and rest his wings; Turtle immediately brought out his healing stone to erase the ache in his shoulders. But it also made Turtle anxious that he couldn't see Darkstalker and he had no idea what the ancient animus would do next. What if he wasn't really leading the NightWings to their old kingdom? What if he was planning to smash the entire tribe into a cliff?

That delightfully morbid image wouldn't leave Turtle's brain as he tried to lie down and sleep. Moonlight poured into their cave from the night sky and from the silver reflections in the sea below. Kinkajou and Moon already had their eyes closed, their tails intertwined. He wondered if he'd imagined it that Kinkajou had maneuvered to be the one sleeping next to him. Her scales were warm, as though she'd been collecting sunshine in them all day, and in her sleep they'd turned indigo and gold, with flecks of citrus green.

Carefully, reluctantly, he eased himself away from Kinkajou's side, and slid out of the cave onto the beach. Sand crumbled around his webbed talons and sharp edges of broken seashells poked his tail. The waves looked as though they were trying to reach out and drag him in, *hissssss shhhhhhhh hissssss shhhhhhhh safe shhhhhhhh hide shhhhhhhhhh.*

He turned his head north, toward the NightWing encampment, and watched. He didn't know how long he sat there, staring at that small patch of stars, but sometime later, he saw a vast shadow blot them out, then soar away west.

Darkstalker's going somewhere. By himself, in the middle of the night.

Which means I have to follow him.

Ice Kingdom

Sky Kingdom

Queen Thorn's
Stronghold

Claws of the
Clouds Mountains

Kingdom of
Sand

Scorpion Den

Jade Mountain

PART THREE

THE LOST CITY OF NIGHT

CHAPTER 16

Turtle glanced up the beach at the cave where his friends slept. But this was just a spying mission. He was the only one Darkstalker couldn't see. Whereas if Darkstalker caught Moon and Kinkajou trailing after him in the middle of the night, there would be some explaining to do, insignificance spell or no insignificance spell.

He rose into the air and followed Darkstalker, feeling as if his heart and stomach had traded places. *Don't be a coward,* he scolded himself. *This is nothing. Eavesdropping with a cloak of invisibility. Sneaking around, which is the one thing you're good at.*

He thought of Peril's fierce lack of stealth, the way she always made the most noise or picked a fight or accidentally blew something up. He missed her. He wondered what she was doing now. Their adventure together, setting out to stop Scarlet and find the rest of Jade Winglet, had felt a lot safer and more fun than this — maybe because he'd known her firescales could protect him, or because his magic had still been a secret from everyone back then.

The three moons lit up a ridge of jagged mountains stabbing into the clouds ahead of them. For a moment Turtle was disoriented, and he turned to look back over his shoulder — but no, there were the Claws of the Clouds Mountains behind him. The ones up ahead rose out of the desert like a wall made of shark's teeth, ending at sheer cliffs along the ocean.

Oh, Turtle thought, remembering the map of Pyrrhia. There was a small peninsula that jutted out at the southwest corner of the Kingdom of Sand. If the continent was a dragon, and that peninsula was a talon reaching out, these mountains were sort of like Turtle's armband. *And nobody has crossed them in hundreds of years?* Turtle wondered. They were quite forbidding; he wasn't sure he particularly wanted to cross them himself.

But that was clearly where Darkstalker was going. At one point, as they flew over land that began sloping up into hills, Turtle felt a sudden buzzing shock, like he'd accidentally grabbed a baby electric eel.

What was that?

There was no way to know, and it was over in a moment. Turtle glanced uneasily down at the ground below him and hoped he was imagining the pale flash of what looked like bones sticking out of the earth.

Up ahead, Darkstalker tipped his wings to soar high over the peaks and Turtle followed, gasping in the thin air.

And there was the Night Kingdom.

Spread out below them, outlined by moonlight, were the ruins of an ancient city that sprawled across the peninsula.

Much of it was hidden within canyons and cliff faces, but at the foot of the mountain, partially built into it, stood a palace, or what was left of a palace. In front of it was an overgrown square paved in marble and studded with bits of toppled columns; a kind of platform had collapsed in the center of it and was nearly submerged in a wild tangle of vines. All around the square were more ruins: once-elegant buildings whose roofs had caved in, statues missing heads, talons, tails, or all three, sculptural details worn away by weather.

Darkstalker's wingbeats faltered as he took in the devastation below him. He slowed to a stop, hovering outside the palace, staring down at the square. Bats flitted in and out of the windows behind him, like dark thoughts scattering into the air.

He feels like he was just here, Turtle guessed. *It's like if I returned to the Kingdom of the Sea tomorrow and found that everything I knew my whole life has been destroyed, apparently overnight. And my tribe was scattered, weakened, with no queen.*

And everyone I ever loved was dead.

The giant NightWing put out one talon and touched the overgrown wall of the palace. Abruptly he turned and flew toward one of the other stately buildings that flanked the square.

Turtle spread his wings to follow and felt a sudden strange chill along his spine.

As though someone was watching him.

He twisted in the air, searching the palace windows. Every shadow was full of eyes, every stirring of air the quiet breath of a hidden dragon.

Was someone still living here? Had some NightWings never left, all those hundreds of years ago?

But no one emerged, and no sound came from within the palace walls.

Maybe he was imagining things. This place was creepy enough to make anyone's scales crawl.

Turtle flew after Darkstalker as fast as he could. At first he couldn't figure out what this new building was. It had at least three entrances, on different levels, although one was blocked by fallen rubble. Turtle also counted five towers, three of them half-tumbled away, and a trickle that looked as though it might once have been a waterfall. Darkstalker flew to the uppermost entrance and paced inside, ducking his head slightly to avoid cracking it on the high ceiling.

And here, in the spiral hallways, there were clues: large rooms lined with tables, broken slates on the floor, displays of awkward, crumbling clay statues that looked as though they'd been molded by dragonets.

Because they were, Turtle realized. *This is a school.*

Why would Darkstalker come to a ruined NightWing school in the middle of the night? If he was searching for something of power, wouldn't it be at the palace? Or if he was looking for something of his own, something he missed, wouldn't it be . . . wherever he used to live?

Turtle realized that he had no idea how old Darkstalker

had been when Clearsight put the sleeping spell on him. He'd always imagined an older dragon, close to the age of the queen he was trying to replace.

Darkstalker stopped at a turn in the corridor, brushed aside cobwebs and dust, and uncovered a painting. It was hard to make out the subject under the accumulated dirt of centuries, but Turtle thought it might have been a portrait of someone.

Darkstalker traced the outer edge of it with his claws for a moment, and then he put one talon on the center of the canvas. Centuries of dust swirled away in a sudden blast, making Turtle's eyes water. He clapped his talons over his snout to stop himself from sneezing.

When he looked up again, blinking away tears, he saw that Darkstalker had used his magic to restore the painting. Now it looked the way it must have looked in his time: brand-new, the colors and lines still sharp.

It was a portrait of a female NightWing, seated with her wings folded back, gazing out at the viewer. Behind her, a web of fiery lines crisscrossed the sky, like a pattern in the stars, with smaller falling stars in between the lines. For the most part, it was not a great portrait; the proportions were all wrong, particularly in the undersized talons and oversized head.

But there was something in her eyes that made you look twice. Something that made you think this dragon truly loved the painter.

Could that be Clearsight? Turtle wondered.

Darkstalker stared at her for a long moment before pulling himself away and continuing on. Turtle followed him through the spiraling labyrinth of the school until finally they emerged in a central courtyard. Classrooms looked out on the courtyard on all sides, and it wasn't hard to imagine being a student here, eating lunch under the trees or practicing your flying.

Turtle had to navigate the tangles of vines, shrubs, and tall grass carefully to avoid getting stuck, but Darkstalker's huge talons crushed all the undergrowth in his path as he strode to a spot under a towering pine tree.

Here he stopped. He bowed his head. His wings slowly drifted down to droop beside him.

Long heartbeats passed.

What is he thinking about? Turtle wondered. *And . . . why here?*

He inched closer, although it made his scales run cold to step through Darkstalker's shadow. It was an eerie, unsettling kind of spying, to stand right in front of a dragon and know he couldn't see you. Also that if he did, you'd be dead.

A silver scale shone on Darkstalker's face, then slipped down his snout to splash on the ground.

Oh, Turtle realized with an awful twist in his heart. *He's crying.*

He did NOT know how to feel about that. Sympathy for Darkstalker . . . he couldn't afford that, could he? Not if he wanted to stay strong enough to stop him.

But this is the real Darkstalker. He's not performing for anyone right now.

He's just . . . really sad.

Turtle glanced around, wishing he knew what to do. Here, perhaps, was a dragon who could be reasoned with. Here was a dragon who might tell the truth, if he had the right audience to say it to.

That idea, combined with the eerie experience outside the palace, led Turtle to a crazy thought.

There was another kind of story Turtle used to read when he was younger.

Ghost stories. Spirits of the dead coming back to haunt those who wronged them. Lost loves lingering around the ones who held their heart in life.

Did Darkstalker believe in ghosts?

Turtle backed cautiously away, scanning the ground for something he might be able to use. Darkstalker couldn't see him or hear him as he moved around — but he'd be able to see something Turtle left behind.

The moonlight glinted off something small and shiny, tucked in the hollow of a nearby tree. Turtle reached in, digging through the moss, and found a stash of beautiful marbles in different colors: blues and greens and silvery blacks. He glanced back at Darkstalker and chose a white marble with a sea-blue heart. It looked like a tiny moon, and he thought it would be the most visible in the dark grass.

Is this stupid? Is this the stupidest thing I've ever done?

He hesitated. But all he wanted to do was see how Darkstalker reacted, if at all; he'd still be as hidden as ever. He'd be careful. Darkstalker might just think he hadn't noticed it before.

He crept forward on trembling talons until he was almost under Darkstalker's nose. He waited until the huge NightWing wiped his eyes and glanced up at the sky. In a flash, Turtle set the marble down an inch from those massive claws and backed away.

Nothing happened for a moment; Darkstalker was still looking at the moons. But then he lowered his head again with a sigh — which caught in his throat when he saw the marble.

He snatched it up in his claws and stared around the garden. His gaze passed right through Turtle, making Turtle feel like a skewered moth.

"Clearsight?" Darkstalker whispered. He cleared his throat and tried again, a little stronger. "Clearsight?"

The wind murmured through the shadows, scattering pine needles across Darkstalker's wings and breathing evergreen air in Turtle's direction.

"Clearsight," Darkstalker said, stepping out into the moonlight, "if you're here, speak to me. Please, please speak to me." He waited with an expression of such hope that Turtle was filled with guilt.

"Then listen," Darkstalker said after a while. "I won't hurt you. I would never hurt you. I forgive you. I know you were scared. I saw everything you were afraid of in that last moment when you — when you put the bracelet on me." He hesitated, and his voice cracked as he added, "I'm sorry I put that spell on you." He closed his eyes and rubbed his forehead with his talons.

What spell? Turtle wondered. *What kind of dragon puts a spell on someone he loves?*

Then he remembered the love spell on Kinkajou and wanted to claw his own face off.

"If you come back to me," Darkstalker said sadly, softly, to the shadows, "I promise I'll never enchant your mind again. I promise I'll listen to you this time. We can choose the best future together." He let out a small laugh. "I could use your help with what you've left me. A ruined city, a weak and broken tribe. You'd be their Queen Clearsight — doesn't that sound all right now? When you can have the crown without anyone having to die? It was just waiting for us, Clearsight."

He started to pace. "You should have to help fix this. Do you see what you did when you betrayed me? It's all gone — our tribe's power, our kingdom. Our beautiful future. You did this to *our whole tribe*, not just to me."

Darkstalker's breath was ragged, his jaw clenched, and his claws ripped at the plants and grass, killing everything in his wake. "Clearsight," he said. "I — I keep looking at all my new possible futures. Millions of possibilities, but they're all empty. They're empty without you. I have no one, Clearsight. All I can see around me, as far as the future unrolls, are slaves and soldiers."

Turtle shivered involuntarily. *Slaves and soldiers. Is that how he sees his own tribe?*

Darkstalker paused again for a long moment, and then said, so quietly that Turtle almost couldn't hear him, "I know you can't be out there. You're not in any of my futures. But please, Clearsight — please come back and tell me there's still hope for us."

The next pause lasted forever and another ten forevers. Turtle's talons were starting to fall asleep, but he didn't dare move while Darkstalker was still listening so intently.

Finally Darkstalker lifted the marble up to glare at it, then clenched his fist shut around it. "I'm a sentimental idiot. You're not here," he muttered. "You could have been, if you'd waited another day or two. I would have made you *immortal*, Clearsight. We could have been together forever." He turned to pace back and forth under the spreading pine branches.

He is immortal, then. Turtle had suspected it, but now he knew for sure. *Invulnerable scales, immortal life. The first spells that any young animus would think of. But no one would actually do them, between the cost to your soul and the unforeseen risks. At least, that's what I always thought.*

"So what did you do instead?" Darkstalker hissed softly. "Did you go back to Fathom? Did you two laugh at the wonderful trick you played on me? Did you let *him* cast spells for you?" He clawed at his neck as though something sticky was clinging to it. "That sneaking serpent of a SeaWing. All high and mighty about protecting his soul and keeping his oath — until it comes to betraying his best friend. Then it's *sure, why not*. It's full speed ahead to sleeping spells and conniving and lies."

He stopped, his sides heaving. "No," he said. "You loved me. I know that was true. Fathom talked you into doing this to me. *He's* the traitor. He's the one I'll never forgive."

Darkstalker hurled the marble at the nearest tree with such force that the trunk split down the middle. Turtle had to scramble out of the way of falling branches, and when he was able to look up again, Darkstalker had vanished into the night sky.

CHAPTER 17

Moon was awake when Turtle got back. She was sitting on the beach, staring out to sea, tracing shapes in the sand without looking at what her claws were doing. A thin thread of light on the horizon hinted at the sunrise about to come, but the cold air smelled like rain.

"Why aren't you sleeping?" Turtle asked, landing beside her.

She gave him a rueful look. "I never sleep well at night. In the rainforest, I mostly slept during the day, and I haven't quite adjusted to a normal dragon schedule." She hesitated. "Although Darkstalker says I'm the one who's normal, and it's the other NightWings who need to fix themselves to match." Her tail flicked sand across the patterns she'd drawn. "And I had a nightmare. *The* nightmare. The one I always have."

"About Jade Mountain falling?"

Moon nodded. "Fire and death and screaming and death. It's not awesome."

"You can't see anything about how to stop it?" Turtle asked. "Any clues?"

"Like something we might find in 'the lost city of night'?" Moon suggested with a sigh. "Not so far. Where have you been?"

Turtle discovered that he didn't want to tell her about what he'd seen — especially about Darkstalker's crushing sadness. She already sympathized with him too much. She didn't need more reasons to want to give Darkstalker a hug. She needed to see him as bad and dangerous so that she'd help Kinkajou when the time came for whatever heroics were necessary.

"Just scouting out the NightWings," he said evasively. "Checking on Anemone." This was partly true; as he flew over them, he had peered down at the NightWings, their black scales blanketing the dunes and the beach where they slept. He'd spotted Anemone down by the ocean, sleeping as close to the sound and scent of the waves as she could get.

"You're a good brother," Moon said.

"No, I'm not!" he protested, and she looked startled at his vehemence. "Don't say that. I'm a *terrible* brother."

"Great heavens, Turtle," Moon said, blinking. "That's not true at all. You're following her to the ends of the continent, aren't you? To make sure she's all right?"

I'm following Darkstalker. I know Anemone's not all right. And that's my fault, and there's nothing I can do about it.

"Trust me," he said. "I'm the worst brother a dragon could possibly have."

Moon studied him for a long moment with a faint frown on her face. "I had a vision about you once," she said.

"About me?" Turtle snorted. "Was I hiding at the bottom of the ocean? Because that's what I see in most of my possible futures."

"No . . . I'm not sure whether to tell you about it," she said. "It was a little scary."

Turtle dug one of his talons into the beach and let the sand fill in over it until it disappeared. With Darkstalker around, probably everyone had a scary future ahead. "I think you should tell me," he said.

"You were on a beach," she said, her voice getting softer, nearly swallowed by the rush of the waves. "And you were attacking Anemone."

Turtle stared at her. "Why would I do that?"

"I don't know," she said. "You had her pinned down. That's all I saw."

"Why are you just telling me now?" he asked.

One of the crescent moons was reflected in her eyes. "I didn't want to scare you. I was worried it might happen because you use your magic too much and lose your soul."

Turtle's claws twitched as though they were reaching for someone's throat. He tried to imagine them sinking into Anemone's scales, drawing his sister's blood. The screaming, battered NightWing flashed through his mind again, along with a whisper: *You have violence in you.*

But that was different. I would never hurt my own sister.

His claws curled inward as though they disagreed with him.

"It might not come true," Moon said. "Darkstalker says our visions are only the most probable futures — but things can always go in a different direction."

Turtle jumped to his feet, clenching and unclenching his talons. "I'm sure it won't happen. I'm a bad brother, but not *that* terrible." He didn't want to think about this anymore. He didn't need one more thing to worry about.

Movement on the horizon caught his attention and he looked up to see black wings ascending into the sky. "They're moving. I'll get Kinkajou." Turtle ran up the beach and poked his nose into the cave, nudging Kinkajou in the side.

"Nnnnnnnnnnnooooooooo," Kinkajou mumbled from under her wings.

"Time to go, Kinkajou," he said.

"Go awaaaaaaay, Bromeliad," Kinkajou grumped in her sleep. "You smell like FISH and I don't WANNA train today."

Turtle felt a stab of affection for her — for this grouchy, sleepy side of her he hadn't seen before. She was so real and so kind and so present. She was the opposite of a terrifying vision of his future. "It's me, Turtle," he said, brushing one of his wings over hers. "Come on, Kinkajou, wake up."

"Turtle," Kinkajou sighed dreamily, and clouds of light pink started drifting through her scales.

Turtle pulled his wing back, feeling sick. So Anemone's spell really was working. He knew this wasn't how Kinkajou actually felt about him. She'd be so furious and embarrassed when she found out it was all magic.

But I can't tell her. What if it makes her so angry she takes off the skyfire? And then Darkstalker notices her and terrible things happen?

Is this why I attack Anemone on some future beach? Because I'm angry with her about the spell on Kinkajou?

"We have to go," he said gruffly and whacked her with his tail.

"Who's that?" she yelped, leaping to her feet and turning red with stripes of pale green. "You want my venom, I'll show you ven — oh, hi, Turtle." She shook herself from head to tail. "Whoa, that was a weird dream. My old teacher turned into the NightWing who used to study us." She shook herself again, harder. "Two of my least favorite dragons. Yeesh, anyone would think I'm worried about something."

"The NightWings are moving," Turtle said. "We should get going, too."

"Oh, sure." Kinkajou rubbed her face and then stretched, shifting her scales through a dazzling cascade of colors, from purple to aquamarine to saffron, where they settled. "Turtle, you're looking at me as though I've been stabbed by a stalactite but haven't noticed yet."

"Sorry," he said, backing out of the cave quickly.

They watched the NightWings gather in the sky like storm clouds until the tribe finally wheeled away west, and then Turtle, Moon, and Kinkajou lifted off and followed them.

The landscape looked much the same in the light as it had the night before, and Turtle felt the same strange zap of energy as they flew over that spot in the hills.

"Did you —" he asked his friends, just as Kinkajou yelped, "OW! What was THAT?"

"I don't know," Moon said, glancing down. She fell silent, and Turtle wondered if she had seen the shapes of bones below them, too.

They waited until all the NightWings had vanished over the peaks before flying after them. But as they came up and over the last mountain, they found a dragon waiting for them in the sky.

Darkstalker.

"Moon!" he cried with genuine delight. "I thought my visions were messing with me, but you did come after all!" He did a joyful flip in the air, spreading his wings toward the city. "Isn't this amazing? Look at our beautiful kingdom!"

"Oh wow," Moon said faintly.

In the gray sunlight, Turtle could see that the city was even larger and more ornate than he'd realized the night before — but he could also see more clearly how broken it was, and how time had eaten away at it. The rest of the tribe had swooped down into the ruins, diving through the canyons, exploring their new home.

"That's the Great Diamond down there," Darkstalker said eagerly to Moon, pointing at the overgrown square. "On one side is the museum; over there is the school; and that building is the library. The library, Moon! I can't wait to show it to you. It makes Starflight's little cave at Jade Mountain look like a toad's den. Although it's not in the greatest shape now . . . but surely some of our scrolls must have survived." He poked Moon with his tail, grinning. "I was hoping my visions were right and you'd come. This is great!"

"I'm not staying," Moon said quickly. "I'm going back to Jade Mountain. I just . . . wanted to see it."

"Me too!" Kinkajou volunteered, popping up behind Moon and waving at Darkstalker. "I'm here to see it, too! Moon's best friend, remember?"

"Yes, right," Darkstalker said dismissively. "Well, sure, Moon, if you want to go back to Jade Mountain, that's fine, but you might find that *our* school is much better and more perfect for you. After all, it's where *I* went to school! We had classes in all kinds of things they'll never get to at Jade Mountain. I just have to rebuild it a little, clean it up . . . find some decent teachers." He frowned down at the scattered NightWings below him. "I suppose I could enchant some of them into becoming good teachers," he said thoughtfully.

"But . . . would your school be only for NightWings?" Moon asked. "Or would you invite students from other tribes, like Sunny did at Jade Mountain?"

"Sunny is very sweet," Darkstalker said, "but you saw how that turned out. It doesn't work to throw tribes together and just hope they'll get along, because they won't — they can't. Dragons don't work that way, no matter what tribe they're from."

"I get along with dragons from other tribes!" Kinkajou objected. "Moon is my best friend! Our winglet is awesome!"

"I kind of like meeting the other tribes," Moon said to Darkstalker. "They're not all like Icicle or Flame . . . or poor Sora."

"Well," Darkstalker said, flicking his tail, "maybe one day you can organize an exchange program. But for now we need to focus on educating our own dragonets. We have a tribe to rebuild! There's so much they need to learn. Perhaps once we've solved all the problems within our tribe, we can start thinking about reaching out to . . . other tribes. Anyway, let me give you a tour of the palace!" He tugged on one of Moon's wings and flashed away.

Moon gave Turtle and Kinkajou an apologetic look and went after him. They followed a few wingbeats behind.

"He pays no attention to me at all!" Kinkajou grumbled. "It's like I'm not even there!"

"That's *good*, Kinkajou," Turtle reminded her. "You don't want him to pay attention to you."

"I know," she said with a sigh. "But I don't like feeling as though I've disappeared. Like I'm not important enough to even look at."

"You're very important," Turtle said reassuringly. "You're the hero of the story, remember? You have to fulfill Moon's prophecy."

"That's right!" she said, brightening. "We're here! In the

lost city of night!" She glanced around as though she expected a parade of cheering dragons to pop out of the mountain. "We did it! So . . . did it work? Is the world saved?" She poked his shoulder experimentally. "Does the world feel saved to you?"

"Not even remotely," Turtle admitted, watching Darkstalker and Moon land on one of the balconies of the palace.

"Thaaaat's the right attitude," Kinkajou said.

They swept down to land on the same balcony, carefully avoiding the parts of the balustrade that had caved in. Inside, Darkstalker was walking around what appeared to be a giant bedroom, eight times the size of any sleeping cave Turtle had ever been in.

"These were the queen's rooms," Darkstalker said to Moon. "They're mine now, of course. It looks like she took most of her treasure with her when she left." He blew some dust off an enormous mirror and frowned at it. "It all used to be so clean and . . . perfect. There were grand parties every other night! And things you would actually like, too, Moon — salons and scientific lectures and readings . . ." His voice trailed off as he wandered into one of the side rooms of the suite, where he started overturning empty chests and opening all the cabinets. Moon disappeared after him.

"Darkstalker!" Anemone appeared in the doorway to the hall, her talons covered in white stone dust. "I couldn't find the rooms you were talking about. All the doors look the same!" She spotted Turtle and her mouth dropped open.

"What are you doing here?" she hissed. "I thought you were going back to school. Stop following me!"

"He's not following you," Kinkajou said haughtily. "He's with *me*."

"Oh." Anemone's snout crinkled into a wickedly sly grin. "Aw, that's *wonderful*. That's so, *so* cute. You guys are *so* cute together." She lowered her voice, although not far enough, and whispered to Turtle, "You're *welcome*."

Moon heard this as she came back into the room. She gave him and Anemone a surprised look. Turtle hoped the floor was about to collapse and take him with it.

"Wait, you're here, too?" Anemone said to Moon, lashing her tail. "Do you just keep changing your mind about who you're loyal to? He doesn't need you, you know. He has me."

"We're not staying long," Moon said uncomfortably.

"What is it, Anemone?" Darkstalker asked, slithering back into the main room. Turtle wondered if he was imagining the hint of weary impatience in Darkstalker's voice.

"You said there was a perfect suite for me, remember?" Anemone said, in her wheedling-whining princess voice. "But I couldn't figure out your directions and I can't *find* it."

"Oh dear, I'm so sorry for straining your tiny SeaWing brain," he said. Anemone didn't even look offended; the insult seemed to sail right past her. "Come on, I'll just show you." She jumped out of his way as he thumped past and Turtle noticed that the doors in this palace were so big, Darkstalker didn't even have to duck as he went through.

They all trailed after Darkstalker through the long black marble halls of the palace, many of which opened onto courtyards or balconies or grand halls far below them. Turtle had always thought the Deep Palace of the SeaWings was the most luxurious, imposing castle in all of Pyrrhia, but he guessed that at least five of them would fit inside this place.

Anemone might have been thinking the same thing, because she said jealously, "You know, *our* palace has a lot more artwork. And treasure. *Lots* of jewels everywhere."

Darkstalker paused and ran one claw through the dust on one of the walls. "There used to be artwork and treasure here, too," he said thoughtfully. "I'm surprised the queen was able to take so much of it with her." He paused. "Unless she didn't." His eyebrows drew down menacingly. "Unless another tribe came in here later and looted the palace."

He whirled toward Moon. "Which tribe would you say is the wealthiest?"

"The wealthiest?" Moon said. "I don't know — I mean, how would anyone know that?"

"Which tribe has the most treasure?" he asked edgily. "What would you guess? I don't need exact numbers. In all those scrolls of yours, which queens buy the most extravagant things? Which castles are the most full of jewels?" He shot Anemone a suspicious look.

"Um . . . all of them, except the RainWings," Moon said awkwardly, "but maybe the SkyWings have a lot, because of Scarlet — and the SandWing treasury was supposed to be one of the greatest in the world, before the war and the whole lie about the scavengers stealing all of it."

"SandWings," Darkstalker hissed. "They barely had any treasure in my time. It must have been them." He rapped the wall with one claw and turned away again. "All right, Anemone, come along."

"*Princess* Anemone," she said, tossing her head.

Darkstalker sped up, whisked around a corner, and threw open a huge set of black doors.

"Here you go," he said with a strange gleam in his eyes. "The perfect suite for you. Decorated with a SeaWing in mind, two thousand years ago. In fact, your own ancestor stayed in these very rooms."

"Fathom?" Turtle blurted.

Anemone looked curiously from him to Darkstalker, expecting an answer. Kinkajou jumped in quickly. "Was that Fathom?" she asked.

"Yes," Darkstalker said. He glanced at Moon and steeled his face, as though hiding his true feelings from her. He stepped through into the main bedroom, his black eyes studying every inch of the space. "This is where our queen put him when she brought him over from the Kingdom of the Sea. To 'educate' me about the perils of animus magic."

"Oh." Anemone stepped around him and sneezed. "Huh. This is it? It's not what I pictured." She peered into a dry, cracked pool in the floor. Her tail bumped one of the tattered, moth-eaten cushions, sending up a halo of dust, and she sneezed again.

"So use your magic to clean it up," Darkstalker said impatiently. "Or better yet, learn how to use a mop and your own claws."

"Where does Moon get to stay?" Anemone demanded.

"Wherever she likes," Darkstalker answered. "If she decides to stay, that is." He turned to Moon with a smile. "Let's go see how the gardens have turned out!"

He bounded out the door again, but Moon lingered for a moment after he left. "I think the room's really nice, Anemone," she said. "It has a balcony and everything."

"You *would* think it's nice," said Anemone. "*You* grew up in a gross muddy fern gully in a rainforest. *I* am a princess. I have always lived in a palace and I've never had to clean my own room! The idea!"

"I've never had to clean my room either!" Kinkajou volunteered. "I mean, I don't have a room. But I have a hammock! Sometimes I shake it really hard to get all the leaves and bugs out. Does that count?"

"Moon!" Darkstalker called.

Anemone stamped her foot. "Why doesn't he want to show *me* the gardens?" She scowled at Moon. "The minute you show up, suddenly you're the only dragon he wants to talk to. I don't see what's so special about you."

"Nothing at all," Moon said. "I'm just the first dragon he met when he woke up. I'd better go." She took a step backward.

"No!" Anemone barked. "If you're so wonderful and amazing, why don't *you* clean my room!" She grabbed a talonful of loose pebbles from the floor. "Turn into a bucket of water and a mop," she ordered, and instantly a long mop and a pail of water appeared in her claws.

She held up the mop and pointed at Moon. "Now go hit that dragon really hard until she starts using you to clean this place — and don't let her stop until I say it's done."

CHAPTER 18

"What?!" Kinkajou yelped.

"Anemone!" Turtle cried.

The mop sailed across the room and rapped Moon sharply on the snout as she tried to back away.

"Ow!" Moon cried, fending it off. "Stop!" The mop evaded her talons and whapped her again. Tears of pain sprang into Moon's eyes and she grabbed the handle, wrestling it down to the floor. "What are you doing?" she shouted at Anemone. "I'm not going to let you hurt me!"

"Neither am I!" Kinkajou yelled. She dashed over and threw herself on the mop, helping Moon pin it to the ground.

"Anemone," Turtle said helplessly. "Stop this."

But his sister was busy scooping up another talonful of pebbles. "Turn into opals and sapphires," she ordered them. "And go distract Darkstalker so he doesn't come looking for her." She opened her claws and a glittering constellation of blue and iridescent gems shot out the door, tumbling over one another in the air.

"There," Anemone said, satisfied. "Now he won't come rescue you. And hey, he did say I should use my magic to clean up. Just stop fighting and do it!" She made a sweeping gesture with one talon and the mop's long handle shot upright, cracking Kinkajou in the jaw.

"Yowch!" Kinkajou roared.

Turtle jumped forward, but he didn't know what to do. Should he cast a spell? Would it be hidden by Anemone's other magic in here? What could he do? Enchant the mop — or enchant Anemone? But then she'd know he was an animus. This seemed like perhaps not the best time to reveal that.

Still, he had to do *something* to help Kinkajou and Moon. What would the hapless sidekick do in this situation?

A heartfelt speech! There was always a right thing to say, wasn't there? Even the sidekick sometimes got a decent useful speech. He could talk her down. She was his sister, after all.

"Anemone, think about what you're doing," he started, his voice cracking.

"Blah blah blah," Anemone said, flapping her claws at him. "Quit your jellyfishing, Turtle. I'll let your girlfriend and her annoying friend go in a minute. I just don't get what Darkstalker *sees* in Moon, do you? She's nobody special. Not like me." A slow smile spread across her face. "Maybe I just need to make him realize that."

Anemone swept over to the dry fountain and fished something out of it — some kind of small device that looked like a telescope and an hourglass stuck together. "What in the moons is this?" Anemone turned it over in her claws for a moment, shrugged, and tossed it aside. She plucked a piece of broken tile out of the pool.

"Turn into an earring," she commanded the tile. "Something really sparkly and cool that Darkstalker would like." A twisty silver snake with ruby eyes appeared in her talon. "Perfect. Now — earring, as soon as Darkstalker puts you on, I want you to make him stop caring about Moon at all. She'll be just another random dragon bothering him. And *I'll* be the only dragon he finds interesting."

"You can't do that to him!" Turtle said. "Can you?" Would a spell like that even work on Darkstalker?

If it did, maybe it would be a good thing — maybe it would help Turtle get Moon away from Darkstalker's influence. Maybe it would keep her safer from him than she would otherwise be.

I should enchant that earring, too! he realized suddenly. *But with what spell? What's the right spell to put on Darkstalker if I had the chance?* Another sleeping spell? Or something to make other dragons see him the way he really was? A spell to make him reveal all his secret plans?

Or . . . a spell that could kill him?

Could I really do that? Is that what he deserves? His brain offered up a flash of lonely Darkstalker in the school gardens last night, missing his lost love.

And then another flash of blood staining his own claws.

Am I a dragon who could kill someone — anyone? Even him?

If I did, would that tip my soul into darkness? Is that the choice I make that leads to me attacking my sister on a beach?

"You — you jackdaw!" Kinkajou yelled at Anemone, coiling her tail around the mop and leaning on it with all her weight. "You overripe melon!" Next to her, Moon was struggling silently. "You're being absolutely horrible!" Kinkajou yelled. "Oh! Turtle, is this her losing her soul? Is she turning evil?"

Is it? Turtle thought with horror. He'd stopped worrying about that after she put on the silver necklace. But if it didn't work . . . or if the spell on it wasn't quite what she thought it was . . .

"Ha!" Anemone cried. "I'm not evil! My soul is protected, remember? I've seen evil — this isn't evil at all. This is just a princess dealing with one of her pesky problems." She held up the earring and dangled it in Moon's direction. "What else should I do with my magic, do you think? Ooooo, I could make him give me the queen's rooms. Or I could make him build me my *own* palace, right next to this one!" She breathed out a contented sigh and touched her necklace. "Life is so much easier now that I can do anything I want."

"I wouldn't be so sure of that," Moon said, looking over Anemone's shoulder.

"Anemone." Darkstalker's menacing voice rumbled like an earthquake rising through Turtle's claws. "Explain yourself." The enormous NightWing stepped through the door and made a gesture toward Moon. The mop clattered to the ground, harmless once more. Kinkajou put one wing around Moon.

Anemone swung around to Darkstalker with a sweet, practiced smile on her face. "There you are! Oh, this is nothing, don't worry. I was trying to clean up and the mop went a bit haywire and these two decided to tackle it. So weird! But look, I found this really cool earring in one of the side tables. Isn't it perfect for you?"

"Liar!" Kinkajou yelled, but Darkstalker ignored her.

He stepped forward to loom over Anemone and she backed into a wall, babbling. "I mean, the king of the NightWings should really wear the best jewelry, don't you think?"

"I don't accept gifts from animus dragons," he growled. "Especially from deceitful, conniving SeaWings. What kind of an idiot do you think I am, that I would fall for a trick like that?"

"It's not a trick," Anemone protested. "It's just a pretty earring. Squid guts, you don't have to be so paranoid." She laughed nervously.

"Spare me your lies," Darkstalker spat. "I heard everything." He uncurled his talon, scattering the dust of gemstones at her feet. "You thought these baubles would distract me so you could hurt Moon." He snatched the earring out of her claws. "You planned to manipulate my emotions. To cast a spell on *me*."

"J-just a little one," Anemone stammered. "I just want you to be *my* mentor and only pay attention to me, that's all."

"Don't be angry at her, Darkstalker," Moon said, her sides heaving as she caught her breath. "She's young. It was just a mistake. And I'm fine."

"I will not have dragons stolen from me," Darkstalker snarled. "Not ever again." He reached one talon toward Moon and Kinkajou and made an odd circling motion with his claws. Instantly Moon stopped moving as though she'd been frozen, staring forward blankly with unblinking eyes.

Kinkajou let out a small gasp and reached toward her friend.

Oh no, Turtle thought frantically. *That spell is supposed to be on Kinkajou, too! Darkstalker's going to notice that his magic doesn't work on her!*

Darkstalker frowned at Kinkajou, then down at his talon. Turtle hissed, catching Kinkajou's attention, and pretended to freeze in place.

Light dawned in her eyes. When Darkstalker reached toward her again, she immediately froze where she was, mimicking Moon's blank stare.

Good, Turtle thought, although his heart was still pounding. *Now hold that. Don't give yourself away.*

Luckily, Darkstalker turned his back on Kinkajou almost immediately, focusing his attention on Anemone. "It's time for you to go, Princess," he growled.

"What do you mean, go?" Anemone cried. "Go where?"

She glanced anxiously at Moon and Kinkajou. "What did you do to them?"

"They don't need to hear this part," Darkstalker said softly. "It's time for you to go back to the Kingdom of the Sea."

What is he doing? Turtle thought in a panic. *Is he putting a spell on my sister?*

"But I don't want to!" Anemone stamped her foot. "I hate it there! I want to stay with you and learn about being an animus!"

"You know all you need to know," Darkstalker said. His voice seemed to be getting colder and darker, like water from the deepest ocean depths curling slowly into Turtle's ears. "You know what Albatross did. You know how easily you could be queen. You know that nobody can stand in your way if you decide to go take the SeaWing throne right now."

"Is . . . is that what you want me to do?" Anemone asked.

"I don't care what you do," said Darkstalker. "I was beginning to think you could be a worthy student. That perhaps I should keep you around, after all. I thought you might be someone who could work alongside me." He glanced at Moon, then fixed his cold black eyes on Anemone. "But I was an idiot to let any affection for you creep in. You are truly Fathom's descendant. You're just as bad as he is. And I don't want you anywhere near me."

"I can't help being Fathom's descendant!" Anemone cried. "I'm sorry, all right? I won't try to cast any more spells on you, I promise!"

"It wouldn't have worked anyway," Darkstalker said,

flicking the earring at her. It bounced off her forehead and skidded across the floor. "None of your spells will ever work on me. I've protected myself from your magic. Now get out. Go kill your mother, if you want. Feel free to kill any other dragons who stand in your way."

He made the circling motion with his claws again. Moon took a breath in, glancing around as though mildly puzzled, and Kinkajou imitated her a moment later.

"You won't be able to hurt Moon anymore," Darkstalker said, sweeping one wing toward the doorway. "So don't even try."

"This isn't fair!" Anemone yelled. "It's not *fair*!" She bolted toward the balcony instead, then turned back, framed by the gray light outside. "I'll show you how special and important I am! You'll see!" She flung herself into the air.

Anemone. Turtle's chest ached, as though all his guilt had become boulders piled on his heart. *This is my fault. This is my fault.*

"I can't believe she did that!" Kinkajou said. "Moon, are you all right?"

"Did she cast any spells on you?" Darkstalker asked gently.

"Not on me, no," Moon said in a shaky voice. "I don't think so. Just on the mop and the earring. Three moons. I didn't realize how upset she was with me. Did you see that in her mind?" she asked Darkstalker.

"A little, but I didn't think it would escalate so quickly either," he said.

"Are you having a vision?" Moon touched her temples. "I have a vision headache, but nothing clear is coming through."

"Or maybe you have a headache because you just got whacked in the head with a mop handle," Kinkajou suggested sensibly.

"No, it's — I think it's some danger in the Kingdom of the Sea," Moon said. Her worried eyes met Turtle's.

Cold terror ran through him. Was Anemone really going back home? Right now? To kill Mother and steal the throne?

She wouldn't do that, he thought, and at the same moment, *this new Anemone might. This Anemone who wants everything, who believes it should be hers — this Anemone who uses her magic for selfish reasons, who wants to impress Darkstalker . . . this Anemone, who acts as though her soul is damaged after all.*

The enchantment Darkstalker did on her necklace — what if it was a lie? What if it didn't protect her soul; what if she'd been losing it, bit by bit, with each spell she cast?

Including the one I asked her to cast on Kinkajou, Turtle thought with a wince.

If that was true, the same thing could be happening to Anemone that happened to Albatross, their murderous ancestor all those centuries ago.

And she could be flying home to follow in his footsteps right now.

CHAPTER 19

"I have to go after her," Turtle said. "My tribe — my family —"

Kinkajou took a step toward him, but Darkstalker was already folding his wings around her and Moon. "*Now* let's go see the gardens," he said. "And put all this unpleasantness behind us."

"But what if Anemone does something terrible?" Moon said to him. "Shouldn't we follow her?"

He looked down at her with sad eyes. "In all the futures I see, following her only makes it worse. You and I are the last dragons she wants to see right now. But there's a good chance she'll get tired after half a day of flying, stop at Jade Mountain, and stay there — safe and harmless. I think that's the most likely future."

Turtle's pounding heart disagreed. *What if everything Darkstalker said to her was a spell and I didn't recognize it? What if Darkstalker has enchanted Anemone to kill Mother?*

To punish us all for being Fathom's descendants . . .

If that's true, there's no way I can stop her.

There's almost certainly no way I can stop her anyhow.

But I'm the only one who can even try.

"Stay with him," Turtle said to Kinkajou, although his voice was shaking. "You have to watch him. I'll go after Anemone."

By yourself? his mind screamed. *Do you want everyone to die?*

He didn't have time to write to Qibli — and Qibli wouldn't be able to help him anyway. Neither Qibli nor Kinkajou could follow him into the ocean, if that was really where Anemone was headed. Only SeaWings could go as far underwater as the Deep Palace.

He stepped onto the balcony and glanced back. Another part of him was screaming *don't leave Kinkajou here! It's not safe! What if he notices there's a spell on her? What if she's not the same when I get back?*

The three dragons were heading out through the main doors of the room. At the same moment, Kinkajou turned to look back at him. She gave him a reassuring smile and flared her wings, letting them turn pink along the edges.

Then she followed Moon out the door and was gone.

And Turtle was aloft. Flying, flying higher, beating his wings as hard and fast as he'd ever flown before.

Could he catch Anemone? If he did, could he stop her from whatever she was planning?

She was smaller than him, but fast, and she might use her magic to make herself faster.

Below him the NightWing city fell away and the mountains whipped past, craggy and jagged like a dragon's spine, peaks reaching out like claws to snag his wings. The air currents were strange in these mountains, falling away in odd places, and he had to concentrate more than usual to stay aloft.

Why couldn't he see her in the sky up ahead? Because she was too small, because she blended in with the pale gray-blue clouds? Where was she?

He burst out of the mountains and veered east, following the same route they'd taken that morning. His wings were tiring already at this pace; there was no way he could keep it up all the way back to the Kingdom of the Sea.

The sea — Turtle looked down at the dark waves pounding the beach below him. Maybe he could swim part of the way home. Maybe that's what Anemone was doing.

He tucked himself into a dive, plunging into the water and nearly caving in his skull on an underwater boulder.

Careful! Careful, careful, be more careful . . . mustn't die before I get there . . . although I might die when I get there.

He found a rip current moving swiftly east and slipped into it, spreading his wings to catch as much of its speed as possible.

Would Anemone actually kill me? Her own brother?

Killing Queen Coral was one thing — that was the only way for the next queen to take the throne, so every princess grew up with that possibility in her mind.

But the rest of the family . . . if she attacked them, that

would have to mean she'd lost her soul, or she was under Darkstalker's control.

My family, Turtle thought, powering himself forward with talons and tail. *My mother.* Coral had never loved him, or been at all interested in him, but he still loved her — the idea of her and the stories she wrote.

My brothers. The whole restless, wrestling, teasing pack of them.

Aunts and uncles and cousins.

My littlest sister. Tiny Auklet.

He couldn't imagine anyone hurting a dragonet so small.

Don't do this, Anemone.

Should he use his magic? Now? Should he try to stop her? Darkstalker might think he was sensing Anemone's magic — but what if he realized it wasn't? What if it made him suspicious?

Drumbeats of panic were thudding around and around in Turtle's head.

He knew this feeling.

He hated this feeling.

The pressure pounded in rhythm with his wingstrokes.

Everything is resting on me. On me. On me. And I will fail. Again. Again. Again.

Searching and searching for Snapper. Knowing his father was waiting. Knowing his father was counting on him. Knowing he couldn't do it. Knowing now what his father's disappointed face looked like, and how all that disappointment would crush Turtle into a nobody.

This was exactly the same, except the disappointed faces would be Moon's and Kinkajou's and Qibli's, and the dragons who died because of him would be his entire family, maybe more; maybe everyone, if Anemone couldn't be stopped.

The current veered north and he went with it, realizing he couldn't see land off to his left anymore.

I want to run away. I want to hide forever.

But he had no choice. Anemone was his responsibility.

Anemone was his biggest mistake.

Once a year, in the Kingdom of the Sea, every two-year-old dragon in the tribe is brought together for a particular ceremony.

At least, it is called a ceremony — the Talons of Power ceremony — but really, it is a test, and smart dragonets who've been listening closely know that's what it is.

Smart dragonets also know exactly what the ceremony is looking for.

When he was two years old, a week before the ceremony, Prince Turtle went out and caught two large fish and a talonful of shrimp. He flew them to a rocky ledge on a deserted island and left them to rot in the sun.

Five days later, he returned and ate them, holding his nose and forcing them down his throat.

The night before the ceremony, Prince Turtle was dramatically, violently ill in the dining room of the Deep Palace.

It was pretty horrifying.

No one wanted to go anywhere near the vomiting prince. He was sent to recover on a small island far away from civilized society, which meant, of course, that he missed the Talons of Power ceremony that year.

Queen Coral wasn't concerned. He was just one of her many little princes, and if he really had any magic in his claws (which was statistically very unlikely), someone would figure it out sooner or later. She decreed that he could be included in the ceremony the following year, when he was three.

But the year Turtle turned three was the year his father went missing — captured by the SkyWings, according to Coral's spies. Queen Coral had spent every moment of that year guarding her new egg so that a princess could finally hatch unharmed. She got her wish: a living daughter . . . but she lost her husband.

The Talons of Power ceremony was canceled that year.

So Prince Turtle was four by the time the next Talons of Power ceremony rolled around. No one had said anything to him about it in over a year. He believed they'd forgotten about testing him. Because why bother? If he were an animus dragon, someone would have noticed by then.

At least, that's what everyone thought.

On the day of the ceremony, Turtle was on his way out of the Summer Palace with a pearl-gathering party when a dark green dragon blocked his path.

"Prince Turtle," the dragon said in an oily voice.

"Whirlpool," Turtle answered evenly, hiding his dislike. Queen Coral adored this particular advisor, and Turtle couldn't figure out why, except perhaps that Whirlpool was an expert at fawning over everything Coral did.

"Have you forgotten what today is?" Whirlpool asked. "Your presence is required at the Talons of Power ceremony."

Turtle's heart thudded hard against the walls of his chest. "Me?" he said. "Isn't it pretty clear by now that I'm not an animus?"

"Still," said Whirlpool, "every SeaWing must undergo the test, especially those in the royal family. If animus power should happen to resurface now, when it is so direly needed, we cannot let it slip past our noses, can we?"

Does he know? Turtle wondered. But Whirlpool always sounded like a know-it-all, even (maybe especially) when he knew nothing.

"All right," he said with a shrug. "Seems like a waste of time is all. I thought the queen really wanted these pearls for Anemone's new necklace."

"The test will be over by midday. Plenty of time for pearl-gathering after that," Whirlpool said, ushering Turtle into the tunnel that led out of the pavilion.

Turtle swam along beside him, his mind paddling frantically. There had to be some way out of this.

He couldn't take that test.

He couldn't let them find out what he was.

If his mother found out — what would she make him do?

Turtle had read every scroll he could find on animus magic. There weren't many, and most of the ones that existed were about Albatross, his ancestor from centuries ago.

Albatross, the one who built the Summer Palace with his power.

Albatross, who went mad and massacred half his family before he was stopped.

Turtle had often tried to imagine what it would be like if everyone knew he was an animus. Would they be terrified of him? Would they always be wondering if he'd suddenly snap and start killing dragons?

Or would they think he could be a useful tool in the Great War that was raging across the sea? What if Queen Coral forced him to use his magic against her enemies? What if she wanted him to do something he didn't want to do?

What if he tried to do it and failed, and dragons died because of him?

One thing was for sure: Everyone would know who he was. Everyone would always be looking at him. He'd never be able to hide or blend in; he would always have eyes on him, waiting and judging and *expecting*.

That scared him a lot more than the idea of losing his soul. He wasn't terribly worried about that. His soul felt fine; he certainly didn't feel like killing anyone, ever. He wasn't even sure he believed the theory that animus dragons lost their souls when they used their magic too much. Maybe Albatross had been naturally crazy and homicidal all along, but nobody noticed.

Still, better safe than sorry. Better a quiet nobody than a big-deal-center-of-attention dragon that everyone thought would do great things.

I'll have to fool the test, Turtle realized. He was four now; surely he was smart enough to do that.

Whirlpool led him a long way, to an island where Turtle had never been before. As they approached, he saw other dragons swimming toward it — parents with their two- and three-year-olds or members of Queen Coral's council who had come to watch.

He wasn't sure why. There hadn't been an animus dragon found in the tribe in centuries, as far as he knew. Surely it would be a very boring ceremony.

The dragonets were gathered on a beach on the eastern side of the island. As Turtle waded up onto the sand, he realized with surprise that there were dragon-made structures around him. The remains of an old pier jutted into the water. Most of the wooden walkway had rotted away, but a few of the pylons still stood, and it clearly led out to where a pavilion had once balanced over the sea.

Farther up the beach, overgrown by jungle vines, ruins rose out of the greenery — walls, a tower, here and there a dragon statue.

"What is this place?" Turtle asked Whirlpool.

"Oh, don't you know?" Whirlpool said in his insufferably

superior way. "What *do* your tutors spend their time on, I wonder. Use your brain, little prince: Don't you remember anything about an ancient SeaWing palace, abandoned nearly two thousand years ago?"

Turtle looked around again, resisting the urge to smack Whirlpool in the snout with his tail. Two thousand years ago . . . that was around the time of the massacre.

"The Island Palace," he breathed.

"It's the *Island* — oh," said Whirlpool, realizing what Turtle had said. "Yes. That's correct." With a faint air of disappointment, he oozed off toward the top of the beach, where Turtle's uncle Shark was pacing and glowering at everyone.

This was where the massacre had taken place. Turtle felt an eerie chill flood through his scales. Nine dragons had died here, the victims of Albatross's magic, most of them members of the royal family — his ancestors. If anywhere in the kingdom was haunted, this would be the place. He imagined restless ghosts, stepping through puddles of blood on the verandas, reaching with translucent talons toward the living . . .

"Hey," Octopus said, breaking Turtle's trance. "What's *she* doing here?"

Queen Coral came swooping down from the sky, but Turtle knew that wasn't the "she" his brother meant. Octopus was talking about their sister, little Princess Anemone, the dragonet clinging to Coral's neck. A harness bound the two of them together; Turtle had never seen them without it.

"She goes everywhere Mother goes," Cerulean whispered. "You know that. They're here to watch the ceremony, like everyone else."

But he was wrong about that. Coral landed on the sand, shook her wings, and looked around triumphantly at the assembled council members.

"I want Anemone to be tested with the other dragonets today," she announced.

"Anemone!" protested Turtle's cousin Moray, who was old and on the Council. "She's not even one year old yet!"

Queen Coral smiled fondly at her daughter. "Yes, but she's very precocious. And I have a *feeling* about her. I just know how this story should go."

Princess Anemone slid off the queen's back in a move that was almost graceful, except she got tangled up in the harness and ended up flopping onto her side in the sand. Growling softly, she struggled to her feet and wrestled the harness back out of her way.

Next to Turtle, a three-year-old dragonet twitched forward, as if he wanted to go help her but he wasn't sure he was allowed to. His scales were grayish-blue and there was a nick on one of his ears which Turtle recognized. That was Pike, who had a reputation for fighting too hard in training classes and hurting himself by accident.

"All right, here we go," Whirlpool said, smacking his front talons together wetly. "A coconut for each dragonet, please."

A few older dragons moved between the dragonets,

passing out coconuts. Turtle looked warily down at his. *This could be the instrument of my destruction,* he thought. *This harmless-looking snack could betray me and change my life forever.*

"We'll start on this end," Whirlpool said, stepping over to the line of dragonets. "You three, loud and clear: Tell your coconuts to float into the air, then return to your claws."

The three dragonets on the end dutifully spoke in unison, issuing commands to their coconuts.

Nothing happened.

"You may go," Whirlpool dismissed them.

As they slipped back into the water with their parents, Turtle felt his heart racing as fast as his mind. Whirlpool would be looking right at him. He'd have to say exactly what he'd been commanded to say. How could he fool the test?

Enchant it now, he thought. *Before he gets here.*

He sank his claws into the coconut shell. *Coconut,* he thought, *don't move. No matter what I or anyone else says to you, you are now a completely normal coconut who can never be enchanted.*

Would that work? He had experimented so little with his power, because of the need to keep it secret. He knew he could enchant things by thinking about it, without having to speak aloud. But he wasn't sure if spoken spells were stronger and might overpower a thought spell. He also wasn't sure it was possible to enchant an object to be enchantment-resistant.

What else can I do to distract them?

His gaze fell on Anemone, sitting up the beach, beside their mother. She held a coconut, too, studying it and turning it between her talons like a large opal. Queen Coral was watching her as though Anemone had been carved out of sea glass, perfect and shimmering and sharp. Her eyes were full of all the things Turtle feared: grand plans, dreams, ambitions, expectations.

In Queen Coral's story of the world, of course her one surviving daughter would be magical. Of course she would be the first animus dragon to hatch in hundreds of years. She would be chosen — she would be a savior for the whole tribe.

That's it. An idea hit Turtle like a lightning bolt.

If the tribe already has an animus . . . then they won't need me.

As quickly as it had struck, his excitement faded. The type of enchantment he was imagining — no one had ever tried it before, as far as he knew. It was probably impossible. Almost certainly impossible. Insane, in fact. Especially since he couldn't touch her or speak out loud — it would have to be a thought spell from a distance, and those were difficult enough, even when they weren't immensely powerful requests.

But the words were forming in his head, unbidden, and he realized he was going to try. If it was impossible, it wouldn't work, and he'd be in the same current as before.

If it *did* work . . . Whirlpool would be happy, Anemone would be even more special, Queen Coral would be ecstatic . . . and Turtle would be safe.

I enchant my sister Anemone to become an animus dragon, too.

Anemone, become an animus dragon.

I enchant you to have talons of power.

"Turtle!" Whirlpool barked in his ear. Turtle jerked back, catching his tail painfully on a giant conch shell.

"Sorry," Turtle said. "What?"

"It's your turn." Whirlpool nodded at the coconut, and then at the two dragons beside him. "Pike and Octopus are waiting."

"Oh, yes." Turtle fumbled his coconut out in front of him and took a deep breath. He heard the other two mumbling along as he spoke to it. "Coconut, float into the air and then return to my claws."

Was the coconut trembling, or was that his own fear traveling through his arms? Did it feel lighter in his talons, as if it was about to lift off?

Oh, please, Anemone, use your magic, Turtle wished desperately.

A piercing shriek suddenly cut the air, making half the dragonets jump and drop their coconuts.

It was Moray, one talon outstretched to point at Anemone — and the coconut that was slowly drifting up into the air over her head.

Whirlpool turned to stare, and Turtle took the moment to grip his coconut forcefully once more. *Stop moving, you hairy idiot. I enchant you to be a normal coconut! A coconut that would never float anywhere, by all the whales!*

The coconut seemed to nestle closer, warm and heavy and still in his claws.

"I was right!" Queen Coral cried. "Anemone! You're an animus! You really are!"

No one looked more surprised than Anemone, who stared up at the coconut in awe. With the sun shining behind it, it seemed to be glowing, and so did all the pinkish-white and pale blue scales all over Anemone.

"I'm *magic*," she whispered.

"The test is over!" Coral called. "Whirlpool, we've found our animus! Look!"

"But shouldn't we —" Whirlpool gestured faintly at the remaining dragonets, then shrugged. "Quite right, Your Majesty. All of you are dismissed!"

Turtle exhaled softly.

He couldn't believe it. It *worked*. He'd turned his sister *into an animus dragon.*

So now he was safe. His magic was his own. He could keep being quiet, ordinary Turtle on the outside.

But had he done the right thing? What if he had ruined Anemone's life by protecting himself?

He hesitated at the edge of the water, watching his sister. She certainly looked pretty happy. Queen Coral threw her wings around Anemone as her council crowded closer, murmuring excitedly.

Would the queen have reacted the same way to finding out *he* was an animus? Would he suddenly be the one she loved, the center of attention all the time?

Would he have ended up with a harness like Anemone's?

He shook a crab off one of his talons. *Remember, that's exactly what I don't want,* he told himself.

This would have been Anemone's life anyway. Really, it wouldn't be any different; she'd still be special and beloved. She'd probably adore having animus powers.

What about her soul? a part of him whispered.

He pushed away the guilt. *Probably a myth,* he told himself. *Someone will make sure she's careful with her magic,* he told himself. *She'll be fine,* he told himself.

Turtle slipped into the water quietly, unnoticed by anyone, and swam away, leaving barely a ripple on the surface of the ocean.

CHAPTER 20

Turtle thought of Kinkajou, of Qibli and Winter, of Peril, as he flew and swam, flew and swam without stopping. He wished he had his friends with him. Peril would be able to stop Anemone, either with her firescales or her blunt honesty. Qibli would have some brilliant plan, or Winter would be able to fight her.

Not him. He had no plan, no fighting skills, no firescales.

I could try honesty. I've never given Anemone the truth before.

I'm not sure she'd be very grateful for it.

The current took him north to a river, which turned out to be Winding Tail River, snaking through the mountains. Whenever it was too shallow to swim, he flew; when the night unleashed brutal gusting winds, he swam.

The windstorm was still going when he had to leave the river sometime the next day; it was hard to tell whether it was morning or afternoon, with the sun swallowed up by clouds, and only a dim gray light filling the sky from horizon to horizon. The landscape below him was equally monotonous; this was the Mud Kingdom, dreary and swampy and bog-riddled.

He let himself stop for a moment in a grove of mist-shrouded trees, so he could use his healing stone on his exhausted wings. Then he replaced it in his pouch and flew on. He was starving, but he couldn't stop to eat. He had to catch his sister.

Another night passed in flying, and the next morning Turtle found himself over the ocean, sunlight sparkling on waves as blue as Tsunami's scales.

Gratefully he dove into the warm water and found a current that was going in the direction of the Deep Palace. As it swept him along, he was able to catch a fish hurtling by and eat it in two snaps of his jaws.

A sense of enormous relief washed over him as he came in sight of the Deep Palace. For one thing, it was home: familiar and comforting in every twist and crevice. For another, it did not look like the site of an ongoing massacre. SeaWings swam peacefully, busily, in and out of the various entrances. Dragonets played around the fins of the soldiers in the gardens. The usual glow of Aquatic conversations danced over the coral and reflected through the palace windows.

No clouds of blood rising from the palace; no dragons fleeing in panic.

If Anemone was here, she hadn't started killing yet.

What if she isn't here? he thought, touching down at the

main palace entrance. He'd look like kind of an idiot if he'd chased her all the way back home for no reason.

But then everyone would be safe, and he wouldn't mind looking like an idiot to make that true.

One of his older brothers was swimming out of the palace as Turtle approached. Fin blinked in surprise when he saw Turtle.

I thought you'd gone off to fancy hugging school, he joked with flashing scales.

I did. I'm just stopping by to say hi, Turtle said. He couldn't stop himself from adding, *And what does that even mean, hugging school?*

Where all the tribes of Pyrrhia will learn to hug out their problems, of course, said Fin, grinning like a comedic barracuda. *Who are you here to say hi to? Nobody's even noticed you're gone.* He laughed and thumped Turtle's shoulder hard enough to make Turtle spin in the water.

Oh, thanks very much, Turtle responded, righting himself. *Have you seen Anemone today?*

HERE? Fin looked alarmed. *She's supposed to be with you! Do not tell me Pike has lost her. Mother will pop off all his scales one by one.*

No, no, Turtle said. *She snuck away from school and I thought she might have come here. But you haven't seen her?*

Fin shook his head.

Where's Mother? Turtle asked. Maybe he should warn her. Although he didn't want her to kill Anemone on sight, which would be the logical reaction. Could he explain everything that had happened? Darkstalker and everything else?

In Auklet's favorite place, Fin said, rolling his eyes and nodding at one of the gardens beyond the palace. *As usual.* He spread his wings to swim away.

Fin — Turtle started. His brother turned to look at him. *If you do see Anemone in the next day or two . . . maybe keep your distance. Just in case.*

You're freaking me out, little brother, Fin said, frowning.

I'm worried about her soul, Turtle admitted. *But I hope I'm wrong.*

Fin blanched, no doubt remembering all the Albatross stories as well. *I've been meaning to do a mapping excursion to the Outer Isles,* he said. *Maybe now would be a good time for that.*

Maybe, Turtle said, adding the sequence of glowing scales that indicated high anxiety. *Maybe take our brothers with you.*

All of them? Three moons, Fin flashed, a shadow of a grin reappearing on his face. *It'll be more like an invasion than a scouting trip.* The grin vanished again. *Thanks, Turtle.*

He swam off at top speed and Turtle headed for Auklet's garden.

As he got closer, he realized why this spot was her favorite. Here, a few vents in the ocean floor sent jets of warm bubbles shooting toward the surface. When he was a little dragonet, he'd loved playing in them, too.

Queen Coral sat beside the bubble sprays, watching her littlest daughter with a smile on her face. She held a slate loosely in her talons, but she wasn't writing on it. At the end of her harness, Auklet was somersaulting and giggling and pouncing at the bubbles as they shot by.

Mother, Turtle flashed as he sidled up beside her.

Oh, hello, she flashed back, glancing at him briefly. She didn't seem to recognize him as the prince who was supposed to be at Jade Mountain.

Turtle sat down beside her, at a loss for words. Where should he start? Would it be wise to warn her about Anemone? What if his sister wasn't really planning to challenge her? After all, she should have easily gotten here before he did. So where was she?

Maybe Darkstalker was right and Anemone was back at the Jade Mountain Academy right now, eating fish and bossing the other SeaWings around.

If so, he didn't want to get her in trouble with the queen.

But if Coral and Auklet *were* in danger . . . shouldn't he warn them? He looked up at the dark ocean overhead, wondering if a soulless Anemone was out there somewhere, circling like a shark.

Isn't she perfect? his mother flashed. It took Turtle a moment to realize she was talking about Auklet. The queen nodded at the happy dragonet. *I was convinced I was cursed. I thought I'd never get even one living daughter — and now I have three.* She caught a wayward bubble in her talons and smiled. *And I'm not afraid anymore. That's the most amazing part. I know the assassin is gone, so I can just . . . be happy to* be with Auklet, *instead of being terrified every minute that I'm about to lose her.*

I never told you how sorry I was, Turtle blurted. He clapped his wings shut. This was not at all what he had meant to say.

For what? the queen asked.

For the eggs that died, he said miserably. *When I was looking for Snapper. When the other guard got sick, and I couldn't find Snapper anywhere, and Dad was so upset with me.*

That was you? She looked at him more closely and he flinched back. But it wasn't anger in her eyes, or even disappointment.

Was it . . . pity?

Your father felt terrible about that, she said. *Especially once we found out that Snapper had snuck off to the Summer Palace and wasn't even here. Oh, I made sure her death was a little extra painful for that.*

What? Turtle wasn't sure he'd followed her Aquatic correctly. *Snapper wasn't — what?*

She was supposed to stay in the Deep Palace in case she was needed, but she left, Queen Coral said. *That's why you couldn't find her here. Didn't you know that?*

No, Turtle said. *No one ever told me that.*

I thought Gill was going to tell you, Coral mused. *Maybe he didn't get a chance before . . .* She trailed off.

Turtle's mind was spinning as if it was caught in a whirlpool. He couldn't have found Snapper that day. Not in time to help his father, if she was all the way at the Summer Palace.

It wasn't his fault. It wasn't his failure. And his father knew it before he died.

Maybe he forgave me, Turtle thought, the first hopeful thought he'd had about his father in years.

Sorry nobody told you, his mother said unexpectedly. *You were such a little dragonet, and you tried so hard.* And then, even more unexpectedly, she put one wing around his shoulders and pulled him closer.

Turtle's heart was definitely going to explode.

What's your name again? she asked. Which almost wrecked the moment, except that nothing could do that.

Turtle, he said. *It's Turtle.*

She smiled down at him. *I'll remember it this time.*

He smiled back. *Holy mother of scavengers. She knows who I am. She cares about my feelings.*

And I didn't even have to be a hero. I'm just me, Turtle. Her dragonet who tried his best.

He leaned into her and thought about heroes and stories and misunderstandings. He knew he still had to go find Anemone to do something heroic and possibly impossible. He knew Darkstalker was still out there, and he hadn't yet tried his best to stop him, but he would.

But for now, for this moment, he let himself just be Turtle, under his mother's wing, where he'd always wanted to be.

CHAPTER 21

All too soon, a SeaWing messenger came from the palace looking for Queen Coral. *A dragon from the Talons of Peace is here to see you,* he reported. *News about changes in the Sky Kingdom, he says.*

The queen made a face at Turtle and Auklet. *Official business,* she said. *We have to get back to the palace, Auklet.*

OK! The little dragonet spun through the bubbles one last time and swam over to her mother. *Turtle!* she cried, recognizing him. Auklet threw her arms around his neck and hugged him tight.

He hugged her back, thinking, *I won't let anyone hurt you, little sister.*

See you soon, his mother flashed. Turtle watched them swim inside. His heart ached but his wings felt stronger than ever. He was going to find Anemone and stop her, no matter what it took.

I know the truth now. The coral was trying to take me to Snapper — it only seemed like it didn't work, because it was trying to get to the Summer Palace.

The coral! He could use that to figure out where Anemone was. A thought that really should have occurred to him a couple of days and a very long flight ago.

He prayed that it would point south, toward Jade Mountain. Maybe it would lead him all the way back to the safety of school.

The tiny red tree felt fragile and brittle in his talons, as though it might snap at any moment. "Anemone," he whispered to it. "Where is my sister?"

It wriggled in his talons, pointing up and away from the Deep Palace, but not south. He let it pull him into one of the swift currents that spiraled out to the islands.

For a while he swam steadily, and his spirits rose with every wingstroke away from the palace. She wasn't lurking there, lying in wait for his mother. Whatever Anemone was up to, maybe no one had to die.

Left! The coral suddenly insisted, tugging him up out of the current and up, up, up to the surface. Turtle had to pinwheel fast with his wings and tail to stay with it. Cascades of green-blue bubbles exploded around him.

It was leading him to an island. He could see the shape of the land ahead of him, but he didn't recognize it — not until he popped out of the water and saw the ruins jutting out of the jungle.

The Island Palace. The place where the animus test had taken place.

Where he'd cursed his little sister with his own power, so he could stay hidden.

And there was Anemone, digging a hole in the beach with her claws, muttering furiously to herself. Wet sand covered her webbed talons and plastered her tail so she looked half–MudWing.

Turtle floundered forward in the surf as the waves tried alternately to toss him onto the sand or to drag him back into their arms. The sun was unexpectedly bright in his eyes. Somehow he'd expected to confront Anemone deep underwater, or in the rain; this idyllic beach scene didn't fit his idea of an animus showdown.

"Anemone," he gasped, staggering onto the beach. The coral practically dragged him forward so it could tap Anemone's tail.

His sister whirled around, her face contorted with fury.

"You BORING LUMP OF KELP!" she yelled at him. "You ruin EVERYTHING! Why can't you leave me ALONE?!"

"You're my sister," he said. He let his wings rest on the sand and tried to catch his breath as he tucked the coral away. "I'm worried about you."

"Are you?" she scoffed. "Or are you worried about what I might do?"

"Um," he said. "That too?"

"Well, you can't *stop* me," she said mockingly, "so there's really no point in you being here. Go back to your loser friends and your hypnotized girlfriend."

"You're the one who put that spell on her!" Turtle flared. "I didn't ask you to!"

"Because you're a wimp who's afraid to even try for what he wants," Anemone said. "But I'm not like you. I'm getting exactly what I want and deserve, and I'm getting it today." She turned back to her digging.

"What are you looking for?" Turtle asked.

"Something Whirlpool said he hid for me here," she said. "Go away, Turtle."

"Anemone," he said, "I'm afraid Darkstalker's put a spell on you."

She laughed bitterly. "Well, that would be ironic."

"I mean, I think he's enchanted you to kill Mother and maybe Auklet and the rest of our family," Turtle explained.

"Oh," she said and laughed again. "I don't need to be enchanted to want to do *that*, big brother. I think anyone who met you all would feel the same way."

"But I think this is his vengeance," Turtle said desperately. "For what Fathom did to him."

"Maybe," Anemone said with a shrug. "But if I do it, I'll be Queen of the SeaWings, and then he'll have to respect me — and if that's what he was hoping for, maybe he'll be proud of me, too."

"How can you not care?" Turtle demanded. "Is it your soul? Maybe he didn't enchant that necklace to protect it, after all. Maybe you've been losing it all along, piece by piece."

"That whole idea of the soul is ridiculous," Anemone snapped. "Good dragons do bad things and bad dragons do good things all the time. Nobody has an entirely good soul to start with. It's just stupid to think that it's like a block of stone and my magic is chipping away at it. It doesn't make sense." She smashed her tail into the sand, cracking seashells and frightening small crabs in every direction. "Where IS it? If he was lying to me, I swear I'm going to hunt down Whirlpool's drifting corpse and kill him again."

"Again?" Turtle's ears twitched. "What? Again? Anemone, what do you mean?"

"I'm the one who killed him the first time." She gave him a scornful look. "Did you really think he 'accidentally' fell into that pool of eels? We figured out that he'd been trying to kill Tsunami. And then he realized how powerful I was and he was going to tell Mother and Blister." She shrugged. "So I took care of him."

Three moons. Turtle had been worrying about Anemone all this time — worrying about what she might do, about how the magic he'd given her might affect her — and yet when she did do something big and terrible, he'd missed it completely.

"Oh!" she said, spotting a gleam of metal in the sand underfoot. She pounced on it, digging furiously, and finally reared back with a triumphant "Aha!"

In her talons was a dagger as long as her forearm, curved like a claw and gleaming wickedly sharp along every edge.

"Three moons," Turtle whispered. "*Anemone.*"

"Whirlpool wanted to be king pretty badly," she said, turning the dagger to catch the sunlight. "I think he was hoping to shape me into a darker dragon by making me cast all those 'practice' spells. He wanted me to go evil and try for the throne. He told me he'd hidden a perfect weapon here, ready for whenever I needed it — for whenever I wanted to challenge Mother." She smiled at it. "I think it'll work fine on little sisters, too, don't you? And big ones, for that matter."

"But you can't," Turtle said, feeling sick all through his scales and bones and muscles.

"Sure I can," she said, widening her blue eyes at him. "I won't make Orca's mistakes. I'll enchant this thing right now to be a perfect killing machine. It'll never miss. It'll go straight for Mother's throat first. Then Auklet, Tsunami, you . . ." Her eyes narrowed. "Moon. Maybe Kinkajou, too. Why not? He did say *anyone* who gets in my way."

This was it; this was the breaking point. His speeches weren't working. He had to do something. Even if it meant Darkstalker found out about him. He had to *do* something.

His talons closed around the nearest seashell, fan-shaped, pale pink and white like Anemone's scales. "I enchant you to break every spell Darkstalker has cast on Anemone the moment you touch her," he said, and flung the seashell with all his might. It bounced off Anemone's side and she jumped back, blinking and startled.

"What the —" Anemone yelped. "Are you out of your mind?"

"Necklace," he said, reaching out one arm. "Come to me." The silver collar around Anemone's neck snapped off and flew into his talons. "I enchant you to be powerless from now on," he said to it, and threw the necklace as far out to sea as he could.

Anemone's claws went to her throat. "But —" she said. "How —"

"Dagger," Turtle commanded. "Turn to sand forever."

The dagger collapsed in Anemone's talons and scattered into the wind.

Anemone stared at him.

"I'm an animus, too," said Turtle. "I'm sorry, I should have told you sooner."

"That's *ridiculous*," Anemone cried. "*You?* You're nobody! *I'm* the SeaWing animus!"

"You are . . . but that's because of me," Turtle said. "I'm so sorry, Anemone. I'm the one who made you an animus. Right here, the day of the Talons of Power ceremony. I didn't want anyone to find out about me, so . . . I distracted them with you. And everything that's happened to you since then is all my fault."

"No!" Anemone screamed. "It's *my* power! You can't just take it; you can't just say it's yours! *You did not create me!*"

She launched herself at Turtle and slammed him onto his back in the waves. Her claws slashed the side of his throat and pain blistered through his gills.

"You didn't make me and you can't stop me! I can still kill her!" she yelled. "I can kill her with my bare claws! I can kill her with anything! I can make daggers out of seashells; I can poison the drops of water around her snout! I can enchant her pearls to choke her or her stupid narwhal horn to stab her in the heart!"

In shock, Turtle fought back, throwing her off him. She skidded onto the beach and he leaped after her, pinning her down into the sand.

This is what Moon saw, he realized. *This fight.*

A jolt of relief made his heart pulse wildly. *But I haven't lost my soul. I still don't want to hurt Anemone.*

Her scales were slippery under his claws and sand sprayed up into his eyes, stinging and blinding him. She sank her teeth into one of the webs on his front talons and he roared with pain.

He'd thought breaking Darkstalker's spells would change her. He'd thought he was setting her free. *Why didn't it work?* Anemone thrashed and stabbed at his underbelly, sending more fiery bolts of agony along his scales.

"Knock my brother off me!" Anemone shouted, flinging one talon out at something behind Turtle.

He turned and saw a huge rock lever itself out of the sand. It shot toward him like an attacking SkyWing.

Turtle ducked and rolled off Anemone, covering his head. "Disappear!" he shouted at the rock. With an odd thudding sound, the boulder vanished out of the air.

Anemone leaped to her feet with her wings spread. "All the crabs on this beach!" she shouted. "Attack Turtle! Do it now!"

The sand erupted as hundreds of crabs came swarming out of their burrows, from tiny hermit crabs up to massive talon-sized red monsters with snapping claws. Blue-gray pincers popped out of the sand right below him and clamped down sharply on one of his front talons. Turtle yowled and jumped back and felt more explosions of pain as claws dug in all along his tail.

"Waves!" he called desperately. "Wash these crabs out to sea!"

The sea pulled back, as if mildly offended by the order, then came rushing in all at once in a huge tidal wave. Turtle felt himself slammed to the sand and through the water he saw Anemone clawing to stay on the beach. All the crabs were caught up and tumbled about and carried away, sucked out into a hissing, foaming ocean.

He didn't have a moment to catch his breath before seashells began pelting him, each one aiming to stab between his scales. *Death by a thousand cuts,* he thought, trying to wipe away the blood running into his eyes.

Turtle tried to duck away, scrabbling through the sand for something he could work with. Here — and here — two sand dollars washed up by the wave. "Protect me from the shells," he said to them, and they shot into the air, warding off the attacking seashells like tiny flying shields.

"Anemone, I don't want to fight you!" he yelled.

"Then you shouldn't say stupid things that make me want to kill you!" she yelled back. "Swallow him up!" The sand suddenly collapsed under him, dropping him into a sinkhole, and then immediately began pouring back over his head. Turtle flailed around in a panic. He did not want to die by drowning in sand. He did not want to be buried and forgotten here on this beach. *Leaving Auklet and Mother unprotected from Anemone. And the rest of my friends enchanted by Darkstalker. And Kinkajou under that awful spell forever.*

He reached out with his magic and wrenched an entire palm tree out of the ground. It came skidding across the sand toward him, nearly plowing through Anemone before she jumped out of the way, and stopped with its fronds hanging over the hole. Turtle sank his claws into the sharp-edged leaves and dragged himself out, talon over talon.

The sand behind him made an ominous *GLOORRRP* sound and tried to suck him back down. "Let me go!" Turtle shouted at it. A flurry of sand exploded upward, then settled into a normal, noncarnivorous beach dune.

Turtle clutched the trunk of the palm tree, panting heavily. This fight was uneven; she was willing to use lethal force, and he was not. He refused to kill his little sister.

A faint whistling in the air warned him to look up.

Something enormous was crashing down toward him — a piece of stone wall from the ruins of the Island Palace.

"Crush him!" Anemone screamed. "Don't stop until you hit him!"

"Stop!" Turtle shouted.

The projectile wobbled for a moment, but it didn't stop. It kept coming, faster and faster.

"Shield me," Turtle cried to the palm tree. He leaped off and covered his head.

There was a muffled smashing, cracking sound, and when Turtle looked up, he saw pieces of tree raining down around him. The wall rebounded off the broken palm and leaped for him again.

It won't stop until it hits me. That's the spell. Turtle grabbed the nearest thing he could reach — a shell that once housed a hermit crab — and whispered, "Make my scales as hard as diamonds. Make my bones unbreakable. Make me impossible to hurt, no matter how hard that thing lands on me." He wrapped his claws around the shell and crouched with his eyes screwed shut.

I'm going to die, I'm going to die, I'm going to die.

The block of stone slammed into him with such force that it left an imprint in the sand. It felt like the entire Deep Palace landing on him. For a moment, he couldn't breathe.

But he felt no pain — and he was still alive.

"Get . . . off . . . me," he croaked at the stone block when he could form words again.

Its original mission complete, the block obligingly lifted away and clunked down in the sand beside him.

Seaweed, Turtle thought dizzily, wondering if he was about to lose consciousness, *go wrap Anemone's mouth shut so she cannot cast any more animus spells — neither by voice or thought, as long as you are touching her. But make sure she can still breathe.*

From the muffled shrieks he could hear, he guessed that his spell succeeded, but he couldn't move yet. He had to lie there, waiting for everything in his body to realize that it still worked.

A moment later, claws raked viciously across his nose and he jerked up to find Anemone standing over him. She had so much seaweed wrapped around her snout that she couldn't see over it; she kept turning her head from side to side to glare at him with one eye and then the other. Only her nostrils were still visible, and they were flaring with fury. She clawed at him again and he stumbled back . . . before realizing that he'd barely felt them.

He blinked down at his scales, which were a mess of blood from the seashell cuts.

His sister leaped forward again and tried to slice her claws across his throat — but they ricocheted off as though . . . *as though my scales are as hard as diamonds.*

Turtle's talons were empty. Where was the shell he'd enchanted? Why was the spell still working on him if he wasn't holding it?

Because I wasn't that specific, he realized. With most of his spells, he worded the enchantment to work as long as he was holding or touching or wearing the animus-touched object. *But with this one, I just told it to make me impossible to hurt.* It was like the healing spell on Kinkajou, or the feather that fixed Flame's scar. The effects were permanent, no matter what happened to the object afterward.

He'd never really thought about the difference before. His mind spun to the spells Darkstalker had cast on his

NightWings. They were all object-dependent. If Darkstalker took away their objects, his subjects would lose those powers.

He must know he could make them permanent, but he's choosing not to.

With a sickening lurch in his stomach, he tried to remember how Anemone had worded the spell on Kinkajou.

Did she say "as long as she has this rock"? Or did she just say "make her love Turtle"?

Was the enchantment permanent? Even if Kinkajou took off the skyfire?

He couldn't remember.

I'm so sorry, Kinkajou, he thought with a wrench of agony.

Turtle realized that Anemone was glowering at him. Her sides were heaving, slick with sweat and sand and seawater.

"Anemone," he said carefully. "Please listen to me."

She gestured to her snout like, *Have you given me any choice?*

"I'm not going to kill you," he said, "and I would really like you to not kill me. Can we talk without attacking each other?" He sidled a step toward her. "I'd like to think we can work this out with words instead of violence or magic."

She rolled her eyes at him. Which wasn't a *very* reassuring yes.

"All right," he said, "let's try this. Seaweed, I want you to wrap around Anemone's arm instead — but still, as long as you're touching her, she cannot use her magic in any way. And stay put until I remove you," he added hurriedly.

The long strands of dark wet seaweed began smoothly unrolling from his sister's snout and transferring to one of her forearms instead. Anemone scowled down at the make-shift handcuff as though she was thinking about cutting off her arm to get her magic back.

"You are *so* annoying," she snapped at Turtle as soon as she could speak again.

"And you're very powerful," he said. "But I can't let you go kill Mother. Or Auklet, or Tsunami, or anyone else. I don't believe you're that kind of dragon."

Anemone threw her wings up in the air. "Of course I am! I have to be! It's my stupid destiny to kill the queen. That's what princesses do. And I'm even worse because I'm an animus so I'm *going* to turn evil anyway, no matter what I do! I should just *do* it and be evil and be *done* with it already."

"You don't have to be evil!" Turtle cried, appalled. "Not every animus is evil. I'm not evil!"

"But you will be," Anemone said accusingly. "We both will be. That's what happens to animus dragons. Unless you're Darkstalker and you're soooooooooooooo smart."

"Fathom wasn't evil," Turtle pointed out.

"We don't know that," Anemone said. "First of all, what he did to Darkstalker wasn't exactly the kindest thing in the world. And then he disappears from history — who knows what else he did with his power?"

"There were lots of animus IceWings who didn't go evil either," Turtle said stubbornly. "And the SandWing from thousands of years ago who disappeared — Jerboa — as far as we know anyhow. And Stonemover."

"So my choices are evil, missing, or fossilized?" Anemone said. "That's appealing."

"I think a spell to protect your soul could work," Turtle said. "I just don't trust Darkstalker to cast it for you."

"It won't work. It's already too late for me." Anemone shook her head. "Ever since Whirlpool died, I see him all the time — in my dreams, in the faces of strange dragons, everywhere. I keep seeing those eels going after him. I see all the dragons I've hurt. Now Moon's there, too, and I hate what I did to her but I also feel *proud* of it. Isn't that twisted? Whatever soul I had, it's long gone, so protecting it wouldn't be much use."

"Maybe losing your soul isn't the right way to describe it," Turtle said. "Maybe it's more like . . . the more you use your power for bad things, the more you feel like you're entitled to use your power for anything. It makes it harder to go back — only forward into more bad things." He hesitated. "But . . . I think you can go back. I think anyone can choose to do good, or be good, no matter what happened before. I think you just have to try really hard. And that means stopping yourself before you do even worse things."

She growled softly. "I suppose you mean like killing a bunch of family members."

"Well, yeah," he said. "That's one example."

She looked down at her talons. "So what do I do instead?

What if I can't stop myself and you're not here next time to wrap me in enchanted seaweed?"

He hesitated. "Do you want me to take it away again? Your power? I don't know if it'll work . . . but I could try. If you don't want to be an animus anymore."

"But then what would I be?" She spread her wings and talons, leaving a trail of droplets from the dripping seaweed. "Animus dragons are rare and special. I like knowing that I'm powerful. I *want* to be that powerful. Who would give away their own magic like that? I'm just . . . scared of it, too."

"I know," he said. "I feel the same way."

"Really?" she said. "Because you don't *act* like you want to be powerful."

Turtle opened his mouth to answer, then closed it again. She was right. He didn't act that way. But he did want to be an animus. It was the one thing that made him special, even if only in secret. He'd never give it up either.

"I've cast a spell to hide myself from Darkstalker," he said. "I think we should do the same for you, in case he does try to enchant you to do something evil."

"Ohhhh," she said. "That explains a lot. I mean, I was like, sure, Turtle is boring, but Darkstalker really acts like he doesn't exist at all! So weird! Now I get it."

"Aren't I less boring now that you know I'm an animus?" Turtle protested. He poked at his armband to pop out one of the last skyfire rocks. "You'll need this, too, so he can't read your mind." She took the rock and held it up so the deep sparkles in it could catch the light.

There was a strange twitch in the air, like someone pinching the world around them. Turtle glanced up at the sky nervously. "Maybe we should also enchant something to make Darkstalker forget about our explosion of animus spells. He must be wondering what's going on."

"He — is that how he always catches me doing magic?" Anemone trailed off with a shiver.

"He can sense animus spells being cast," Turtle said, nodding.

"Then let's do that first," Anemone said, alarmed. She grabbed a palm frond. "Hey, leaves, erase all the — *yikes!*" she shrieked as the entire beach shuddered violently underneath them. "Erase all our spells from Darkstalker's memory!" she shouted as fast as she could.

The air was suddenly pressing in on them, as though they were being squeezed into an invisible chest. Turtle's ears popped painfully and he staggered toward Anemone.

"Did it work?" she yelled, and Turtle realized there was a dark, high-pitched whistling sound drowning out all other noises.

"I don't know — I don't see why — it should —" Turtle's gaze fell from the gathering clouds to his sister, and he was hit by a sinking realization. "The seaweed!" he cried. He leaped forward and sliced through the wrapping of seaweed around Anemone's arm. "It didn't work because your magic was blocked!" There seemed to be infinite thick sticky layers of seaweed and they wouldn't come off fast enough, no matter how he stabbed and peeled at them.

"You do the spell!" Anemone shouted, but the wind was now screaming along with the sound and sand was blowing fiercely in their faces like the entire beach was rising up to attack them. Turtle clasped his sister's talons, folded his wings around her, and held on tight.

Suddenly there was a bending, warping feeling to the universe, and Turtle heard Darkstalker's voice as clearly as if he were standing right next to them.

"Bring them here," Darkstalker growled. "Every animus dragon in all the seven tribes. Bring them here to my throne room right now."

The world collapsed inward, into darkness, and unfolded again into pale sunlight streaming through tall narrow windows across a vast black marble hall.

Outside the windows: the mountains of the Night Kingdom.

Inside the hall, staring down at them: Darkstalker, wearing a crown made of twisted metal with sharp points.

CHAPTER 22

Turtle gave a startled gasp and glanced around. *All the way across the continent. He just summoned us like a tray of shrimp.*

There were still cracks of darkness in the air, like it was a scroll that had been folded and wrinkled too many times. The cracks hissed and sparked, spitting out Turtle, Anemone, Stonemover, and right behind Darkstalker, an unfamiliar SandWing.

The SandWing met Turtle's eyes, her face a mask of startled terror, and then she vanished again in less than a heartbeat. She was gone so quickly that Turtle thought he might have hallucinated her — that perhaps she was a double image accidentally reflected by the teleporting cracks. Especially since no one else acted as if they'd seen her, too.

Was that real? He sat down, rubbing his eyes. A splitting headache was trying to splinter his skull into small pieces.

"I enchant this room so that no one can cast any spells while they're in here except me," Darkstalker growled. He loomed over Anemone. "Where is your neckband?" he asked.

"I lost it," she said. "I'll make another one, don't worry."

"Someone gave you skyfire, I see," he said, tapping the top of her skull. "Did you kill your mother?" Turtle guessed from his tone that he already knew the answer.

"No," Anemone said, lifting her chin defiantly. "What do you care anyway? Why'd you drag me back here after you just ordered me to go away?"

Darkstalker hissed. "Who were you fighting, Anemone?" he asked. Turtle flinched guiltily. A scratch behind her ear was bleeding and there were scratches along her sides from Turtle's claws.

"No one important," she said. "I was winning until you interrupted, though, by the way."

"Those were battling animus spells," Darkstalker said. "And every animus in Pyrrhia should be here. Which means . . ." He whipped his head toward Stonemover. The NightWing lay awkwardly on his side, still encased in stone, but looking very odd without his cave around him. His talons twitched feebly as though he might be trying to right himself.

"Stonemover," Darkstalker said. He tipped Stonemover onto his talons and leaned over to hiss in his ear. "Tell me the truth. How many dragons are in this room right now?"

Turtle tried to wave frantically, to get his attention, to hold up three claws or mime to keep his secret or *something,* but he wasn't fast enough, or Stonemover was too slow.

"Four," Stonemover said, sounding puzzled.

"I knew it," Darkstalker cried. "There's another one.

There's someone hiding from me!" He seized a sword that was hanging on the wall. "Bring me a dragon our hidden animus cares about very much. Alive, for now."

"No!" Turtle cried, but the sword was already whipping out the door. *What can I do? I can't cast any spells in here. Do I have anything I can use?* He scrabbled open his pouch, all banged up and covered with sand, and searched inside, trying to think. The coral finder. The slate. The healing stone. His hiding stick.

The slate — Qibli! He pulled it out and wrote as quickly as he could.

DARKSTALKER KNOWS ABOUT ME. TRAPPED IN THE NIGHTWING PALACE. HELP!

As soon as he'd written it, he erased it. He couldn't risk Darkstalker finding out he'd sent a message. *Please see it soon, Qibli,* he prayed.

"Hidden?" Stonemover coughed, bewildered.

"Yes," said Darkstalker. "One of the dragons you can see is a coward. Planning against me in secret."

"I think he's smart," Anemone said sharply. "He knew right away not to trust you. He knew there was something seriously wrong with you. You think everything you do is right. You think you're so perfect that you don't even care about the dragons around you. You're the only one who gets to decide what happens to everyone else."

"By all the MOONS," Darkstalker growled. He pointed at Anemone. "Enchant this dragon to obey my every command. Now shut up," he barked at her.

Anemone's mouth snapped closed. She touched her snout, looking startled and outraged and terrified all at once.

No! Turtle felt the cold marble hall pressing in on him. *That's the same spell he put on his father. He can make Anemone do anything he wants now.*

"That's better," Darkstalker said. He paced around her slowly. "You know, I've always had so many questions about animus power. Maybe now, with you and Stonemover both under my control, I can test out some of my theories. For instance, is there a limit to how many spells one can cast in a day? What happens when two animus dragons try to enchant something at the same time? And of course . . . how many spells does it take for a dragon to turn evil?" He stopped in front of Anemone, smiling down at her. "For you, my dear, I'm guessing it won't be very many more."

Turtle was transfixed with horror. This was exactly what he'd been trying to save Anemone from. It hadn't even occurred to him that Stonemover was one of Darkstalker's puppets already. *Maybe that's what he meant when he said his talons weren't his own — maybe he sensed Darkstalker taking them over.*

Oh, Anemone. How can I save you?

A clattering sound came from the hall outside and they all could hear a voice coming closer.

"This better be important! Summoning a dragon with a *sword* in the middle of *suntime*, I mean, someone has the manners of an orangutan! I am MOVING, quit pointing that — yourself at me!"

Oh no, Turtle thought. Despair poured over him like wet sand.

Kinkajou bounded into the throne room with the sword hovering menacingly in the air behind her. She was indignantly tangerine from horns to tail, and Turtle's heart leaped at the sight of her.

"Hello, King Bossy," she said to Darkstalker, flicking her wings back. "You could have sent a dragon to ask me *nicely*. It's pretty rude to wake someone up with sharp weapons, I have to say."

Darkstalker slid over and stared at her thoughtfully for a moment. "Really?" he said. "Somebody cares about *this* dragon?"

"Hey!" Kinkajou squeaked. "That's so unnecessary!"

"All right," Darkstalker said with a shrug. "Cowardly animus," he said, raising his voice. "You see that I have your . . . unimpressive little RainWing." Kinkajou scowled at him. "So now would be a good time to reveal yourself, unless you want to see her sliced to pieces." He hooked the sword out of the air and swept it around to point at Kinkajou's throat in one graceful move.

"No!" Turtle shouted, taking a step toward her.

"Don't do it," Kinkajou said. She closed her eyes. "Stay hidden. You can stop him — you *have* to stop him."

"Not by myself," Turtle said. "Not without you."

"Yes, without me," she said. "I know you can. Oh, *monkey* brains — does this mean *I'm* the hapless sidekick? Blorg, that is so lame. Better than the wailing victim who needs rescuing, though. Make sure nobody writes me that way when this story becomes an epic poem, all right? And I would definitely like to be the hero next time, please." She glanced down at the sword and shivered slightly. "I mean . . . in my next life, I guess."

"Kinkajou." Turtle couldn't breathe. Was this what drowning felt like for other dragons? "The story doesn't make sense without you. You're the whole point of it, for me."

"Do please stop talking," Darkstalker said to her. "Last chance, animus. In ten seconds, this babbling dragonet dies."

Turtle took his hiding stick out of his pouch. It was so ordinary. Unremarkable, boring, nothing anyone would ever notice. Kind of like him.

But it held some of the most powerful magic in this room.

And it was the only thing that might still be able to save the world.

This wasn't the heroic story he'd dreamed of as a dragonet. He wasn't standing at the gates to the palace fighting off attacking hordes with a spear. He wasn't defending his kingdom with valiant strength, and he might still be the idiot who died while the real heroes saved the day.

But this was his chance — a chance to be a different kind of hero. One who stood in the way; one who got noticed, so that someone else could live. Heroes don't have to stab the bad guy in the heart or save the whole world. Maybe it was enough — more than enough — to save his sister and Kinkajou.

All he had to do was stop hiding.

"Anemone," he said urgently. "I don't know if this will work, but if it does — get out of here as fast as you can. Go find Qibli and make him help you." He closed his claws around the stick and took a deep breath. "I'm not going to leave you in danger anymore while I hide. But it means you have to be the hero now."

Turtle glanced down at the stick again; his heart was pounding and his insides were threatening to dissolve into sand. But he couldn't hide anymore. For Kinkajou, for Anemone, for everyone.

He tossed the stick through the air to his sister.

For a moment, as it was airborne, Darkstalker's head snapped up. Perhaps a thousand new futures were crowding into his mind; perhaps he knew for a moment what was about to happen, and he saw what he was about to lose, and where it might lead.

But then Anemone caught the stick in her front talons.

And then Darkstalker saw Turtle, and whatever future he had been looking at was forgotten as his eyes flashed with fury.

"Fathom!" he snarled. A blast of flame shot out of his mouth and enveloped Turtle in fire.

Blistering heat scorched over Turtle. He threw himself to the ground with his wings over his head. "I'm not Fathom!" he shouted. "I'm Turtle!"

Kinkajou screamed and leaped at Darkstalker's head. Her talons wrapped around his snout, her wings beat at his ears, and she reared back, opening her mouth wide. Jets of black venom shot from her fangs and landed *splat sizzle ssss* across Darkstalker's face and in one of his eyes.

Darkstalker roared and threw her off. Kinkajou landed on the floor and skidded halfway across the room.

"OW! MOONFIRE AND STAR VOMIT!" Darkstalker shouted, clutching his face. "HEAL, by all the snakes!" He lifted his talons away and Turtle saw that his scales were undamaged, but there was a black hole where his eyeball had been. A moment later it filmed over, and a new eye started to grow into the spot.

My accidental invulnerability spell worked, too, Turtle realized, stretching out his wings. The fire had not burned him. He was unharmed.

He stood up and looked around frantically.

Anemone was gone.

She'd escaped in the chaos, small enough to fit out one of the narrow windows. He hoped she was on her way to Jade Mountain right now, clutching his stick, erased from Darkstalker's memory. He hoped it would keep her safe. If Darkstalker didn't know she existed, he couldn't control her. As long as she stayed hidden, she could still be free.

He also hoped he could trust her. Would she do the right thing, now that she was free? Would she know what the right thing was?

He darted over to Kinkajou, who was struggling back to her feet. "Are you all right?" he asked, trying to help her up.

"Oh, you're not a pile of ash!" she said. She collapsed to the floor again. "That is such a relief. I'm going to lie here and be relieved for a minute. Don't mind me."

"I wish you would stop getting yourself hurt," Turtle whispered.

"Me too!" she said. "Talk to the bad guys! Tell them to stop hurting me!" She tried to move one of her wings and winced. "Ow ow ow."

"Here," Turtle said, giving her the healing rock. "This might help." He glanced over his shoulder, saw that Darkstalker was still holding his eye shut, and pressed the entire pouch into her talons. "Pretend this is yours," he whispered. "Maybe something in here can help."

"I'm scared for you," she whispered back.

"Just making sure you get to be more than the dead side-kick," he said. "You're a lot more than that to me."

"I love you, Turtle," she whispered, softer than ripples in a still pool.

"You don't really," he said, feeling his heart break a little more. "Anemone put a spell on you to love me. I'm so sorry."

"Oh," she said. "That's . . . not cool. But I *feel* like I love you, and I'm afraid this is our tragic good-bye, so don't argue with me."

"My apologies, Kinkajou," Darkstalker rumbled behind Turtle. "I didn't mean to hurt you. Although, in my defense, you did melt my eyeball."

Turtle turned and found himself face-to-face with Darkstalker. Those black eyes were seeing him for the first time since Darkstalker swarmed out of the mountain.

"It's all coming back to me," Darkstalker rumbled. "Turtle. Yes. Moon's friend. Fathom's descendant. You look exactly like him. I believe I had a whole plan for you, before you muddled it up by hiding like that." He tapped Turtle lightly on the nose. "Surprisingly clever, especially for you. I would never have guessed you had it in you."

"Whatever you're going to do to me," Turtle said, "please let Kinkajou go."

Darkstalker chuckled. "I would never hurt a ball of fluff like her."

"Ball of fluff!" Kinkajou protested. "I just melted your eye! I'm totally terrifying!"

"Kinkajou, shhh," Turtle said, nudging her sharply.

"No, I promised Moon I wouldn't hurt her friends," Darkstalker said thoughtfully, "and she's very fond of both of you. Of course, she doesn't know where you are," he said to Turtle, "so, for the time being, let's stick you in the dungeon, until I decide how you can be useful."

Darkstalker bent down and took Kinkajou's chin in his talons, looking into her eyes. "As for you: I enchant you to forget about everything that happened in this throne room today. You'll wake up from your suntime in an hour and carry on with your day as though everything is normal and Turtle is not here."

Kinkajou went very still. Her eyes flicked from Darkstalker to Turtle.

His spells don't work on her, Turtle remembered. This might be the one thing he'd done right.

She nodded slowly and took a step back. Her expression was full of questions, but Turtle knew she couldn't ask any of them without giving away that Darkstalker's spell hadn't worked.

"Go on now," Darkstalker said. "Turtle and I need to have a little talk."

Kinkajou gave Turtle an agonized look, bowed her head, and flew away. She still had Turtle's pouch. Maybe something in there would help her, if she could figure out what any of it did.

"It's unfortunate for you," Darkstalker said to Turtle, "that you look so much like Fathom." He spread one wing around Turtle and steered him toward one of the side doors. "I have very good reasons to hate him, you know. It's going to make it hard to look at you. Although I suppose if you're locked away deep in my darkest dungeon, we can avoid that problem."

When we leave the room I can cast a spell, Turtle thought. *But what? Something to help me escape . . .* His mind raced.

But just before they reached the exit, Darkstalker paused and regarded Turtle pensively for a moment. "I wouldn't normally do this," he said. "I always think an animus could be useful in some way, if handled correctly. But you managed to trick me once, and that makes me a bit nervous about you, so, I'm sorry."

Darkstalker cupped his talons around Turtle's face. "Enchant this dragon to lose all his animus power right now," he said, "so that he shall never be able to cast a spell again."

Turtle caught his breath, and caught it again, gasping with disbelief. A strange sensation scraped over his scales, like a powerful scrubbing brush scouring him clean.

It was gone. The faint tingling in his claws that had been there from the second he hatched. He'd never even known what it was — never guessed that it was a sign of animus magic. And now it had vanished forever.

He'd always thought he was ordinary, but he'd never *been* completely ordinary until this moment.

"Don't be too sad," Darkstalker said. "To be the most powerful animus in the world, you have to be the smartest — and that was never going to be you anyway, was it? Now all the pressure is off. You don't have to come up with something brilliant to stop me. Isn't that a bit of a relief, really?"

Turtle's tail dragged on the floor as two NightWing guards led him away to the dungeon.

Caught by Darkstalker. Imprisoned, just as he had feared his story would end for so long. And worst of all, stripped of his magic as well.

But Anemone was safe. Turtle had finally atoned for the Talons of Power curse he gave her on the beach.

And Kinkajou was safe. And Qibli was out there, ready to help.

Between the three of them, maybe they could stop Darkstalker.

He had to cling to the thin hope that they could, because if they didn't . . . there was no one else.

~ EPILOGUE ~

In the Kingdom of Sand, three explosions rocked the markets at three different oases, timed to go off simultaneously. Dragons wearing black hoods and gold medallions stamped with a bird symbol were spotted fleeing the scenes. In the streets and tents and towns of the kingdom, SandWings muttered and growled to one another. *Who is doing this? Why isn't Queen Thorn keeping us safe?*

In the Kingdom of the Sea, a class of young dragonets on an overnight trip was terrified half to death by a pale phantom that dove from the sky. It swept around the island where they were camped, hissing and snapping, and at least five of the dragonets swore it glared at them with beady black eyes. Rumors spread quickly that the tribe was being haunted . . . by the vengeful ghost of Albatross.

And far to the north, in the Ice Kingdom, in the midst of a blizzard, Winter's brother Hailstorm stood before the wall of rankings, shivering with fever. His claws brushed over the last spot, where Winter's name had been not long ago.

Why is this happening to our tribe?

Are we being punished for what happened between me and Winter?

A dragon trudged through the snow toward him but had to stop halfway, his body wracked with deep, lung-churning coughs.

"Is there news?" Hailstorm asked. "Are my parents any better?"

"No," the other IceWing wheezed. "They're getting worse. But there's something else — someone else."

Hailstorm waited through another storm of coughs. "What is it?" he said finally. "What's happened?"

"It's Queen Glacier," said the other dragon. "She got the plague first, three days ago."

"I know," said Hailstorm. The world was swimming before his eyes. Heat blurred his vision, pounded through his blood.

"I'm sorry, sir. It's over," said the messenger. Snow covered his wings, his tail; snow piled up around his talons, consuming him from all sides. He bowed his head as though he was ready to sink into it and become a part of the frozen landscape forever.

"The queen of the IceWings is dead."

DISCOVER WHERE IT ALL BEGAN . . .

WINGS OF FIRE

LEGENDS

DARKSTALKER

TURN THE PAGE FOR AN EXCERPT

"There's a storm coming. Does that make a difference to your moon superstitions?"

"I don't think so, but it doesn't matter. He'll be out before it gets here. Look how strong he is." A moment, a pulse where they almost shared the same emotion, and then she added, "They're not *superstitions*, by the way. You don't have to be a rhinoceros nostril just because you don't understand something."

The danger flashed before him again. Time to fight harder. He dug in his claws and squirmed, pushing in every direction at once.

The light, the light, the light wanted him out, wanted to run its talons over his wings, drip through his scales, fill him with silver power. He wanted that power, too, all of it, all of it.

CRACK-CRACK-CRACK.

The walls fell away.

The moons poured in.

Three silver eyes in the sky, huge and perfectly round, with darkness all around them. It felt as if they were sinking into his chest, melting into his eyes. He wanted to scoop them into his talons and swallow them whole.

He was in a carved stone nest lined with black fur, at the peak of a sharp promontory. Another egg sat quietly in the nest, nearly camouflaged against the fur and the shadows.

Below him stretched a vast landscape of caverns and ravines, glowing with firelight and echoing with the flutter of wings. It looked as though a giant dragon had raked the ground with her claws, digging secret canyons and caves into the rock all across the terrain, some of them stretching toward the starlit sea in the distance.

After several heartbeats he realized there were two large dragons behind him, their wings drawn tight against the wind that buffeted them all. One was black as the night, one pale as the moons. He glanced down at his scales, but he didn't have to see their color to know he belonged with the dark one. That was Mother. She sparked with anger from snout to tail, but there was immense room inside her for love, and she adored him already, heart and soul. He could feel it. It filled him like the moonlight did, setting the world quickly into understandable shapes in his head. He loved her, too, immediately and forever.

The danger came from the white dragon. This was Father, some kind of partner to the dragon who cared. The newly hatched dragonet could hardly look at him without seeing a spiral of confusing flashes: pain, fury, screaming dragons, and blood, everywhere, blood. This white dragon had done something terrible that haunted him, and he might do worse someday. Father's mind had patches of damp, rotten vileness all over it.

The dragonet immediately wanted to turn him into a fireball and blow his ashes away. But inside Father, hidden under layers of ice, pulsed a small, warm ember of love for Mother. That was the thing that saved him.

Wait and see, thought the dragonet. He did not understand yet that he could see the future. He had no idea what the flashes meant. He couldn't follow the paths that were unfolding in his brain; cause and effect and consequences were all still beyond him. But in his mother's mind he found the idea of hope, and in his father's mind he traced the outline of something called patience.

He could wait. There was much still to come between him and this father-shaped dragon.

"Darkstalker," said Mother. "Hello, darling." She held out her talons and he climbed into them willingly, content to be closer to that warmth.

"Darkstalker?" Father snorted. "You must be joking. That's the creepiest name I've ever heard."

"It is *not*," she snapped, and the dragonet bared his teeth in sympathy, but neither of them noticed. "The darkness is his prey. He chases back the dark, like a hero."

"Sounds more like he creeps *through* the dark. Like a *stalker*."

"Stop being horrible. It's not up to you. In my kingdom, mothers choose their dragonets' names."

"In *my* kingdom, the dragon with the highest rank in the family chooses the dragonets' names and the queen must approve them."

"And of course you think your 'rank' is higher than mine," she snarled. "But we're not in your kingdom. My dragonets will never set foot in your frozen wasteland. We are here, whether you like it or not, and he is my son, and his name is Darkstalker."

Father's eyes, like fragments of ice, studied Darkstalker's every scale, and Darkstalker could feel the cold, congealing weight of Father's resentment.

"He looks every inch a NightWing," Father growled. "Not a shred of me in him at all."

Suspicion, hatred, outrage flashing on both sides, but none of it spoken.

"Fine," said Father at last. "You can have your sinister little Darkstalker. But I want to name the other one."

Mother hesitated, glancing at the unhatched egg, which was still black. Darkstalker listened as her mind turned it over, already half detached. She wasn't sure anyone would ever come out of that egg. She was ready to give all her love to Darkstalker, her perfect thrice-moonborn dragonet. All of it, and he was ready to take it.

But Darkstalker knew his sister was in that egg. Alive, but not restless. Quiet. She didn't care for the moons that had called him forth. She couldn't hear them.

Something tingled in his claws.

He could change that.

He could touch her egg and summon her. He knew it, somehow; he could see in his mind how her egg would turn silver under his talons, how it would splinter and crack open as she scrambled out. He could see the beautiful, odd-looking dragonet that would come out, and he could see the moons sharing their power with her, too.

Then they would be the same. She would be born under three moons as well. She would have the same power as him . . . and the same love from Mother.

Which he already had to share with the undeserving ice monster across from him.

No. This was his. All he had to do was nothing. His sister would come out in her own time, tomorrow when the moons were no longer full. Then he would be the only special one.

"All right," said Mother. "If that egg hatches, you can name the dragonet inside. Only . . . remember she has to grow up in the NightWing tribe. It'll be hard enough — just, try to be kind, is all. Think of her future and how she'll need to fit in."

Father nodded, seething internally at being instructed like a low-ranked dragonet in training.

She'll be all right, Darkstalker thought. A thousand futures dropped away before him as he made his first choice. Futures where his sister joined his quest for power; futures where she fought him and stopped him; futures where they were best friends; futures where one of them killed the other, or vice versa. As Darkstalker folded his talons together, choosing to keep them still for tonight, every possible future with a thrice-moonborn sister disappeared.

He saw them blink out, and although he didn't know exactly what it meant, he felt somehow a tiny bit safer, a tiny bit bigger and stronger.

Sorry, little sister, he thought, not in so many words, but with visions of his future cascading through his mind. *This is my mother. Those are my full moons.*

This is my world now.